SCENT
OF THE
JAGUAR

A DEADLY FORCES NOVEL

S. E. GILCHRIST

Books by
S. E. Gilchrist

SCIENCE FICTION/SPACE OPERA ROMANCE

DARKON WARRIORS SERIES:

Legend Beyond the Stars

The Portal

Awakening the Warriors

Star Pirate's Justice

When Stars Collide

Bargain with the Enemy

Touring the Stars

The Slave Trap

MARS ACADEMY SERIES:

Stranded

Cosmic Fire

APOCALYPTIC:

Paying the Forfeit

Storm of Fire

Don't Look Back (Warders of Earth)

Quest for Earth

CONTEMPORARY

Dance in the Outback

Cowboy under the Mistletoe
(A Wingarobba Outback Romance)

The Cowboy's Gift
(A Wingarobba Outback Romance)

Desire for Love

Bindarra Creek Makeover

FANTASY/ANCIENT WORLDS EROTIC ROMANCE

Bound by Love

Bound by Lies

COMING NEXT:

Broken Lies
(A Diggers Ridge Suspense)

Cotton Field Dreams
(An Edge of the Outback Romantic Suspense)

For lovers of adventure, suspense and romance—
this book is for you.

For Erin—it's been a blast. Your enthusiasm for this
project was boundless. Loved our brain-storming
sessions and hours of research.

For my amazing children—
thank you for always supporting me.
Stay strong, follow your dreams
and enjoy every day of your journey.

~ 1 ~

The storm had hit hard and fast, not long after take-off from São Paulo de Olivença, a municipality in the western section of the Amazon Basin. Several passengers had drifted off to sleep, lulled by the drone of the engines and the stuffy tin-can air.

However, an afternoon nap was the last thing on Bernie's agenda. Not with so many anxious thoughts squirreling through her mind. Inside the cramped restroom, she pressed her pounding forehead against the cold glass, recalling her father's phone call. The storm interference had transformed his voice into a bubble of white noise, his frantic words difficult to make out.

She'd only deciphered, 'get to the US Consulate... Jaguar hunting you...' before the call had been cut off and he was gone.

Her father had too much respect for her profession to believe a wild animal would make an archaeologist give up the prospect of a new dig. Especially one as exciting and wreathed in mystery as this. So, the

Jaguar had to be a person. But what *had* he been talking about?

Bernie hadn't waited to find out. Whatever was going on had germinated fear in her father and, as an ex-marine, he wasn't a man easily intimidated.

She'd galvanized into action, leaving messages for the professor and the guides she'd intended to meet up with tomorrow. If she'd been alone, she would have risked continuing her journey to the dig—jaguar or no jaguar—but not when she had her younger sister, Kit, with her.

Within three hours, they were in the air, flying back to Manaus. Now worry plagued her that she'd made the wrong decision by insisting they change their plans. Maybe heading to a remote area of the jungle would have been a safer bet than isolating themselves on an airplane.

The Jaguar could be here, with them. He could be anyone. Waiting to spring his trap, to take her down. Or worse...Kit.

After splashing water onto her clammy face and patting it dry with a paper towel, Bernie exited the cubicle. She paused, shrugging the strap of her compact backpack into a more comfortable position over her shoulder. The plane dipped then levelled out. Her belly rolled, and she pressed a shaky hand to her protesting stomach.

A female flight attendant appeared out of the small galley, a frown marring her attractive features. "Please return to your seat. Didn't you hear the pilot request everyone remain seated until we're through the turbulence?"

"Sorry, I'm on my way now." Giving the woman a

tight smile, Bernie headed down the aisle. She studied each passenger as she passed, her body tense, palms damp.

The guy in the front row gnawed at his fingernails while darting furtive glances behind him. Apparently ignoring him, his companion had her nose buried in a magazine. Across the aisle, a middle-aged African-American couple had their heads bent over a sheaf of papers, their voices low in discussion. The row behind held a Brazilian family of four, the kids tossing potato chips at each other and squabbling. In the next row, two men appeared to be napping while another guy bent over, tying his shoelaces.

Any one of them could be the Jaguar. Her footsteps faltered, her eyes zeroing in on a lean-faced man with dark auburn hair in the process of stowing a duffle bag in an overhead locker. He looked down, the tender smile on his tanned face softening his profile for a moment, before he took his seat and became obscured by the headrest. As recognition hit, her heart stalled for a second before it kicked into high gear.

Zane MacIntosh. He'd turned up at the dig in Mexico last year with a group of possible benefactors then become part of their team for three weeks. How exactly he'd achieved that feat when everyone else had to go through a long-winded screening process, remained a question she'd like answered. Anger and bitter disappointment burned through her with such force, she charged down the aisle to confront him without a second thought.

"You stole that gold amulet and I intend to prove it." She dropped into the seat across the aisle from the man she suspected to be an artefact smuggler. Leaning over, she narrowed her gaze to meet his laughing one, a wicked twinkle in that ridiculously good-looking face. "You're a total low-life. A desecrator of history."

In the murky light, his olive-skin was shadowed, although nothing could mask the flash of white teeth when he grinned or the sexy dimple in one cheek.

"I'm so glad you find this amusing." Her voice dripped with ice as she fought the desire fluttering in her belly.

His grin grew wider, deepening the grooves around that amazing mouth with its sensually fuller lower lip. "Bernie, how wonderful!"

"Don't you dare pretend you're pleased to see me."

"You'd be surprised, sweet Bernie."

"My name is Bernadette. Only family and friends call me Bernie. And *you* are neither." She raised her chin in challenge.

For a split second, the amused glint cloaking his mocha-colored eyes flickered, his smile slipped, and she glimpsed—*wistfulness?* Her heart softened, her body tingling as she remembered the tenderness of his lips from their last encounter. Maybe there were moments when he regretted his life choices. Maybe there was a better man, hidden inside that stealing rogue, waiting for the right woman to chisel him out.

With a blink, she realized she was still gaping as if mesmerized by the very sight of him. Blue blazes, was she mad? She drew back, ruthlessly denying the unmissable tug of attraction, telling herself she'd imagined that soul-wrenching connection. This man was on the wrong side of the law. A thief who could never be trusted.

His polished, impersonal smile back in place, all emotion veiled in those velvety brown eyes, his composure an impenetrable armor. "Are you going to or coming from a new dig? Who's running it this year? Professor Kowalski? What are you hoping to find?"

"None of which is any of your business." Suspicion raised its snarky head at his probing questions.

The way he'd snooped about and his constant dogging of her footsteps still niggled. It wasn't as if she'd been the prettiest woman on the dig. And she'd certainly done her best to ignore him. She'd been there to work not play, but reluctant admiration had stirred when he'd pitched in and shown surprising enthusiasm for excavating.

"I wouldn't be too certain of that, Bernie. You never know when I could end up funding your next dig."

She swept a disparaging stare over his pristine clothes. "With what? Proceeds from stolen artefacts?"

"The person who took your precious bracelet could be anyone. Why focus on me?" His eyes narrowed.

"You disappeared the same morning we discovered the amulet missing. It's not hard to connect the dots. Besides, I've worked previously with the other team members and Professor Kowalski personally vets each person before approving them on sites." There was no way any of them could be involved. A sudden disquiet pricked at her thoughts and she frowned. Finding evidence Zane was responsible had proved surprisingly difficult.

"I wasn't the only outsider on that dig. Neither

you nor your professor had met the businessmen I brought with me. Add in the journalists hanging around and the tourists, and you've got more than one suspect."

"But none left the very morning we discovered it gone," she fired back.

His companion stirred. Bernie snuck a quick peek, but a fleecy, white shawl hid the woman's face. She had to summon every ounce of willpower she possessed not to grill Zane over the woman's identity.

Zane shrugged, drawing her attention to the way his navy polo shirt molded his wide shoulders. "I love the way your imagination goes into hyperdrive on the flimsiest of assumptions. It's fascinating. How is your precious professor, by the way? Still strutting about playing king of the archaeologists?"

"I don't know why you keep demeaning him. I've known him since college when he was head of his department. He's considered top in his field and a remarkably intelligent man. But then, that's something you'd know little about." She raised her eyebrows in a haughty manner.

Zane laughed. "It's because you always bite, my sweet Bernie." He winked, his hooded gaze raking her body. "You look well. Very fit. Must be all that physical exercise."

Heat crawled up her throat. Glaring at him, she shrugged off her pack and placed it in her lap, taking care not to disturb the guy asleep in the window seat beside her.

The plane dropped sharply and pitched to the right before levelling out. Her breath hissed out as she clutched at the armrests. Lordy, she hated flying.

Especially during thunderstorms when buffeted about by powerful winds, and with plane engines making intermittent spluttering noises.

Leaning back, she released her death-grip and folded her arms. She'd hide her terror of flying from this lying rogue, if it was the last thing she ever did. Acting cool, she said, "It won't be long before Interpol hauls you off to prison."

His deep chuckle had her tummy muscles taking flight and her toes curling. He stretched out his long legs, making himself more comfortable. She ground her teeth at his relaxed attitude. He obviously had no qualms flying. And no concern at all that she considered him a criminal.

Her heart beats stuttered. What a fool she was. He could be the Jaguar.

An icy shiver ran down her spine as she buried her disappointment. If only she'd never allowed him to kiss her. "What are you doing here?"

His eyebrows rose at her sharp tone. "Enjoying the comforts of air travel. What about you? Travelling with someone special?"

Her breath caught. He was fishing for information, but whether he sought details about her love life or her sister, she couldn't decide.

Lightning forked through the rain-laden sky. Twisting around, she looked over the whirling propeller protruding from the plane's engine on the wing behind them. Heavy, ominous, purplish clouds surrounded them. As they parted momentarily, she caught a glimpse of dark jungle below.

Heart thumping, she pointed. "Did you see that? Out there?"

"What? The lightning?" He turned and gazed past his companion, still concealed by her shawl. The blind was only partially lowered despite the cabin crew's earlier request to keep them closed. All the glass revealed now was sheeting rain and a sea of gray.

Shoving her pack onto the floor, she leaped out of the seat and leaned over him to peer out the window. "I saw the jungle." When the aircraft rocked, she clutched the armrest and swayed.

"Nonsense. You're imagining things. We wouldn't be flying that low."

Despite his rebuttal, she picked up on a thoughtful note in his tone. As if he'd already considered that possibility. His gaze lifted to hers, ensnaring her in eyes so hot and dark her skin prickled. She drew closer, fascinated by their rich depths and swirling shadows. A man with secrets. The type of man she avoided. So, why couldn't she dislodge him from her dreams?

She clamped her lips closed, her nostrils flaring as she caught the faint, sea-fresh scent of his aftershave beneath the musty odor of recycled air. Heat sizzled, firing an awareness that startled her with its force. Appalled, she straightened. She refused to be attracted to a man she couldn't trust. "Are you calling me a liar?"

"Are you calling me a thief?"

"You are."

Zane folded his arms over the impressively well-toned chest she knew lay beneath his shirt and quirked an eyebrow. "Prove it."

"I intend to."

"I won't hold my breath." He shifted in his seat to stare into her face. "Instead of playing detective, Bernie, you should channel all that fire and energy into other avenues. How about we continue where we left off in Mexico?" His voice lowered to a deep purr.

How typical of him to remind her of the night she'd succumbed to the temptation to taste his lips. Even toyed with the idea of taking him up on his suggestion of a guaranteed satisfying—his words— sexual encounter.

For long, burning minutes, she'd reveled in the exquisite sensual touch of his hands roving her body with an artistry that had painted amazing fantasies in her mind. His kisses had been wings, beguiling her to dizzying heights, sending her senses soaring beyond anything she'd imagined a kiss could be. And she'd devoured every single one.

The hunger of her response still astonished her. Judging by his teasing smile and the roguish glint in his eyes, he remembered too well how she'd all but catapulted into his arms.

For the first time in her life, her body had ignored her rational self, throwing aside her misgivings over his charm and good looks. Lordy, she could well have ended up with her back against a crumbling ruin while he claimed her body. Hardly ideal surroundings, but she'd been completely consumed by the inferno his touch had ignited. Then a squeal from one of the tourists as she'd been lowered into the cave had brought Bernie to her senses. Blast him, he'd invaded her dreams ever since.

He reached out and pressed his thumb against her

lower lip. Her body liquefied. He winked. The man had no shame. She clenched her jaw, irritated beyond measure that she could still feel the imprint of his touch shiver across her skin. As if she'd been marked as his for all eternity.

"I'd prefer to be burned at the stake."

He chuckled. "I'm glad you like it hot, babe. That's something I can deliver on."

"You're impossible." Scowling, she compressed her lips together, curbing her smile. His laugh was infectious, the glow in his dark eyes alluring. His proximity infused her body with excitement and her heart with dismay. Why did he have to be a thief?

His companion stirred. "Zane? Aren't you going to introduce your friend?"

The small overhead light switched on. Cheeks flooding with heat, Bernie met the twinkling, periwinkle-blue eyes of an elderly woman with a bob of soft white hair framing a smiling, round face. The shawl had fallen around her shoulders. It was hard to judge the woman's exact age. Her smooth pale skin had few lines and the chic, pale pink pantsuit she wore was expertly cut, revealing a slim figure. Not a girlfriend then.

Ignoring her flood of relief, Bernie tugged at the wrinkled mud-brown, thigh-length tunic she wore over black lycra leggings. She shuffled her feet, clad in a pair of thick socks and black canvas shoes, recalling how her impeccably-dressed mother would sigh every time she set eyes on her. Bernie preferred to dress for comfort and the situation rather than to please others. Thankfully, her mother had realized long ago that attempting to turn Bernie into a society fashion-plate was a lost cause.

"I'm sorry if I woke you."

"Think nothing of it, child. I take my catnaps when I can." In one graceful movement, the older woman pushed the shawl aside and offered her hand. There was no disdain in the way she studied Bernie, her smile warm and friendly.

"Mother, this is Bernadette Ashford. Bernie this is my mother, Elizabeth MacIntosh."

"You have a mother?" She squeaked, staggering as the plane jolted, narrowly avoiding landing in his lap. With a weak smile, she shook his mother's hand.

"I didn't hatch out of an egg," he drawled.

"Actually, I thought you'd sprung from the pits of hell, fully formed with horns and tail," she snapped. The plane rocked, and she gripped the headrest.

His mother laughed. "I like this girl, Zane. Why have you never mentioned her?"

Cursing the heat that flooded her cheeks, she muttered, "We hardly know each other." Her eyes fused on the devilry dancing in his.

He grinned and cocked an eyebrow.

"Call me Elizabeth," the older woman said, her voice warm, curiosity shining brightly from her pretty eyes.

Bernie's attention shot to the window when brilliant light zig-zagged through the moisture-laden clouds, giving her a glimpse of terrain that definitely should not be visible. Her breath seized. "Zane, look."

His gaze followed hers. "Tree tops. Bloody hell. We *are* flying too low. Excuse me, Mom." He reached over to shove the blind up fully, and scrutinized the rain-soaked scene outside. The edge of his polo shirt

11

rode up, exposing the golden-brown skin above the waistband of his chinos.

Bernie suppressed the sigh that trembled on her lips and wrenched her gaze from his tempting firm buttocks, blocking out those blasted erotic fantasies that would *not* stop tormenting her.

A massive shudder shook the plane. It dropped for several heart-pounding seconds before levelling out again. Legs giving way, she flopped into the seat she'd appropriated, hoping Zane hadn't heard her frightened squeal.

A flurry of words about turbulence burst through the intercom accompanied by a blast of static. Overhead, the lights suddenly blacked out, leaving the plane filled with gloomy shadows until the floor emergency lighting switched on. Icy fingers stole her voice.

"I don't like this." Zane stood up to look over the headrests toward the front row as a tsunami of anxious murmurs from the other passengers flowed through the cabin.

Bernie leaned sideways and looked for the flight attendants. She saw them huddling close as they spoke, their faces pale in the illumination of the galley light. Clearly there was something terribly wrong.

She looked towards her window, but the shutter was pulled closed. She was reluctant to reach across the man who, incredibly, appeared to still be asleep. Whatever he was on, she could do with some right about now. The plane shook violently, like a rat in a terrier's mouth. Everything rattled. The noise competed with the shrill whine of the engines, setting her teeth on edge and her belly into freefall. A couple of rows forward, an overhead locker sprung open, and a pile of baggage and packages tumbled down. A male passenger swore as a book hit him on the head. The book skipped along the floor like a pebble over water.

Too late to return to her own seat, blind terror a heartbeat away, Bernie snicked on her seat belt. The plane rocked from side to side as if pummeled by a giant fist, flinging her around like she was weightless. From the rear, a woman shrieked, and a child cried out to his mother.

A flight attendant rushed down the aisle, requesting everyone remain seated with their belts on, brushing off the volley of queries fired at her by several of the passengers. Bernie tracked her progress to a jump-seat at the rear of the plane. She craned her neck, scanning the passengers, desperate for a glimpse of Kit.

Zane, his face grim, captured her stunned gaze when he spoke. "We're landing."

"But where?" Heart racing, she leaned forward to see past Zane and his mother.

Lightning lit the sky. She swallowed as it revealed the shadowy mass of the Amazonas jungle through a veil of torrential rain. A craggy outline indicated a small mountain or the edge of a range to their right. When the plane banked and turned in that direction, she realized the pilot must be hoping to find a flat, cleared area in which to land rather than risk crashing through the jungle canopy.

The intercom crackled. "Remain seated. Brace for emergency impact."

Zane murmured something to his mother, who appeared remarkably calm considering the circumstances. He raised her hand to his lips and Bernie glanced away. Thief or no thief, he didn't need her prying on his private moment.

Turning, she shook the young Latino guy beside her awake. Loud vibrations erupted through the cabin combining with the cries of the passengers and competing with the rapid galloping of her heart.

The turbulence worsened, tossing everyone around like marbles in a blender. She peered down the aisle again, frantic to spot Kit's familiar face, but failed. The plane dived into a steep decline, engines protesting as it battled the gusting wind and raging storm. Bernie's heart missed several beats as she clung to the armrests, ramming her feet against the floor to stop herself from sliding off the seat. Possessions became missiles, flying through the cabin.

Ducking her head to miss being struck, Bernie prayed her sister would be safe. The choice they'd made to travel separately to put their pursuer off their scent no longer seemed like a good idea. If they crashed, she wanted to be by Kit's side.

Oxygen masks fell from overhead and danced crazily in front of her face. She snatched one, hands trembling as she fumbled with the strings. It broke, the mask falling uselessly to the floor.

A jolt and shudder rocked them as the landing gear cranked down and the plane engaged the turbulence head-on. She recalled the sight of the ridge and worried her lower lip with her teeth. From her previous excursions into the Amazon, she was certain the area west of Manaus was flat. If that was the case, where had the pilot taken them?

Please, Kit, stay where you are and don't move.

"The flaps are lowered," shouted Zane. "But we're coming in too fast. And way too steep. Hold tight."

Heart pounding fit to burst, Bernie nodded, fear stealing her voice as she wrestled with sickening dread. The plane jerked, throwing her forward before it appeared to level out. Only her belt restrained her from smashing her head on the seat in front.

A male voice roared over the intercom, *"Brace, brace, brace."*

"Kit!" Bernie fumbled with her clasp, fighting off Zane's hand as he tried to stop her.

"No," Zane yelled above the whine of the engines as the plane's thrust slowed. "We're about to land."

It's too late. I should never have allowed myself to be side-tracked by this thief.

Zane reached across the aisle, pushing her head forward. At the last second, she snatched up her backpack and crunched over it, assuming the crash position and squeezing her eyes shut.

"Brace," screamed the flight attendant.

Oh God, I'm going to die. The faces of her parents, her sister, her half-brother flashed across her mind. She thought of her father's warning. *I'm sorry, Father. I failed to keep Kit safe.*

The aircraft bounced once, twice. The third time the plane's wheels miraculously remained on the ground. The brakes were applied, emitting a horrendous screech and vibrations rocked the plane. The forward momentum didn't cease. The plane slewed to the side, tilting on an angle. People screamed.

Bernie's breathing seized, her heartbeat thundered in her ears. Zane reached over, giving her leg a quick pat, the pressure fleeting comfort.

The plane kept sliding, shuddering from nose to tail. The grating sound of tearing metal filled her ears until she couldn't think past it. Maybe that was a blessing. Blankets and bags continued to spill from the lockers. Then the aircraft tipped nose forward, seeming to pick up speed, as it careened downward.

She pitched forward. Terror strangled her throat. Her fingers gripped the armrests like claws, body rigid as a board to stop herself from falling through the cabin.

Kit, oh Kit, please live.

Holding on, she bounced as the plane skidded and bumped over rough terrain. The noise assaulted her hearing. She feared the plane would splinter apart at any moment. People cried, some prayed. The stench of vomit and sweaty terror assaulted her nostrils.

The plane plummeted. Down, down. Shaking and rattling. Until it slammed into something solid.

Then it felt as if the plane's tail end flung into the air. For one horrifying second, Bernie was airborne and thought the craft would somersault onto its roof. It dropped back down with a bone-shaking crash. She fell hard against the back of her seat which disengaged under the impact, smashing her onto the row in front. Pain sliced through the top of her head, agony ripped at her right leg.

The horrendous screech of metal rent the air as something smashed onto the plane making it shudder one last time as the engines shut down. Silence as dead as a cemetery filled the cabin.

Her head throbbed and whirled. Blackness shrank her vision. Then she fell into nothing.

~ 2 ~

"Bernie! Bernie!"

The male voice was insistent, urgent. Was there something she had to do? Something she'd forgotten? She wanted to sleep. Wanted to stay where it was cool and safe. Where she didn't have to think and feel. But the voice wouldn't stop. She wanted to slap away the irritation, tell the voice to leave her alone, but her hands wouldn't move, and her tongue felt glued to the roof of her mouth.

She stirred, gasping at the shaft of pain that snatched her breath before it left her throat. Sticky liquid dribbled down her face. The metallic taste of blood filled her mouth. She coughed and fought to control her nausea. Gentle hands moved over her body, but there was nothing sexual about their touch.

Kit. Jaguar hunting you. The dig. Random thoughts flitted in and out of her mind, too fast for her to catch.

"Bernie, wake up. We have to get off the plane," a guy shouted over a constant drumming noise.

She knew that voice. Zane? The artefact smuggler.

Plane. The crash. Kit. Her gritty eyes sprang open. She forced her mind to concentrate over the pain pounding into her skull. Staring into Zane's frowning face as he unclipped her belt, she struggled with panic. Rain slapped incessantly against metal, a beating drum that kept time with the pounding in her head.

A shudder racked her. Kit. Where was Kit?

"My sister," she mumbled, her lips trembling, tears stinging her eyes.

A large bump on Zane's forehead was swelling quickly and a patchwork of grazes and red marks adorned the left side of his face. There'd be some interesting bruising later.

"Where does it hurt?"

"Apart from everywhere?" she croaked. "My right knee feels like it's been wrenched on the rack, but I can walk. My head is aching, and I feel really ill."

"No time for that, sweetheart. You can be sick later. I need your help." His lips thinned, he turned his head and examined the carnage. "This isn't going to be easy. We must check for survivors and help everyone off the plane. I'm concerned that the blasted thing may slide to the bottom of this ravine. Something is blocking its path. It could give way at any moment though." Zane touched her cheek, the contact brief yet speaking volumes. "Are you up to it?"

His touch had the power to rip away the fear gripping her soul. He was right. This was no time to huddle in a ball and weep and wail. She could do that later. After she'd found Kit and ensured she was safe. "Damn straight, I am."

Her strength and determination returned. Her churning gut settled. She wiped the tears from her face with the back of her sleeve and scrambled onto her knees. Zane helped her up. The plane sat nose-down at a sharp angle. Balancing against the back of a seat, she held onto another to steady her shaking legs. A putrid mix of body fluids, petrol fumes and toxic smoke burned through her senses. Pinching her nose, she covered her mouth with her hands.

The emergency lighting still worked, throwing tiny pools of yellow illumination over a scene that could have come straight from one of her worst nightmares. What was once a streamlined interior had transformed into a mangled mess of broken seats, piles of luggage, strewn clothing and debris, interspersed with bodies. Most of them, thankfully, were moving and groaning, their clothes stained with blood and gore.

A weeping, fair-haired woman and a man with a young boy clinging, monkey-like on his back, edged around the remains of two seats and climbed slowly to where she remained frozen by the enormity of the catastrophe.

Zane hoisted himself up, holding out his hand for the woman to grab as a wince of pain contorted her face and she slithered down the back of a crushed vinyl seat. "Easy does it. One step at a time and you'll be fine."

"Cheers, mate." The man behind her threw Zane a grateful glance.

Bernie shuffled to the side out of the way as they moved past, slipping and sliding their way down toward the flashing emergency exit sign.

"Your mother?" She stole a cautious glance to where the older woman had been sitting. Relief whooshed from her lungs when there was no sign of a crumpled body and no blood oozing between the seats.

"She's helping the crew." He nodded towards the flashing light.

Bernie squinted through the gloom and dust to where a small group of people milled near the exit. Zane's mother and a male flight attendant were steadying the blonde woman as she climbed awkwardly onto the chute. Her partner lifted the kid to sit behind her. The boy wrapped his arms around the woman's waist and her partner hopped on behind. They disappeared from view. Several passengers scrambled over the ruined seats, making for the exit. A few struggled with their hand luggage, ignoring the command to leave everything behind.

Snapped wires and piping swayed, casting eerie moving shadows over the shambles. Bernie's gaze shot toward the rear of the plane. Her breath hitched, horror tightening her throat. She croaked, "Where are the seats?"

"A tree fell across the plane's mid-section." Zane's voice was heavy with grim meaning.

The poor souls who'd been sitting in those rows had little chance of survival. Dark blood trickled along the aisle.

Gulping, her hands curling into fists, Bernie averted her gaze. Dread was like a live thing crawling through her mind. Was her sister dead? No, she'd never accept it. Kit had to be alive. She'd know otherwise. Their bond had always been close despite the age gap of four years. Forcing herself to move, she shut her mind down on the 'what if's' screaming inside her head. Somewhere in this wreckage was Kit. She had to find her.

She firmed her trembling lips. "My sister's behind that mess."

"We can search for her as we go."

Nodding, she surveyed the blockage. Her nails dug into her palms, bile bubbled in the base of her belly. "Kit was sitting in row nine around the middle of the plane, but I know she would have moved further back if she'd seen two empty seats. She likes stretching out."

"You weren't sitting together?"

She hesitated. How much should she reveal? "Taking this flight was a last-minute decision. We had to accept whatever seats were allocated."

"Strange. I didn't get the impression the plane was that full."

"Are you really going to argue the point? Here and now?" She glared, inwardly shrugging off the unsettling reassurance his presence gave her.

His eyebrows rose. "I was making an observation."

She wrenched her gaze from his quizzing eyes and shuffled forward. "I propose we begin checking the rows closest to where the tree is and work our way towards the front of the plane."

"My thoughts exactly." He hesitated a moment then said in a gruff tone, "You certain you're up for this? If not, I'll assist you to the chute."

"Absolutely. Stop wasting time, unless you want me to lead the way?"

He growled a curse as he climbed his way up the plane, testing each seat for a foothold before settling his full weight on it. Steadily, he cleared a path by pushing cases, shattered laptops and clothing out of their way.

The storm blanketing the sky and the dark density of the surrounding jungle limited vision inside the plane.

Terror her sister lay trapped drove Bernie forward. Her head whirled and throbbed from where she'd connected with the seat, and her knees trembled. The stifling humidity of the jungle permeated inside the plane, heightened the increasing stench. She sucked in air, her lungs wheezing at the thickness of it. Sweat formed a damp, itchy film under her thick hair.

In a few minutes they reached the spot where branches and a massive trunk barred their passage. Leaves rustled. She tugged on Zane's polo shirt to snag his attention. A snake could well have landed inside the plane and be about to strike.

They exchanged a fraught glance. Zane nodded, motioning with his hand for her to back away. With around seventeen venomous snake species abounding in this region, she wasn't about to argue.

Groping behind her with one hand, she climbed one row away from the trunk, eyes straining to see past the blockage. But it was impossible see past the tree.

He hunkered onto his hands and knees. "Bernie, there's someone caught under this seat. Can you find me something to use as a lever?"

Kicking aside a blanket and someone's discarded jacket, she spied a gleam of metal between the debris. Bending down, she swiftly pulled out a seat rail that had worked loose from the floor. "Will this help?"

"Better than nothing." He switched on the flashlight in his cell phone, playing it slowly over the shattered seats.

Her gaze followed the bright beam, her heart skipping a beat when she saw the pale gleam of exposed bone, ragged flesh and blood. The rail fell from her numb fingers with a clatter.

"Damn. He's not breathing." Zane gave a heavy sigh as he reached for the rail. Crouching lower, he angled his head until his face was almost on the floor while he directed the light. His voice gruff, he added, "I can see at least three more bodies. One's a woman, I think. Whoever they were, they had no chance of surviving with this tree on top of them."

For three long seconds that lasted a lifetime, his words rebounded inside her head.

"Kit!" She hurtled past him to claw at the branches. But there was no way through.

3

Zane gripped Bernie by the waist and hauled her, kicking and screaming, from the plane's crushed mid-section—a crude make-shift coffin for far too many passengers. His shin caught the side of a hard-shelled suitcase and stung like the devil.

"Get a grip, Bernie," he shouted, then cursed himself for his careless tongue. A little sympathy might have been a better strategy, but blast it all, he wasn't feeling that chipper himself.

Fury blazed from eyes that burned like deep-blue fire in her white, tear-stained face. Fury, grief and resolute determination. Her chin rose, her fists fell to her sides. Bernie froze him with her icy glare. Joan of Arc couldn't have looked as regal.

This was some woman. All tart tongue and fierce resolve blazing in eyes of such a brilliant turquoise, he could gaze into them for eternity. And that went nowhere close to how the siren in her called to him at the most primitive level.

With regret as sharp as a tiger's claws, he recalled that missed opportunity in Mexico. But he shook off the emotion with the irritation of a dog flicking off fleas. His well-honed instinct for danger that had saved his ass on more than one occasion, now yelled inside his head to get as far away from the plane as possible. But, bloody hell, it was hard going attempting to lug this little tigress over a mountain of spewed luggage and damaged seats.

Her elbow connected with his nose, making his eyes water.

Right. That does it.

"Bloody hell, Bernie, I know this must be difficult for you, but we have to get out of here. Do you understand?"

Eyes glazed, chin jutting with determination, she seemed to stare right through him. He had to shake her from her personal world of pain, bring her back to their need for survival.

Dragging her closer, he clutched a fistful of silky, dark-brown hair and pressed his lips against hers. As a kiss, it was woeful, his usual suave foreplay skills deserting him as hunger exploded. That first touch swept aside every other thought in his head. All he could think of was more. More her. A sharp pain assaulted his left ear, leaving it ringing. His hold loosened, and he blinked in surprise as those pillow-soft lips wrenched away.

"What is wrong with you?" Bernie swung her fist in his direction.

He ducked and felt the whoosh of air on his face as her punch missed him by mere inches. Holding up his hands, he quipped, "I surrender," hoping to defuse the tension crackling between them and the heaviness in his pants.

He couldn't believe he'd lost control so easily. *Him.* Mr Discipline personified, who always single-mindedly pursued his quarry, no matter the distractions. The easy-come-easy-go type of guy who never lied to a woman, but never gave her a backward glance either as he walked out the door. How could he? When his sole focus in life centered on locating his biological mother's killer.

Then personally transporting the bastard to face the justice he deserved.

"You wouldn't listen to reason." He managed a careless shrug, feeling lower than a slug when fresh tears glistened in her eyes and she glanced away.

That moment when he'd first laid eyes on Bernie should have warned him. She'd been tipping a bucket of water over her dirty, mud-encrusted body as she'd stood beside a partially excavated wall. He'd been instantly drawn to her side. Lusty fantasies firing his rampant imagination, fueled by the way her thin, damp shirt had clung to a pair of tempting breasts as she raised her arms to push aside her wet hair. Then one glance at her intriguing face and he'd been captivated.

Over the three weeks he'd been on the dig, he'd been lured to her side by her inquisitive nature and passionate enthusiasm for her work. But he suspected it was the steady integrity shining from her beautiful eyes that had really chipped a crack in his well-guarded heart. He'd been hard pressed to retain focus on his goal.

Her refusal to take his flirting to the next level had

been for the best. When sanity had prevailed, he'd quickly realized she wasn't a one-fling woman. The keepers were women he maintained a wide distance from. His adoptive mother and sister were the only keepers in his life plan.

Zane cleared his throat. "Your sister probably exited via the rear escape hatch. No doubt she's outside. Waiting for you." Taking hold of her hand, he ignored her attempt to tug free. "I'll go first to break your fall, in case you slip."

"I don't need your help."

Good. She was well and truly snarky now. Her determination to show him up would fuel her energy and get her off this death trap. "Give me a mule any day. So much less stubborn than a pig-headed woman."

"You're such a sweet talker. I'm surprised you aren't surrounded by a harem."

"There are so many in my harem, I couldn't afford the plane tickets."

With something between a snarl and a choked-off chuckle, she ripped her hand free and cautiously lowered one foot, searching for solid purchase.

Amused despite their perilous situation, he dropped the subject and began the climb to where the front chute offered escape.

Escape to nowhere. The view from the windows revealed little more than rain and trees. They could have landed anywhere in Brazil. Trekking back to civilization or finding help would be no easy task. And there were bound to be injured passengers, some of whom might be unable to help themselves. What a right, royal cock-up.

"Zane!" came his mother's voice.

Pausing, he raised his hand to give her a reassuring wave. After one long look, she broke her gaze and allowed the flight attendant to maneuver her onto the chute and out of the plane. The tension in his shoulders released. Thank God, she'd suffered no serious injury from the forced landing. His mother was one tough lady.

A crack like a cannon shot reverberated through the cabin. The plane shuddered, and he guessed another tree had fallen, possibly from a mud slide sweeping it along in its path. A terrifying growling noise exploded from the jungle amidst the rustle and crack of branches. It sounded like a cross between a jet engine and enraged animals. He swung around, searching for the source. "What the...?"

"Howler monkeys," said Bernie.

He glanced over his shoulder to check her progress. "Monkeys! Sounded like a stampede of King Kongs."

"Recognize your relatives, do you?" Her lips twitched.

"Here. Let me help," said a male voice.

He dragged his eyes away from Bernie, to find a middle-aged African-American guy extending his hand. "Cheers."

The man assisted him over a pile of luggage which had broken free from its restraints in the front cargo area and spilled out into the small walkway beside the hatch.

"Delroy Lewis."

"Zane MacIntosh." He shook hands, sizing up the older man.

Well over six-foot-five with a shaven head, silver strands in his stubble betrayed that he was probably between fifty and sixty years of age. Smooth mahogany skin, a wide smile, the flattened nose of an ex-boxer and a jawline as solid as granite, Delroy appeared to have little fat on his big body. He looked like a good man to have in a tight corner.

"New Yorker?" Zane queried with a slight smile. He turned, planted his hands around Bernie's waist and lifted her down. As soon as her feet hit the floor, she peeled off his fingers like she couldn't get rid of his touch fast enough.

"Hell man, no way. New Jersey is where the good Mrs Lewis and me have lived close on thirty-six years." Delroy peered into the shadowy cabin, his smile fading. "Those poor souls. Anyone else left...I can't even say it, man."

Zane met his concerned gaze. "I believe we're it. We've checked each row down to where the tree sliced the plane in half."

"Then let's get out of this metal box." Delroy looked at Bernie. "This your lady?"

Zane shook his head as he introduced her. "Just someone I know. Bernie, meet Delroy."

"It's a pleasure." Delroy nodded towards Bernie. "You okay, ma'am? You look a mite peaky."

"Bad day." Bernie managed a brief smile.

Delroy sighed. "Ain't that the truth."

The flight attendant touched Delroy on the arm. "Your turn now, sir." He waved him forward to where the yellow escape chute flowed out the open hatch.

"Be seeing you now." Delroy folded his arms across his chest and slid out of sight.

After scooping up a duffle from the floor beside him and tossing it down the chute after Delroy, the flight attendant cast a questioning glance towards Zane.

"Problem?" Zane pulled Bernie towards the hatchway.

"The cockpit door is jammed and there was no response when I knocked."

"Still, we need to check."

"Yes, sir." Relief resonated in the flight attendant's voice.

"If the door's blocked from the inside we may be able to access the area from the cockpit window. Or at least determine if anyone is alive. We can decide what to do from there." Zane eyed Bernie. "Time to say goodbye, sweetheart. We men have work to do."

She rolled her eyes, ensured her pack was snug over her shoulders and slithered onto the chute and out the hatch. When she reached the bottom, she swung a hand out, grabbing a thick vine and stopping herself from sliding further down the mountain side. *Clever girl.* A sense of pride flooded him. His girl. No, he wouldn't—couldn't—allow himself to think that way.

Delroy helped her to her feet. Satisfied she was in no immediate danger, Zane eased past the shaky flight attendant and gripped the edge of the hatch, hoisting his upper torso up until his chest rested on the hatch jamb. Craning his neck, he attempted to see inside the cockpit through the side window. Too far.

Rain slapped steadily onto his body. He flicked the water from his eyes with a quick shake of his head.

"The plane's nose has crumpled on impact. We could smash through the windscreen. Is there a fire-extinguisher handy?"

"There is one attached to the cockpit door. I will go," the flight attendant said.

Seconds later, Zane heard the scrapes and thuds of luggage being thrown aside.

"I have it," came the flight attendant's breathless response.

"Excellent. We'll do this from the ground, but make sure you stand off to the side. Be ready to run. We won't have a lot of warning if the plane begins to slide." He lowered himself back into the plane and eyed the flight attendant. Wiping water from his face with his forearm, he smiled and extended his hand. "Zane."

"Juan Felipe." The guy bobbed his head, his gaze darting around the cabin.

Juan appeared close to breaking point. If Zane wanted to help the pilots, he needed to move fast before the guy went to pieces. "You first. I'll follow with the fire extinguisher."

"Good. Good." Juan hesitated then gave a nod before launching himself down the chute.

Before following suit, Zane scrutinized what he could see of the plane's interior. "Can anyone hear me? Anyone still on board?"

Silence greeted him. Nothing moved. Clenching his jaw, he rolled his shoulders to rid himself of that frisson of fear running over his skin like a platoon of skittish spiders. If his mother or he...or Bernie...had been in rows eight to eleven...

He pushed the thought from his mind. There was

still work to be done before they could consider themselves safe. The sooner he was out of here, the happier he'd be. Turning away from death, he moved towards life.

A few seconds later, he hurtled down the chute and grabbed for the vine that had steadied Bernie earlier. His feet almost slid out from under him in an ankle-deep slush of sticky mud and leaf litter. Staggering, he regained his balance and squinted through the pelting rain.

He spotted his mother applying a sticking plaster to the gash on Bernie's forehead. Chatting at the base of a tree, they looked up as if sensing his gaze. His mother smiled. The taut stillness to Bernie's pale face told him she had yet to find her sister. He winked, satisfaction swelling his chest when a spot of color bloomed on her pale cheeks.

Those bloody monkeys were still making a racket in the canopy above. Frogs croaked incessantly while overhead thunder rumbled. Wiping water from his face, he noticed Juan rising onto his toes, attempting to see into the cockpit. But the cracked glass, a spider's web of damage radiating over the windscreen, prevented.

Zane squelched over. "Hate to tell you, mate, but you're not tall enough. Stand back while I have a crack at that window."

With a palpable air of relief, Juan shuffled aside. "What can I do?"

"Give me a leg up?"

"Of course." Juan bent his knees, interlocking his fingers together.

Zane placed one foot into the make-shift step and

braced himself against the plane's surface with his other. Raising the extinguisher, he rammed it against the glass.

A couple more cracks appeared, but the windscreen remained intact. Zane struck it again and again, each impact shuddering through him and he struggled to keep his balance.

Breathing deeply, arms aching, he paused. The force, while denting the glass further, failed to break through. *Shit!* This could take a while and any second the wreck could plummet further down the mountain.

"Zane? What's going on? What are you doing?" called Bernie. "The pilots—"

"Stay away," he yelled over his shoulder as he raised the fire-extinguisher and rammed the glass again.

"I can help."

"No, ma'am, I believe this is where I come in," said Delroy. "Hey, you two guys, come on over here. We've got a man down."

From behind him, Zane heard the suck of mud and squish of sodden leaves as heavy footsteps moved forward.

"I'll get a branch and hit the glass from the other side," said another man in an unmistakable Australian drawl.

The same man who'd been with the blonde woman and little boy. Someone tapped Zane on the leg. He looked down. Bernie, covered in a see-through plastic rain poncho with hood, stared back at him. Beside her stood Delroy and the young Latino boy who'd been sitting in the window seat opposite, his baseball cap twisted around so the peak faced backwards.

Mud and leaves coated their lower trouser legs and obscured their footwear. Rain had soaked their clothing so that it stuck to their skin, in heavy, dripping folds. If only this bloody weather would ease up.

"This here's Ricky." Delroy gestured towards the boy.

Ricky nodded. "Hey, man."

"Think they're still alive in there?" Delroy inclined his head towards the cockpit, a grimace on his face.

"I have no idea, but we can't leave without checking." Zane slapped at a bug crawling up his arm.

"I hear you, buddy."

"Hoist me up. Then Juan and Ricky can help our Aussie friend do likewise."

"Not a problem."

Zane leaped to the ground, nodded his thanks to Juan, who then moved carefully around the massive tree that had stopped the plane from sliding further down the ridge.

Delroy flashed him a grin. "Ready?"

"Go for it." Two strong arms wrapped around Zane's thighs. Staying as still as possible and keeping his body stiff, he let Delroy lift him into the air. He waited until the Australian was in a similar position, a thick branch clutched in his hands then nodded. Together they whacked at the windscreen. Not having to worry about sliding off the wet plane, Zane utilized his upper body strength. The glass gave way under their combined onslaught.

Seconds later, both men had pushed the windscreen back inside the cockpit. Zane called over his shoulder, "I'm going in."

Delroy's grip tightened around Zane's legs then he gave him a push. Zane landed belly-down on the crumpled nose of the plane.

"Here! Use this."

A jacket plopped beside him. Zane threw Bernie a lightning smile to show his thanks. He placed the jacket over the framework of the window to protect his hands and body from any remaining shards of broken glass. Swinging his legs around, he lowered himself into the dark cockpit. He fished his cell phone from his pocket, knowing the flashlight could well use up what battery life he had left. But he had to check.

From outside the plane came a male voice, ordering everyone to make their way back up the side of the ridge to the runway. A good decision in Zane's opinion. With luck, they could find shelter to wait out the storm until help arrived.

The acrid stench of death caused his nose to twitch and he held his breath, trying not to gag. The pilot's body was jammed in between the seat and the crushed control panel. His head lolled lifelessly on his shoulders.

Poor bastard. Gritting his teeth, Zane placed his hand on the man's neck. No pulse. He frowned. Strange. Despite the tropical heat, the body had already begun to cool.

A groan shifted his attention. He turned around to find the co-pilot staring blankly at him. Something about the fixation of his gaze made Zane uneasy, but before he could analyze the co-pilot's expression, the man squeezed his eyes shut.

Zane swept the light from his cell phone over the co-pilot's body, noting the rapid rise and fall of his chest. He called out, "Co-pilot's alive, but I'll need some help getting him out of here."

"No worries, mate," said the Australian then nimbly dropped into the cabin. "Tai Miller."

"Zane MacIntosh."

"I can stand," rasped the co-pilot, opening his eyes and turning a gray face towards Zane. He hissed as Zane unclipped his belt and began to press lightly over his torso, checking for any obvious injuries. "I think my collarbone may be broken."

Together Zane and Tai assisted the co-pilot through the cockpit window into the waiting hands of Delroy and Juan. Tai climbed out while Zane took a few seconds to study the remains of the cockpit. He had a niggling feeling he'd missed something of importance. But whatever the bloody thing was, it eluded him.

Shaking his head, he hoisted himself out and slid down the metal surface to land in the mud. Thunder rumbled overhead, and rain continued to bucket down from the gray sky. He and Delroy gripped the co-pilot around the waist. They struggled over the twisting roots of a massive tree and shin-high vines that lay tangled in the leaf litter to where a group of passengers waited.

After propping the co-pilot against a section of wing that had ripped from the plane, Zane moved aside. His mother gently positioned the man's arm into a sling with the bandage Bernie handed her.

"Thanks," the co-pilot muttered.

"Was the transponder still working?" Juan asked.

Zane tracked Bernie as she shrugged her backpack onto her shoulders and headed to the young couple.

She crouched down to speak to their young son who was crying and burrowing his small body as close as possible to his mother. "Sorry. I didn't check. I can go back in..."

His mother stepped to his side, frowning. "Absolutely out of the question, Zane. That tree could collapse any second and you'd be trapped inside."

Using a cotton ball soaked in antiseptic, she dabbed at a large cut on the back of his hand he hadn't noticed. The sting effectively swallowed any objection he'd intended to raise.

His mother zipped up the small first-aid satchel she always carried in her handbag. "We've got quite a few injured passengers."

"How bad?" He glanced around, his gaze again seeking and finding Bernie who walked about, head lowered as if searching for something on the ground. She bent and picked up a three foot-long, sturdy-looking branch, jabbing it against the ground as if testing its strength. A walking stick and a good way of thumping the ground to ward off snakes.

She glanced up, catching his stare. A little sparkle had returned to her eyes and her face had lost its haunted expression. His shoulders relaxed. Maybe she'd found her sister alive and well. He winked, grinning when a smile tugged at her lips before she marched off, head held high.

Juan stood ten or fifteen yards away speaking with a tall, well-built guy, the female flight attendant and a very pretty woman with reddish-brown hair wearing a flimsy-looking dress so wet it stuck to her slim body. Juan gestured toward the co-pilot while the big guy pointed toward the runway.

The woman's gaze appeared to be fixed on Bernie. Could this be her sister? But if so, why hadn't they rushed over to greet each other? Bernie glanced over at the other woman, then noticed him watching and smartly turned her back.

He stroked his jaw as he recalled her demeanor before the plane crash. She'd held her body tensely and had appeared to study the other passengers in a manner that suggested wariness. He didn't know her that well, but his instincts told him she wasn't a woman who was easily frightened.

Damn it all to hell and back. Something was up, and he meant to find out what. But for now, he had more pressing matters to attend to. "How are the other passengers, Mom?"

"Several have cuts and bruises. One has a sprained wrist and another a twisted ankle. I suspect more than one may have broken bones. I'm worried about the little boy's mother. She has no obvious injury, but her color isn't good and she's in considerable pain. I believe there's a doctor on board. Perhaps once we find cover, she can be assessed properly."

"Some shelter from this bloody rain would be good. How's that cut on Bernie's face? She was bleeding quite badly in the plane."

She patted his shoulder. "Don't fret. Your Bernie is all sorted. The bleeding had stopped by the time she got out. I cleaned and taped her wound. She's a very determined young woman."

His Bernie indeed. He rolled his eyes. "Try obstinate and opinionated."

"How interesting." His mother smiled then bent to

pick up a pack of plastic-wrapped water bottles someone had thrown off the plane.

Around them, people began to move, their forms merging with the rain then disappearing into the mist. Curses and squeals mingled with the boisterous monkeys shaking branches and howling, the frogs croaking, the squawking of parrots and the constant splashing of the rain onto leaves and into deep puddles.

"Let me take that, Mom." Smiling, he relieved his mother of her burden.

She picked up a duffle bag stuffed with thermal space blankets and together they followed a small knot of passengers scrambling through the mud and fallen branches up the hillside.

He heard the low murmur of Bernie's voice as she spoke with the Australian couple. A quick glance assured him they were close behind. Bernie dug her sturdy branch deep into the mud, an arm around the blonde's waist while the woman leaned heavily on her. Tai had the young boy clinging to his back, no doubt their son. The anxious looks he gave his wife worried Zane. Just how badly injured was she?

He hoisted the bubble-wrapped plastic bottles under one arm and looped his other around his mother's waist. "Hold onto my belt, Mom. I don't want you slipping."

The pilots would have sent out a mayday call. Coupled with the plane's transponder and the wonders of radar, it would only be a matter of hours before they'd be airlifted out of the jungle and on their way to civilization. They'd all be safe.

Reaction began to set in, sucking the energy from

him and he still had to climb to the runway. His normal line of work entailed extricating himself from dangerous situations. He'd lived through quite a few near misses, but this was different. This time, more than *his* life teetered in the balance.

~ 4 ~

The climb to the top of the ridge had Bernie's heart pounding hard against her ribcage as she struggled to fill her lungs with oxygen. Humid, thick air clogged her throat. Doing a boot camp workout inside a sauna would be more comfortable and a hell of a lot easier.

Her knee throbbed and the lump on her head ached, but she suspected they were minor compared to Cheryl Miller's injuries. Every second or so, Cheryl would grunt and gasp. But she didn't cry out or ask to rest. Her intent gaze remained on her husband, Tai, and their son, Cody, as they struggled up the hill ahead.

Thunder crashed through the sky and rain drenched the earth. Bernie's shoes were caked with mud, each step collecting more, making her feet unbelievably heavy. Several times, she staggered, off-balance.

Despite the rigors of the ascent and her ever-increasing certainty they'd landed somewhere close to the Colombian border, her spirits were hopeful.

Kit was alive. They'd both survived.

The other passengers were on their feet and moving to the runway where hopefully they'd find shelter while they waited for rescue. With a little luck, if he'd been on the plane, the Jaguar had been sitting somewhere in rows eight to eleven and had died in the crash.

Not a nice thought, but the heightened stress in her father's voice had left her with little doubt, he considered the personal threat close to the mark of DEFCON 1. And until she was certain the threat was no longer an issue, she had no intention of allowing her vigilance to slip.

With a start, she realized Zane and Tai were crouched on the edge of the ridge waiting, eager to assist. She sighed with relief and eased Cheryl into Tai's arms before taking Zane's hand and allowing him to pull her onto the plateau. She waited several beats while she regained her breath and her legs stopped shaking, before she moved. Shrugging her pack into position, she rammed her stick into the ground and rose to her feet.

"How's your knee?" Hands on his hips, Zane squinted at her through the rain.

"Fine."

"And your head?"

"Sore, but I'll manage."

He snorted, but refrained from further comment. He slipped his hand under her elbow and steered her over the deeply gouged runway. She pretended not to notice, thankful for the help.

When she looked along the runway, she shivered, her eyes zeroing in on the path of the plane as it had careened along the plateau to the point where the wheels had lost traction sending it sliding over the edge.

Luck or their guardian angels had been busy today. A few yards to the left, and the downward slope was completely vertical. If the plane had gone over there...

"Welcome to Airport Amazonas. Hot tea and scones will be served directly." Zane swept his hand in a wide arc.

Bernie's heart sank. The passengers crammed together, huddled beneath a zinc-aluminum roofed structure supported on rickety thin sapling posts. A few bags and one or two crates lay discarded in the mud nearby. One man sobbed quietly into his hands. Those who wore wet weather gear had elected to stand in the rain. Few spoke, many hugged their waists as if holding onto their tattered composure.

Shivering in her thin dress which stuck to her skin like plastic wrap, her sister stood not far from a tall muscular man. Delayed shock? A chill from the rain? Bernie started forward, intending to grab a space blanket for her, when she was pulled up short by Zane's voice.

"Any idea where we are exactly? I'd ask the co-pilot, but he appears to be quite disorientated. Must have hit his head."

After sending Kit another glance, Bernie shaded her face with her hand to ward off the rain. She turned around slowly, looking down at her watch then at the horizon. "I'd say close to the Colombian border and nowhere near Manaus."

"I thought as much. That's an interesting gadget."

"It has an in-built compass and it's solar powered." Even she could hear the pride in her voice.

Zane glanced at the cloud-covered sky. "I can see that's going to come in real handy today." He waggled his eyebrows.

She laughed. "It has a battery life of several months."

"Not bad." He crooked his index finger in front of her then pushed up the sodden sleeve on his left arm. "But *I* have a Garman Tactic Bravo with GPS. It also supports GLONASS. That's the Russian version of GPS."

She wanted to chase that smug look from his face. Still GPS... "I know what GLONASS is." Eagerly, she examined the amazing high-tech watch which looked tough enough to withstand a hammer strike. This could be exactly what they needed right now. "That's excellent news. Have you checked our position?"

"I would have, but I was waiting for you to climb to the runway." Grinning, he wiped water from the lens, pressed some buttons and muttered under his breath.

"Well, do you have a signal?"

The grin slipped from his face. "I'm not connecting with any towers. It could be the storm, or we may be out of range. I couldn't get reception with my cell phone and no one else has managed to get through either."

"No big deal. Then we wait for rescue." Shrugging, she pulled the hood lower over her face and wandered closer to the shelter.

Elizabeth broke away, snapped up an umbrella to cover herself and approached. "Bernadette, Zane, I believe there is something you should know. A doctor has examined the co-pilot. His name is Nyle Beaumont. He has a twisted ankle and a broken collarbone. Possibly mild concussion as he seems confused. The doctor thinks Cheryl has internal injuries and shouldn't be on her feet." She indicated the soggy ground. "The poor girl can't lie in the mud."

"We'll make a stretcher..." Zane paused as the flight attendant's voice shouted something unintelligible.

Bernie glanced up to see the guy disappearing into the sleeting rain, Kit trotting after him. "Where's Juan heading off to?" *And my sister.*

Elizabeth smiled. "I believe someone said they saw headlights on a road leading up to the runway."

"That's a relief." Bernie debated for a couple of seconds whether she should run after Kit.

Zane glanced at the rickety shelter. "If our rescuers are in a truck, a stretcher will make it less painful when we load Cheryl into the back."

"Good thinking." Bernie slapped Zane on the back. "There's a clump of walking palm growing on the opposite side of the runway. If we can find and break off two long stilt roots, we can use them as the framework for the stretcher. Or we may be able to knock down a smaller palm and use the trunk. Come along."

She marched off, her feet making sloppy noises as she stepped from a puddle of water to a pile of sticky mud to gravel. Once she reached civilization, she would treat herself to a new pair of shoes. A long massage. A soft bed with crisp cotton sheets. A pot of hot tea. Maybe those scones Zane had spoken about. Her tummy grumbled. She shouldn't have considered scones.

Since the runway was narrow, it didn't take long to reach the other side.

"You sure this will work?" Fruitlessly wiping water from his face, Zane stared at the long roots of the tall palm tree with a dubious expression.

No way would she mention how the inner parts of the roots were used by tribal men as an aphrodisiac. Based on her brief experience with him, Zane had no problem in that area. "Trust me. The hard part will be breaking off the roots."

"That's easy. I've got it covered." He dug in his pants pocket and took out a Swiss army knife.

"How did you get that onto the plane?"

"My charm."

"Let's see if you can charm those roots off then. Mind you pick the youngest-looking of the bunch. They'll be less likely to snap under any weight. And watch out for spiders and—"

He spun round and chucked her under the chin with his knuckle. "Orders. Orders. Orders. How about a kiss instead?"

"Hah! It'll be a sorry day in heaven and hell, if I'm ever that desperate. Which I won't be. Now, are you going to do some actual work or—" A gunshot echoed from down the hillside stopping her in mid-sentence. Someone screamed. Bernie jumped, her breath catching momentarily. "Was that a gun?" Her voice perilously close to a shriek.

"Bloody hell!" Zane stared through the rain. "A rifle, I believe, and it came from the road below. Quick, Bernie, give me a hand. Something tells me Cheryl needs that stretcher damn fast."

Jaw tight, she squinted through the rain to where

small group of people milled about looking down the hillside. After spying her sister—seemingly okay—Bernie set to work, quickly ascertaining two likely specimens. "*Hurry*, Zane."

"I'm working as fast as I can," he snapped, sawing away with his knife while he twisted and turned the root trunk until finally it came away from the palm. Quickly they worked on another.

Tension wound her tighter and tighter, but she stood her ground, resisting her desire to rush to her sister's side. The gunfire had ceased along with the sound of an engine. They still had time to escape.

Escape... Oh God, why did she think they needed to escape? There was nowhere to go. They were surrounded in all directions by jungle. Civilization could be hundreds of miles away.

The Jaguar. This was a dangerous region. Remote. Within reach of the border. No way could that landing strip be an official one. It was probably used by drug traffickers to run their illegal goods in and out of Colombia.

Her imagination could be running riot, a reaction to the stress of the day, her father's message totally unrelated. The Amazon teemed with danger, and not only of the predatory four-legged type. More likely whoever was on the road had taken a pot-shot at a real jaguar. Or a wild boar.

Pain spiked across her forehead as wild thoughts tumbled through her head.

Unable to stay where she was a moment longer, she straightened. "I'm going to find out what happened." Leaving Zane to carry the poles across the runway, she sprinted through the rain in the direction where she'd last seen Kit.

As Bernie sloshed through the ever-widening puddles, she heard a guy bellowing for everyone to head for the plane. Something about mercenaries.

And her knees almost gave way. Not people here to help, but hired thugs bent on God only knew what.

A couple loomed in front of her, one tugging the smaller along. *Kit.* Panting, she hauled her sister into her arms, holding her tight.

"We need to get out of here." Kit raised tear-drenched eyes.

"Go. I'll catch up with you as soon as I finish here. We have an injured woman who needs help." Bernie kissed Kit's cheek.

They broke apart. Kit followed the bulk of passengers scrambling over the ridge and down the treacherous descent to the crash site. Jaw clenched, Bernie made for the shelter. As soon as everyone re-grouped near the plane, she'd join her sister. And she'd make damn sure they remained together until they were rescued.

A few passengers lingered around Cheryl, propped up in her husband's arms. Delroy had his hand on the shoulder of the woman next to him—probably his wife, Pearl—and nodded as Bernie came closer. Pearl had a crumpled handkerchief pressed to her face, eyes wide in terror. Elizabeth had also remained behind. She'd drawn the little boy aside, showing him a small odd-shaped rock she'd found.

Zane shot Bernie an intent glance as she crouched down to examine the stretcher. "No need to explain. Everyone is already up to speed."

"Almost finished?" She bent closer, fingering the

length of duct tape he'd wrapped around the space blanket that lay between the two poles. "Where did you get this?"

"Found it in one of the duffle bags someone brought up from the plane."

"I don't understand why they shot at us."

"No idea either. All I know is we need to get away from here. Fast." He yanked at the last knot. "There. That should to it."

"Not bad. Where did you learn to do this?" She fished a handkerchief from her pack and blew her nose before tucking it away.

He managed an easy shrug. "Bernie sweetheart, it's amazing what you pick up on the internet. I'm a chronic browser when I'm taking time out from my harem."

Although casual, his tone carried a faint undertone of evasion. *Yes. Definitely a man of secrets.* She turned to Cheryl. "I'm sorry, but you'll have to be strapped in or you'll slide off as we climb down the mountain."

Cheryl gave Bernie a determined nod. "Do it."

Bernie looked up. "Anyone have a spare belt?"

"You can use mine." Delroy immediately removed his belt and handed it over.

Cheryl's chin wobbled as she managed a brave smile. Her husband leaned down and rubbed his cheek against her hair. "Some honeymoon. I never should have suggested the Amazon."

"Oh, Tai, this was my dream too."

Tai looked around. "We're ready."

Zane tested the knots again, then stood. "All good. Let's move."

"I'm hearing you, buddy. Come on, little lady. Let's get you settled on this thing and we can all be out of here." Delroy patted his wife's hand and strode forward.

Thunder erupted in a long, low rumble. As it faded, the groan of straining truck engines grated over the plateau. Several more shots rang out.

They rushed to secure Cheryl on the stretcher. Zane and Tai each took hold of a front pole with Delroy taking both rear ones.

Zane said, "On the count of three. One, two, three." Carefully they rose to their feet. "Let's go, gents."

"One sec, please, Zane." Bernie covered Cheryl with a spare space blanket, tucking it under her hoping to shield her from the rain.

"Cody, you be a good boy for the nice lady," Cheryl croaked through cracked lips.

"I will, Mommy." Cody took Elizabeth's hand.

"Don't you fret, Cheryl. I'll see your lad safe to the plane. Let's not dally." Elizabeth set off with the young boy, snapping down her brolly to use as a walking stick. They clambered over the ridge, her voice as she spoke to Cody gradually fading from earshot as they descended.

Bernie glanced around. "I'll grab the last of the gear that's left here. Pearl? Can you please give me a hand?"

The older woman stuffed her damp handkerchief into her equally sodden handbag, closing the clasp with something of a defiant snap and nodded. Fearful and in shock, but obviously a woman with no intentions of hanging around to die.

Just like me.

Bernie crammed another blanket into her backpack and popped spare water bottles into the pockets either side. Picking up several bubble-wrapped water bottles, she stowed them under one arm, then hesitated, wondering what it was she'd forgotten.

The murmur of voices as the others progressed slowly down the side of the ridge, faded. Alone, she studied her surroundings before scooping up the few empty water bottles scattered on the ground, thinking she'd make use of them later to catch the rain. The many footprints in the mud filled rapidly with water.

The groan of straining engines grew louder. Or was that merely because the rain had eased? She'd thought the trucks were stuck and unable to traverse any further to the runway. Unless the soldiers had found an alternate route.

"Bernie," bellowed Zane from somewhere down the mountainside.

"All right, all right. Keep your pants on," she muttered, then sighed. Zane without his pants on had been a fantasy that had teased her dreams far too often. *Drat the man. Remember, he's a thief.*

As she turned away, she caught sight of a piece of white paper on the ground. She snatched it up, her curiosity piqued by the handwritten words, some blurred where the rain had cause the ink to run. No time to look. No time to read. Not when there were men with guns shouting at the end of the runway.

Tucking the paper into a waterproof pocket on her pack, she readjusted her gear and set off. Using her stick, she slid and slipped her way down to the crash site.

"Sweet mother, you took your time. What the hell were you doing up there?" Zane appeared out of the misty rain and shook her arm.

"What's going on? Where is everyone?" Ignoring him, she pulled away, scanning the area. *Where's Kit?* She caught a glimpse of her sister, a bulky pack strapped on her back, climbing over the roots of an enormous fig tree. The next second, she was swallowed by the dense jungle.

Keep going, Kit. I'll catch up with you soon. The other passengers had taken off as well, leaving Zane all but tapping his foot as she carefully picked her way through the mess.

Luggage lay strewn among bits of twisted metal, many ripped open, the contents scattered. It appeared they'd been rummaged through, probably to look for anything useful. A sudden barrage of shots from an automatic rifle cut through the rain and jungle sounds. The monkeys went ballistic, shaking trees and howling their fear.

Who were the soldiers shooting at? Other passengers? No, that couldn't be right. Everyone had rushed back to the plane. Then she remembered seeing a few passengers run to the opposite side of the runway. Nausea gripped Bernie's gut as she swallowed hard over rising hysteria.

"The mercenaries are close. Come on, Bernie. Stop day-dreaming." Zane gave her a not-so-gentle shove in the small of her back. "We're all heading down the side of the mountain then veering left until we find the road. With luck, we'll come out below the trucks. The mercenaries will make for the plane first then probably fan out through the jungle, hoping to herd us into a bunch. We can't be found napping."

"The road could lead to a village."

"True, but some guy thought the village could be under their control."

"Maybe, but honestly, that road could lead anywhere. How's Cheryl?"

"Struggling, but she's one determined cookie. Another bloke, Colin, took my place on the stretcher. I told them to keep moving while I waited for you. We can catch them up easily enough. It'll be slow-going carrying that stretcher." Zane shook his head. "Enjoy your nap up there?"

She huffed a breath. "I was making certain we hadn't forgotten anything or left anyone behind."

"Yeah, well...about that." Zane rasped a hand along his jaw and prodded her back with the other. Again. A not so subtle hint for her to move. "Some passengers weren't on the let's-get-the-hell-outta-here agenda. They set off to meet the mercenaries, hoping to bribe them to lead them to safety."

"Oh, no!" Horror liquifying her belly, she stared at him.

"Let's hope for their sakes, they have it right."

"I need to find my big pack. It's got some essentials we may need."

He reached his hand around his back and patted the large, waterproof canvas duffle strapped to his shoulders. "Got mine. Some bright spark had the right idea tossing luggage out of the plane."

With Zane at her heels like an agitated terrier, she located her pack, wedged beneath the shattered wing.

"I'll give you a hand." Scooping up a thick branch

off the ground, he slipped it beneath the wing. Bracing his legs, he lifted the metal sufficiently for her to tug her pack free.

"My camp pot and mini lantern are crushed. Blast, my hammock's missing, too. Must have fallen out," mourned Bernie, rifling through her bag's contents and tossing aside the ruined articles. Looking up at Zane, she sighed. "Thank heavens my first aid box isn't damaged. We're going to need it. At least, I can pack in some water bottles and blankets, if you can find more."

"Sure. Although, it's going to make your pack heavy."

"Won't be a problem."

A few minutes later, she was ready to roll. Shifting her smaller pack to her front, she heaved the larger bag onto her back.

"Any idea how far to the road?" she asked, picking up her stick.

"None." Zane rolled back his wet sleeve as they set off and checked his watch. "Five-thirty. We need to make it there before nightfall. With this storm, full darkness is going to hit us sooner rather than later. We have to find the others and decent shelter within the next hour. If we don't, we'll be at risk of walking straight into those thugs' arms."

"Agreed. In the morning, we can work out a new plan."

The thought of her sister, alone in the jungle, hunted by vicious killers hardened her resolve. Renewed strength coursed through her veins, like an injection of adrenaline. She had one hour to find Kit and somewhere to hide.

~ 5 ~

Zane held aside a large palm leaf for Bernie, wishing he could see more than a few yards into the gloom of the dense undergrowth. Wanting to reserve battery power, he'd switched off the apps on his phone and secured it inside the jacket he'd pulled over his soaked polo shirt. Shadows deepened, twilight waned, and nightfall lurked, as much a predator as any jungle animal.

Tamping down his impatience, he carefully measured each step he took over the maze of hazards covering the jungle floor. Twisting roots, some as high as his thigh had to be climbed over. Hidden under layers of bracken and moss lay deep holes that could easily snap a bone.

The people strung out ahead left an easy trail to follow, marked by broken palm leaves and deep footprints in the sticky mud or where they'd waded through knee-high foliage, crushing the undergrowth. A path that could also be easily followed by the mercenaries.

Water ran down his collar, trickling along his spine and he longed to be out of this constant rain. Not that that would happen any time soon. His cramped thigh and calf muscles told him they were still descending, although the slope had lessened considerably. A peek at his watch revealed thirty minutes had passed. They had to be near the bottom or, at least, close to the road.

The humidity formed a thick mist they could have done without. The constant chirpings of birds had faded as they looked for sanctuary from the coming night. Those hair-raising monkeys appeared to have moved elsewhere. The frogs continued to croak, along with crickets and he constantly swatted at the mosquitoes buzzing around his face and hands.

Their footsteps seemed louder, as did their rapid breathing. Sweat coated his face and stung his eyes. He longed for an air-conditioned motel room set to sub-zero temperature.

"You're very quiet," said Bernie, her voice low.

"I'm thinking about what I'm ordering for tomorrow's breakfast."

She snorted. "At least you're not the whining type."

"No way. This is the perfect opportunity to seduce you. With these romantic surroundings, I can't possibly fail." He tossed her a grin over his shoulder.

"Dream on." She laughed.

"Hush." He held up a hand and peered through the foliage. "We've found the road."

They crept past a prickly, low-growing palm with fronds that scratched the backs of his hands before emerging directly on an embankment above a rutted dirt track.

Bernie moved to his side. "I was hoping for civilization."

Zane caught the bitter bite of disappointment in her voice. "I was hoping for a king-sized bed."

"Where has everyone gone? I thought we were meeting up on the road."

"I'm guessing they're hiding somewhere close."

"I hope so. I don't fancy attempting to find anyone in the middle of the jungle at night. Too many dangers plus it will be easy to pass by someone and not even know they're there." She sighed. "I doubt this track leads to much. But maybe the others have decided to follow it anyway."

Hands on hips, she peered up the side of the mountain then down to where the track petered off into the distance, rambling and winding as it followed the contours of the rough terrain.

He touched her hand. "We're almost at the bottom of the ridge. I hate to tell you this, Bernie, but the odds are that the mercenaries are based somewhere along this road."

From further up the mountain-side, came the rumble of an engine and the unmistakable grating sound of gears changing.

"Damn! They're heading our way." He shot a hand out to stop Bernie from stepping onto the road.

On the opposite side of the road, Delroy stepped out from behind a tree, arms wind-milling above his head. "Hey there. Where you two been? Get on, over here." He made urgent gestures.

Zane herded a reluctant Bernie in front of him. She

scrambled down the slope, looking up and down the track as she jogged across the muddy road. *Her sister. Of course, she'd be looking for her.*

They reached where Delroy waited and Bernie asked, "Is everyone from the plane here?"

"Sorry, sweet girl. Most folk have scattered."

Bernie bit her lip before turning her face away.

Zane wanted to reach out to reassure her, but he knew she wouldn't appreciate the attention right now.

"It was bedlam here a few moments ago. We heard the trucks coming and everyone panicked, running all over the joint." Delroy shrugged, worry lines creasing his forehead. "Follow me. The others are a little way up ahead."

They pushed through dense ferns, huge trees, and palms of all shapes and sizes then waded through shin-deep water, stumbling over the stony ground, ankle-deep in decomposing leaf litter and fallen branches. A stench of decay mingled with the humid, misty air. But at least they were sheltered to some extent from the raging storm although rain still streamed through the canopy above to splash onto their bowed heads.

A few minutes later, they caught up with a group of people huddled beneath the shelter of trees. His mother, the Miller family, the Lewis', Colin who'd taken his place on the stretcher, and a couple of new faces. Ricky and a dark-haired Latino woman whose attractive face held a scowl, propped up the injured co-pilot. Apparently, not everyone was keen to help out.

The ground here appeared to be elevated, as little water covered the sodden grass and fallen leaves. The downpour eased to drips and the mist thinned.

Shadows had lengthened, and the gloomy light revealed pale and weary faces. He doubted they could travel much further tonight.

"I heard the trucks. Are the soldiers on the move?" asked a tall, bony woman with fair hair. She stared at him with small, watery eyes framed by dark-rimmed glasses.

"This here is Rhoda Bloomfield. We found her and her daughter, Tatum, sitting beside the road and persuaded them to come with us," Delroy said, gesturing with his thumb.

"Evening, ladies." Zane nodded.

Mrs Bloomfield's expression remained stony, offering no response to his greeting. A thin blonde teenager sat on a log, rocking to and fro, her face hidden behind her hands.

"I think we should make for the village." Mrs Bloomfield crossed to her daughter's side and placed a hand on her shoulder.

The kid shook it off and sprang to her feet. "This is your fault. You should have left me with Dad. It's your fault he left us. You're an ugly old cow and I hate you."

"That's enough, Tatum. The courts granted me custody. And just as well." Mrs Bloomfield sniffed. "Your father should never have resigned his job and moved to this terrible place."

"He wants to save the rainforest. And so do I."

"He's a fool. Until you've finished your education, you'll live with me."

"I want to live with Dad. It's your fault we were on that plane. It's your fault I'm going to die!" The teenager's voice rose to a piercing shriek.

The hairs on Zane's neck rose. *Sweet mother.* The kid was loud enough to be heard in Rio. "If you don't keep quiet, we'll all die here."

"Mommy, I don't want to die," wailed Cody from where he sat on the stretcher beside Cheryl. His father picked the little boy up, cuddling him close and crooning reassurances.

"Now look what you've done." Bernie glared at Zane so hard, it was a wonder he didn't turn to stone.

He tamped down his exasperation. "I'm sorry. Look, people, I know we're all tired and worried, but we need to keep our heads. The situation hasn't changed. We've got thugs searching for us. Whether it's a game to them or they intend to ransom us, I have no idea. All I know is that we need to stay hidden and quiet until help arrives."

"You think the search team will find us?" Delroy wrapped his arms around his wife.

"They'll certainly start looking once our plane fails to make the scheduled landing." Zane turned to the co-pilot. "Nyle, they can lock onto the plane's transponder, right? Were you able to send off a distress call before we landed?"

Nyle licked his cracked lips and raised a shaking hand to his head, pressing his fingers against his forehead. "I think so. I don't remember much about what happened."

"You mean you don't know if you sent out a mayday call?" Bernie said, disbelief clear in her voice.

"Shit. My head is pounding. I told you I don't remember." Nyle pulled away from Ricky and the dark-haired woman supporting him. He swayed on his feet.

The woman snorted and stalked off to stand beside Colin, where she leaned into his side and whispered into his ear. Colin frowned and shook his head.

"What's the last thing you remember?" Zane eyed the co-pilot narrowly, recalling that moment inside in the cockpit. There was something he'd noticed, something he should remember, but what the devil was it? The more he searched his memory, the more it slipped away.

"Engine malfunction." Nyle sighed and slowly lowered his head to look at the ground, as if his strength ebbed. His shoulders rounded. "Manuel...the pilot..." He stopped, obviously remembering the poor bastard was dead, then added in a thick voice, "Manuel didn't believe we'd make Manaus. He punched in the co-ordinates of this runway and we turned the plane around. I think...I think it was while we were descending that he had the heart attack."

Nyle glanced around, his veiled eyes meeting the scrutiny in Zane's. "I botched the landing. Manuel was making terrible noises, but I couldn't help him. The landing took all my attention. I don't remember anything after that until I came to when you were getting me out of the plane. Thanks, by the way."

"It wasn't only me. Tai, Delroy, Ricky and Juan helped," Zane pointed out.

"Of course. Thanks all." Nyle nodded.

"It's getting late." Bernie stepped closer to the stretcher and Cheryl. "We have to find shelter. Everyone is exhausted. We can't risk blundering about in the dark in case we bump into those thugs."

"I agree." Zane looked over at Bernie, noting the tight pull of her lips. He could only imagine how worried she must be over her sister's non-appearance. "We need shelter. Any suggestions?"

He had a few of his own, but for the time being, he preferred to have all and any comments on the table before they made a decision. And Bernie, bless her, had a clear head on her shoulders. With her jungle experience, her ideas were bound to be excellent.

She didn't disappoint. "Everyone stay here. I'll scout around for a tree big enough for us to hide inside."

"Huh? Inside?" Delroy cocked his head.

"Yes. You'll understand once I find one. No time for explanations." She shouldered off her backpack and unzipped a side pocket, bringing out a small LED flashlight. Flicking it on, she added, "I suggest everyone keeps the chatter down to zero. Zane, you and Delroy should mount a watch a few yards away from the rest of us."

He saluted, and the teenager giggled. Even the co-pilot cracked a faint smile. Glad to have lifted the dismal mood, Zane dropped his bag to the ground and gestured to Delroy. "I'll watch the road, if you'll watch the jungle. Bernie?" He waited until she turned and meet his gaze. "Don't stray too far."

She gave a short nod before striding off, ducking her head beneath a low-growing branch. Within seconds the soft squelch of her footsteps faded. The urge to drag her back to the relative safety of the group made his fingers twitch. She wouldn't listen, anyway. He had to trust in her expertise and hope she wouldn't meet any trouble.

After another reminder for the group to remain watchful and quiet, he slipped through the jungle, back-tracking over their trail until he came to the roadway.

Crouching, he made certain he was concealed then settled down to wait for her return.

~ 6 ~

It took longer than Bernie had hoped to find a suitable kapok tree. By the time she struggled back to the group, her tiredness had become bone deep, matching her worry and her aching knee. Because no matter how diligently she looked under palms and around the bases of trees big enough to provide hiding places, she'd discovered no trace of her sister.

She could only hope Kit and the other survivors had gone to ground until morning. And meanwhile, she had people she needed to see safe for the night.

When she ducked under a king fern and stumbled into the clearing, everyone gasped. For a second she thought she heard the click of a gun being cocked and froze.

"It's me...Bernie." She swept her flashlight over the now familiar faces.

No one held a gun, although Elizabeth had her umbrella gripped as if ready to strike an intruder's head.

I'm hallucinating. Bernie shrugged off her crazy notion. "I've found somewhere we can shelter for the night. I'll fetch Zane and Delroy, and we'll move out."

"Why not stay here? Its reasonably dry, I'm tired and my head is pounding." Rhoda Bloomfield's jaw jutted forward in a belligerent manner. Tatum glared through a swath of limp hair with an almost identical expression to her mother's. That woman and her daughter spelled trouble.

Through gritted teeth and too damn weary to argue, Bernie kept it simple, "We're exposed here. Everyone gather up your gear."

She pulled her backpack over her shoulders and headed through the undergrowth. Four minutes later, she'd rounded up her two sentries. With Zane, Delroy, Colin and Tai on stretcher duty, the others carried the packs and duffle bags after wasting a full minute on grumbles and protests.

Silent they shuffled along, through puddles of water, past branches and ferns crawling with leeches and insects, and over twisting tree roots. The rain had eased to a drizzle and, in the distance, thunder rumbled.

By the time Bernie located the tree again, she could almost feel the frustration and fatigue blasting from the others, although no one raised their voice to complain. Too tired, no doubt.

"We're here." She swept her flashlight over the enormous kapok tree with its thin, plank-like buttresses spreading over the ground around them. "See there, where the buttresses form a tunnel? We can use palm tree fronds to spread over the top and the sides which will give us a cave for the night and keep out any animals." And hide them from criminal eyes.

"What about Cheryl?" His son cradled in his arms, Tai came to stand beside her.

"The stretcher should fit inside fine. This tree is perfect. Most of the buttresses curve out from the main trunk. If we cover all of them, there will be plenty of room for us to spread out and get a decent rest."

"Thanks, Bernie." The sadness in his smile drove darts into her heart.

"I'll show you where I want Cheryl. Everyone will need to hunch down a bit to get inside." Guiding the way with her flashlight, she wriggled between the high plank buttresses and indicated the trunk base. The leaf litter here was dry and she'd already made certain no animal spoils lay on the ground. No way did they need a tapir or a jaguar to return and find them occupying its home.

They lowered the stretcher carefully and Tai deposited his sleeping son next to his wife. Cheryl rested her hand on Cody's hair, before closing her eyes. Pain had carved lines into her face, making her look older than her twenty-five or so years. If help didn't find them soon...

Blinking away hot tears, Bernie shuffled from beneath the tree. With the aid of her flashlight, she showed the others what palms to use and how to weave the stems to form a thick roof over the buttresses and sides. Another thirty minutes and everyone was snug in their makeshift cave. She wedged the flashlight into a crack in the tree trunk and switched it on.

Zane passed around bottles of water, asking everyone to be sparing with their consumption, while his mother handed out apples and bags of nuts she'd unearthed from a duffle bag.

Elizabeth muttered as she examined the contents. "Thank heavens, there's a roll of toilet paper in here."

"I think we should set a watch," Zane said.

"Probably a good idea." Delroy spoke around a mouthful of apple.

"What's the point? There's nothing we can do against armed men."

Bernie recognized the high-pitched voice as belonging to Colin—he of the prominent Adam's apple, nervous twitch near his left eye and what looked like a thermal insulated container strapped to his backpack. He appeared to be travelling with the Spanish-American woman, who'd introduced herself as Melanie Enriquez.

"If we stay quiet there is every likelihood they'll walk straight past us," Bernie said through her teeth.

Colin whined on. "If we'd stayed on the road, we'd be at a village by now."

"Here now, you heard what the man said. Ain't no good reason to believe we'd find a friendly welcome there."

"You don't know for certain, Delroy. The rest of the passengers may already be there enjoying a hot meal, while we're sitting here surrounded by insects and soldiers."

"Colin, if the others have made the village and are safe, then we don't have no need to fret. Help will be coming up that there road in the morning."

"Do you really think so, Mr Lewis?" With her back

to her mother, Tatum leaned over to peer at her legs. "I'm scared, and something just bit my ankle."

"Probably an ant," Bernie said in her most soothing voice and pushed back her poncho hood. Opening her main pack, she dug deep, coming out with a large vial of a murky-looking substance. "If anyone has any clothing that will cover themselves more, now's the time to put it on. Then rub this ointment over any exposed skin. It will help stop insect bites."

"Ew. Looks disgusting. What is it?"

"It's a concoction my sister made from natural products. It may be smelly, but there's nothing in the ingredients that will harm you, Tatum. Even people with very sensitive skin can use it." She handed the vial to the teenager who took it between her finger and thumb.

In the dim light, her scrunched up nose spoke volumes. Tatum unscrewed the lid and sniffed. "This is awful. It smells like a skunk. Or a raccoon."

"Then it must be good for you," came Tai's easy tones. "We'll give it a go when you're finished, Tatum."

Shaking her head, Bernie retrieved another vial, this one filled with a powder-like substance. "Shake a little of this around the perimeter of the branches. It should keep most of the insects away from us for the night, especially the army ants and spiders."

"This place sucks. I want to go home," wailed Tatum.

"Oh, be quiet. Your voice is like a nail gun ramming my head," snapped Melanie.

Tatum pulled a face while Rhoda adjusted her glasses to glare at the other woman.

Bernie pulled out a clear plastic bag. "These are salt tablets. Everyone should take one or you'll end up suffering cramps from the humidity."

"Babe and I have our own supply." Melanie's tone implied she had no intention of sharing her stash.

"We've also got our own and a few to spare, if anyone needs them," said Zane.

"Great, thanks." Bernie handed tablets to Tai, Delroy, Ricky and Rhoda.

Zane, who'd settled beside her, leaned close. His breath ruffled her damp hair when he spoke. "You may want to conserve your flashlight."

"I'll wait until everyone has finished dressing and using the ointment then turn it off. I've spare batteries in my pack."

"How tired are you?"

She tensed. "I've still got some miles left in me."

"I can't wait to take you for a road test." He chuckled.

Glad the gloom hid the rising heat in her face, she play-punched his arm.

"Seriously." His voice flattened. "I suggest we scout further down the road. See if there *is* a village not too far and, if so, check it out."

"What are you whispering about?" snapped Colin. "If there's a problem then we all need to know."

"Lower your voice, man," growled Zane. "Bernie and I intend to see where that road leads."

Delroy folded his arms over his wide chest. "Good idea. I'm with you."

"Thanks, but I prefer that you stay and lend a hand here if need be." Zane checked the time on his luminous watch before pulling his sleeve down to conceal the face. "We'll follow the road for one or two hours and if we find nothing, head back. That should give us a few hours' sleep before morning."

"And then what? We can't stay here forever," shrilled Rhoda.

"True, Mrs Bloomfield, but let's take it one step at a time. I suggest everyone tries to sleep. Maybe you, Delroy, and Tai can take it in turns to keep an ear to the ground. And remember, everyone keep quiet."

A few minutes later, Bernie pulled her hood back over her head then crept out from their hideaway. She stretched, working out the kinks in her back while she waited for Zane, who'd paused to speak to his mother and retrieve the flashlight, before joining her.

When he slipped his hand into Bernie's, she didn't protest. It made sense to assist each other as they made their way over the treacherous ground towards the road using the thin beam from the flashlight as a guide. Every so often, she paused to leave a sign only she and Zane would recognize. Their special trail of breadcrumbs—like a branch bent a particular way, plucking orchids and wedging them in tree cracks, even arranging a bundle of sticks. Doing so, slowed them down, but even with a compass, finding their way back would be difficult in the dark of a jungle, if not impossible.

"The road should be just ahead," Zane murmured in her ear.

He handed over her stick he'd been using. They waited several beats, listening for the sound of trucks or footsteps over the pattering of raindrops. Reassured no one lurked close by, they pushed through the last couple of yards of palms and bushes until they emerged by the roadside.

No shouts of discovery. No pounding of feet. Bernie swept the flashlight over the embankment and the rutted track. "We should keep off the road and close to the jungle's edge."

"I agree." Zane checked the time. "We need to cover as much territory as possible."

Nodding, she set off, lighting the way, her ears straining for any alien sounds—like trucks, jaguars, wild boars. Her eyes examined the mud and the deeply rutted track, looking for footprints or any sign of her sister.

As children, they'd often left secret markers for each other when playing at being explorers in the grounds of the governor's residence. Markers like those she and Zane had left to find their way back to camp.

When their parents divorced, and Bernie and her sister had moved to England with their mother, she'd considered herself too old for such games. Now the memories of those carefree days flooded back. She hoped Kit remembered them too.

But no matter how hard she looked, she found no indication Kit had passed this way. Or was still alive.

Judging by the length of time they'd been half-walking, half-jogging, Bernie estimated they'd journeyed about five miles when they heard the grating sound of a generator.

"Do you think we've found the village?" Shivering, she stopped, heart pounding, her skin slick with sweat despite the steadily falling rain and drop in temperature. Her body trembled from the effort of their trek, her knee throbbed bone-deep and her head ached. *What a terrible day. And I still haven't found Kit.* Swallowing over the knot in her throat, she tilted her face to the dark sky and allowed the rain to wash away fresh tears.

"Can't tell from here. We need to get closer. Let's move into the jungle and work our way forward away from the road."

"Agreed." Keeping the flashlight angled low to illuminate a few feet ahead, she merged into the undergrowth, Zane close behind, his presence warming her through the plastic of her rain poncho.

The noise grew louder and up ahead, every so often, light glimmered through the jungle. The foliage thinned out until they could see where trees had been cut down to form a clearing.

Bernie flicked off her flashlight, stowing it in her small backpack.

"Not much of a village, is it?" Zane pushed down on a palm leaf as large as his torso then peered over the top. "Damn. Looks like a mercenaries' camp."

Huddling close together, they studied the five primitive buildings of sticks and palm branches that made up the indigenous village. A small pen cut from saplings contained scrawny chickens clucking softly as they nestled on the ground.

Around two large canvas tents, fires burned in four fifty-gallon drums.

Bernie stiffened, counting three soldiers wrapped in heavy oilskin coats, dozing at their posts. No one moved about, and no trucks could be seen. A tall sentry tower built from raw timber rose from the ground. On the platform, a thug stood beside a searchlight that speared over the village. Apart from him, there appeared to be no one else awake.

"Do you think they're looking for us?"

"Possibly, but if they'd expected company, the sentries wouldn't be sleeping on the job."

"We can't move any closer to get a better look unless we somehow disable the generator fueling that light." Bernie gnawed on her lower lip. "I can't see any antennas or a satellite dish. But that doesn't mean they don't have a radio."

"True. Which means we have to check for ourselves." Zane paused for a moment before adding,

"I've counted the seconds it takes for that light to swing past the tents. If we work our way around the perimeter, I believe I can make it to a tent before the light comes full circle again."

"You're mad. What if you're caught?"

"Then you hightail it out of here and back to the others. And no acting the hero."

She snorted softly. "They'll probably welcome you with open arms. Being a thief and all."

"I'm surprised you haven't accused me of being in league with them."

"The thought has crossed my mind. The jury is still out on that verdict."

"Damn, but you're a pain in the ass." Zane touched her hand lightly. "Follow me and don't make a sound."

She didn't move, resisting his tug on her clothes. "How do I know you're not going to double-cross me? Tell them where I am and where the others are hiding?"

"I could have done that a hundred times already. Are you with me? Or are you going to continue nagging?"

"Lead on, thief." She gave him a not-so-gentle push on the back, positive she could hear his teeth gnashing.

Pleased at having gotten under his skin, she smiled as they eased back into the jungle and steadily made their way toward the tents.

When he'd judged they were sufficiently close, Zane murmured, "Stay here."

She sank to her haunches and lifted a large palm frond while Zane moved to the edge of the jungle and waited for the searchlight to sweep past. Then he sprinted off across the narrow strip of mud to disappear around the side of the tent.

Time dragged by. She was halfway through reciting her favourite Edgar Allen Poe poem, *The Raven*, when someone touched her on the shoulder. Whirling around, she hefted her stick and swung.

"Bloody hell. Bernie, it's me," spluttered Zane from where he'd flung himself sideways to avoid being clobbered.

"Why did you sneak up on me like that?" she hissed and shakily lowered her stick. Her heart thudded like a jackhammer. It took several deep breaths to steady herself.

"You're a menace." Zane picked himself up and brushed leaves and mud from his clothes. "Ow, I think I landed in an ant's nest." Shaking his feet, one at a time, he brushed at his trouser legs.

"Serves you right. Well? Did you find a phone? A radio?" She switched on her flashlight.

"Shush. Let's get out of here." He caught her hand, pulled her deeper into the jungle, whispering, "There was nothing to find. The tents were empty."

"No other soldiers?" She frowned as Zane quickened his pace, pulling her along after him.

"The only soldiers I saw were the three outside the tents and the guy operating the light. The rest must be out searching for us."

"Maybe, if we follow the road, we'll come to another village. A bigger one."

"That's a possibility. But this close to the border, I'll bet my last quid, any place we come to will be swarming with mercenaries." He sighed heavily.

"Bernie, all indications are we've landed smack-bang in drug cartel territory. That was probably their runway we came down on."

He paused to take the flashlight from her and spear her with a speaking glance. "If they capture us, we'll be tortured and executed. And the women, including you, will bloody well wish you'd died in the crash."

~ 8 ~

Early the next morning it took Bernie a good hour, but finally she found sufficient fruit to feed the group before trudging back to the hide. The deep shadows thrown by the dense foliage had lightened, indicating the heavy cloud cover was clearing, leaving behind a humidity that would have done a Turkish steam bath proud. The rain had ceased, although fat droplets fell every so often from the leaves to plop into the deep puddles.

Wiping away the sweat beading her forehead, she dropped her load of *cupuazu, maracuya* and the reddish-pink *goiaba* near Zane's feet and met his furious gaze.

"Where the hell have you been?" Behind his anger resonated concern.

Her heart fluttered at the thought. "Are you always this grouchy in the morning?" She cocked her head and allowed a tiny smile to tease him, pleased when his eyes lowered and locked onto her mouth.

Tension oozed from his stiffly held body when

after a few seconds, his gaze dropped to her bounty. "What's this?"

"Breakfast. And probably lunch and dinner." Pointing first to the oblong, brown fuzzy-looking fruit, she said, "It's late in the season for *cupuazu,* but I was lucky to find a few. The *maracuya* here are like passionfruit and the *goiaba* are excellent sources of vitamins and potassium. I'd hoped to find some *acai* berries, but was out of luck. It's a pity because they're rich in protein." She pushed a lock of damp, tangled hair from her face and indicated the hide. "Is everyone awake? We need to eat and move on."

"You sure none of these are poisonous?" Looking suspicious, he toed the closest fruit.

"My sister is a botanist. Plus, I've been on three digs in the Amazon over the past five years. Mostly, we lived rough, especially if our supplies were held up due to an abnormal wet season."

His jaw worked. "Oh yes, with your precious Professor Kowalski."

"Yes, the same professor whose dig I was on in Mexico. You remember that dig? Where you stole the gold amulet and later sold it on the black market." Suspicion curled like poison in her belly. She leaned back on her heels, hands on hips and nailed him with a disparaging glare.

Zane bared his teeth. "Still barking up that tree? I hate to disappoint you, Bernie, but you're wasting your breath."

"Time will tell."

A spear landed with a thud near her feet. She jumped and spun around then pressed a hand to her racing heart as Ricky and Colin appeared from behind the kapok tree.

"For pity's sake. Ricky, you scared me."

"Sorry," the Latino boy said, but the twitch to his lips belied his apology.

"Weapons are not toys, Ricky." Colin's Adam's apple bobbed and the bunch of spears he carried rattled as he lost his grip and they clattered to the ground.

"Did you make these?" Bernie scooped one up and inspected it closely. Although crudely made from thin branches that weren't particularly straight, the tip had been honed to dig deep into the earth. Quite a formidable weapon, sharp enough to slash through skin and bone.

Ricky pulled the spear from it was embedded in the ground and performed a series of complicated maneuvers, shifting the weapon around his body like a cheerleader's baton. "Your boyfriend's idea, along with the rope."

Zane grinned, the thunder in his face vanishing as he blew on his knuckles. "No need to thank me. *Girlfriend*."

"I wasn't going to." She suppressed her smile at his teasing. His handiwork was impressive, as was the coil of rope lying on the ground. She picked it up. Closer examination revealed it had been made from shredded plant stems, knotted together then twisted around and intertwined with a similar string. She recognized the technique from the tribespeople she'd interacted with on her last tour of Brazil. Now, where had Zane learned to make rope from plants?

Leaves rustled, and his mother emerged from the

jungle, an ashen-faced Cheryl leaning heavily on her arm.

"Pit stop," said Elizabeth, her gaze scanning the clearing in a keen sweep. "Good morning, Bernadette. I hope that's breakfast I see on the ground, because I'm hungry enough to eat the bark off a tree."

Tai and Cody followed. The little boy's face lit up and he raced over to inspect the fruit.

Melanie pushed out from the hide, not bothering to cover her wide yawn. "Did I hear someone mention food?" She scowled at the fruit before lifting her gaze to the canopy above their heads, as if expecting a rescue team to rappel from the sky at any moment with a fully cooked breakfast. "What do you mean this is our lunch and dinner?"

Bernie ignored her. "I'm sure Zane has updated everyone regarding what we found at the village. We've decided it would be useless to go any further in that direction as the road will be swarming with cartel soldiers. If we can locate a river, all we need to do is follow it east until we reach a village where we can seek help."

"Who died and made you queen bee? I vote we stay on the road." Melanie turned to Colin who had begun to pick up the spears. "What the hell are they for?"

"We need to defend ourselves," Zane said.

"A spear against a gun. Like that is going to work." Melanie stalked over to Elizabeth, snatching the roll of toilet paper from the older woman before shoving off into the jungle. The palm frond whipped back with a snap like a gunshot.

"She's not a morning person," Colin offered with an

anxious grin, blinking rapidly behind his thick glasses.

"Or any kind of person." Zane waggled his eyebrows at Bernie.

Grinning, she crouched down and picked up a *cupuazu* then held out her other hand. "Let's eat, shall we? May I borrow your knife?"

"By all means, my queen." He flicked the blade open and passed it to her, handle first, watching with obvious interest as she peeled away the outer skin to reveal the creamy pulp within.

After placing the fruit onto a palm leaf for the others to help themselves, she cut open a *goiaba* and tossed it to Ricky who caught it easily.

He took a big bite, speaking around a mouthful and revealing strong, white teeth in the process. "This is good. That *chica* could be right. We can't go wandering into the jungle with no map and no food. I vote we follow the road."

Zane folded his arms. "It's obvious that runway belongs to a cartel. What if the road only leads to their compound?"

"And what if it doesn't? Cheryl needs medical attention," Tai pointed out as he assisted his wife to the stretcher Delroy had dragged from the hide.

Delroy and Pearl helped themselves to fruit then Pearl placed her marmalade-colored jacket over a fallen log and perched on top. Delroy looked older this morning. Lines Bernie hadn't noticed previously carved across his forehead and bracketed his mouth. Maybe he was as sleep deprived as her.

She glanced over to where Cheryl had closed her eyes, too tired or too weak to partake in the argument raging around her. Her son sat beside her, devouring a *cupuazu*, the pulp smeared around his mouth and oozing through his fingers. He grinned when he caught Bernie watching him. "Easter eggs!"

Laughing, she added, "Yes, it does taste a bit like chocolate."

With sandy-fair hair, bright blue eyes and tiny freckles over his snub nose, Cody was a cute kid if a little on the thin side. Far too young to lose his mother.

"I've already told you people, we make for the road." Melanie, her mouth a narrowed hard line, stalked into the clearing and made for the pile of fruit. She tossed the toilet roll onto the ground, indifferent when it rolled into a puddle.

Elizabeth hissed in a breath and dived for it, throwing Melanie an annoyed glare as she placed the roll onto a branch to dry.

Bernie crossed to where Nyle slouched against a tree trunk, his face gray with fatigue and pain, and handed him a piece of fruit.

Assuming an air of supreme indifference, Melanie chose the largest of the remaining pieces of fruit and joined Colin where she began a heated exchange that ended in Colin obediently eating. He sank onto his haunches, his shoulders hunched like he was guarding his food in a good imitation of an agitated primate.

About to rescind her earlier decision, Bernie frowned, suddenly realizing who was missing. She drew in a deep breath of humid, steamy air into her straining lungs. "Where's Rhoda and Tatum?"

Melanie shrugged, biting into her *goiaba*. "Tatum left the shelter about thirty minutes after you. Her mother took off ten or fifteen minutes later when the kid didn't return."

"You mean no one has seen either of them since..." Bernie checked her watch. "Six thirty? That's fifty minutes ago!"

Zane raked a hand through his hair. "Damn. I didn't realize. I was doing a recon of the camp."

"So what?" Melanie raised her hands in the air. "Who cares? They do nothing but whine and moan. The kid scratched and scratched all night and kept sniveling and crying. I didn't get a wink of sleep."

You are a total bitch. The words bubbled on Bernie's tongue. With the utmost restraint, she swallowed them. Starting a catfight would be a waste of time and energy.

Delroy exchanged a glance with his wife. "The screams last night may have frightened the girl and she's run off."

The knife fell from Bernie's suddenly nerveless fingers. "What screams?" Oh lordy, had it been Kit? "I know I was tired, but I'm certain I would have heard screaming."

"Don't fret, girl. It was before you and Zane returned. It didn't last long enough for me to work out which direction the sound came from, but it sure sounded like a woman." Face grim, he shook his head. "No way could I sleep after that."

"A woman?" croaked Bernie, the blood in her veins freezing colder than death.

"No way! You a fool, Delroy. It was a monkey. They be all around us," scoffed Ricky.

"That would be *Mr Lewis* to you, boy."

Ricky flicked him the finger.

Unable to utter another word, Bernie rose stiffly to her feet and reached for her staff. If Kit had fallen into the hands of those thugs...if she'd been hurt, killed...how could she ever live with herself? *And where was I? Hiding in the shadows with a thief.*

"I'll come with you." Zane scooped up the knife and a spear. His firm tone brooked no argument.

Having him by her side was proving far more reassuring than she'd ever believed possible. Nodding, she looked at each member of their small group, her voice husky as she said, "Everyone stay quiet. It may be a good idea to be packed and ready to leave the moment we return."

"Don't you worry none. We'll get right onto that." Delroy wiped his palms on his trouser legs and moved over to the hide.

"Which direction did Rhoda and Tatum take?"

Rolling her eyes, Melanie sighed and gestured. "That way."

Bernie set off with Zane. In silence, they pushed through the jungle, Zane taking the lead. The trail was easy to follow with broken branches where someone had rushed past in a hurry and two sets of footprints set deep in the mud.

"The scream they heard?" She eventually forced the question past her numb lips.

"It could have been a monkey."

"If we hadn't gone to the village, we could have checked it out last night. We may have been in time to help her."

He stopped and turned around, placing his fingers under her chin, his touch a whisper of warmth on her cold skin. "Don't go there, Bernie. There is no way we can know who was hurt—if anyone—or what happened. If anything."

"But..." Scalding tears burned at the back of her eyes, blurring the concern on his face.

"If your sister is anything like you, she's resourceful. Wherever she is, we'll find her."

"You shouldn't make promises you can't or have no intention of keeping." Bernie found a handkerchief in her small pack and after dislodging his hand, blew her nose. When she finished, she stuffed the crumpled cotton away then realized he hadn't moved.

He stood curiously still, staring at her. An implacable expression veiled his eyes and there was a taut cast to his features that sent a shiver scurrying along her bones. "I always keep my word."

The deep inflection in his soft voice made her wonder whether he referred to something or someone other than her sister. She suspected he did—a man of secrets. A pertinent fact to remember, especially as the blasted fellow had wriggled his way beneath her defenses.

Her composure carefully reconstructed, she raised her chin. "It'll be lunchtime soon. When are you going to get a move on?"

"One day, I'm going to accept that challenge you keep taunting me with." A grin tugging at his lips, he bent lower to examine the ground. "This way."

They walked on, until Zane indicated with a lift of his hand for her to stop. He sniffed the stifling air.

Bernie moved closer, taking a deeper breath of the hot, moist air and gagged. Slapping a hand over her mouth, she worked at controlling her retching.

The pungent stench of a decomposing body was unmistakable.

"Stay here," muttered Zane, before ducking beneath a low spreading palm with spiky branches.

No way was she staying put. She had to see, had to check what or who that stench belonged to. Heart pumping, her body feeling as brittle as dried out sticks, she followed to where Zane was pulling aside a thicket of ferns to reveal two prone bodies.

He fell onto his knees in the dirt and looked up at her. "Looks like a couple of mercenaries. And they certainly didn't die of natural causes."

Relief was as powerful as a punch to her gut. Her legs gave way and she folded, joining him on the ground. Keeping her eyes averted from the dried blood and the industrious insects swarming over the remains, she mumbled, "How long have they been here?"

"Hard to say given this humidity, which would hasten decay. I'd hazard a guess, no longer than a day."

"Could one of them have screamed?"

He shrugged, rubbing a hand along his jaw and scrambling to his feet. He scanned the flattened bracken. "I think there was a struggle over here and by the quantity of blood near that log, they died there and were then moved to their current position."

"But by who? Unless there was a falling out of thieves."

"Hey! Don't look at me that way whenever you mention the word *thieves*. It's losing its fun appeal."

The snappiness in his voice snuffed out her snarky response. She pushed to her feet, wiping the mud off her bottom and said in a milder tone, "Since there are no other dead bodies lying about and no one's popped out from behind a bush to say hello, I bet whoever else was here escaped."

"It's an endless source of fascination to me how you leap to these conclusions without one single shred of concrete evidence."

So much for her attempt to wave the olive branch. The blasted man was having a jab at her. Sniffing, she stomped off to peer under a pile of broken palm fronds. "There's more footprints here."

"You're a regular Miss Marple," he drawled.

"And you are an honorless thief!"

"There. Do you feel better now you've got it off your chest?"

Doing her best to ignore his goading, she hunched over, her gaze tracking the mash of indentations in the mud. "Let's see where these lead to. We might find other passengers."

Zane checked the time. "Half an hour, Bernie. I don't like leaving our lot by themselves too long. They could scatter every which way and we'll waste the rest of the day searching for them."

"I agree."

They set off again, but at a pace made faster as whoever had passed through the jungle before them had cut a wider path. From the corner of her eye, Bernie caught Zane looking at his watch again and knew he was about to urge her to turn back.

A few more feet. Please, only a few more. I know Kit is close by. I can feel her.

Her chest tightened, her throat closed, panic surging like an adrenaline shot. She broke into a jog.

If Kit was in danger, then she had to do whatever it took to help her. Ducking beneath low hanging branches, she pushed her way through thick foliage. God knew what lay ahead, but she had to take the chance that whoever had murdered those mercenaries was long gone.

She faltered when Zane demanded she stop but her gut instinct urged her to continue. She took a few precious seconds to peer around a walking palm before bursting into a small clearing, Zane a few steps behind.

Her gaze immediately zeroed onto a massive tree and she rushed over. From between the twisted roots, she pulled out a large pack which she instantly recognized.

"Look..." Her voice turned thick and gruff. "Kit was here. This is her gear."

She collapsed to her knees, scrubbing at the tears flooding her cheeks. Kit may have been here at one stage, but there was no trace of her now. And Bernie had no idea in which direction to search.

~ 9 ~

Voices raised in anger could be heard from several yards away when they arrived back at the hide.

"Someone has lost their sand bucket and is not playing nice." Zane sent Bernie a loaded glance.

"I wish they'd keep their voices down."

"We could always try gagging them," he said drily.

Her answering smile was brief and he'd bet his last pound, her thoughts were centered on her sister. During their return journey, she'd argued vehemently for continuing to search for the other group.

On one hand, he knew it made sense to catch up with Bernie's sister and her companions. Safety in numbers held a lot of appeal. But burdened by an injured woman on a stretcher and Nyle with his twisted ankle and bunged-up shoulder, Zane doubted that was a possibility. If the mercenaries were hot on the other group's heels, all those thugs had to do was slow down or turn back, and this group would walk straight into their arms. Quite possibly, what awaited them would be torture, then death.

And Zane had no intention of dying any day soon.

Before they'd turned back, he and Bernie had lost the trail of Rhoda and her daughter. Those two could be anywhere by now. It had been a hard decision for him to make, but the two women were on their own. He had to hope that somehow, they'd elude the mercenaries and find safety.

Bernie marched past him to her pack and made a show of heaving it onto her slim shoulders. He knew she'd shoot him down if he offered to carry it, so he rammed down his concern and funneled his irritation elsewhere.

There certainly were plenty of available targets. Except for Delroy who paced the length of the camp, and Tai speaking softly to his wife, the other passengers were all loafing about, chowing down on the last of the fruit and guzzling their precious hoard of bottled water.

Not his mother, of course. She sat on a log with Cody, telling the kid a story about a squirrel and his friend, a badger. The glares she directed at Ricky and Melanie spoke volumes.

"We're supposed to be rationing our supplies." Zane strode over and yanked a bottle from Ricky's greedy clutches.

"Hey man, give over. This humidity is a killer."

"No, you listen. Everyone listen. This is not some picnic we're on. Until we find a village and help, no more eating or drinking whenever you feel like it. And keep quiet."

Melanie curled her lips into a snarl. "We've held a vote and we're taking the road to civilization."

"I told you..."

"Whatever."

She waved a hand in the air so abruptly Colin, who sat on the ground scribbling away in a small notebook, shied like a startled horse and dropped his pencil. The guy had a serious problem with his nerves.

Melanie huffed. "No one cares, Zane. If you and your nerdy girlfriend want to stay lost in this jungle forever, go for it. The rest of us are off to that village."

Zane sucked in a sharp breath, his gaze travelling around the group. Delroy stopped walking, but avoided returning his gaze.

"Who else thinks the village is our best chance?" Zane said.

Colin didn't answer, simply tucking his pad and pencil into his shirt breast pocket. But he looked at Melanie, as if she spoke for the both of them.

"Sorry, Zane, but I can't *not* risk finding medical help for my wife." Tai met his eyes steadily. "If your mother, Bernie and yourself want to part company with us, that's your choice. Although, I'd prefer if we remained together."

"Any sign of that woman and her daughter?" asked Nyle.

"We found tracks, but lost them further into the jungle. They were heading east."

"Damn." Shoulders slumped, Nyle reached down and slapped at an insect near his ankle.

"We can always follow the other group. Maybe catch up with them," Bernie piped up.

Zane could have taken her by the shoulders and shook her until her teeth fell from her head. Didn't she realize the folly in giving people too many choices? But another division in opinion didn't eventuate. The others were dead set on that bloody village.

He scooped up the last *goiaba* and stuffed it into his duffle before crossing to his mother. "I believe we should stick together. At least until we make the village."

"I agree, but the village is *not* a good idea. Drug runners are difficult to deal with, and I doubt they'd honor any agreement to take us to safety no matter how much money we offer." His mother touched his hand, gazing into his face. "Lead the passengers to the road, then we can take our own path."

He shook his head. "I can't do that, Mom. With the stretcher and Nyle's injuries, they'll need every able-bodied man to reach the village."

"That's their choice." Her eyes grew diamond hard. "I won't lose my son because of their stupidity."

"Bernie is hell-bent on finding her sister," he muttered, his gaze seeking and finding the only other woman apart from his mother and sister who had the power to terrify him with her choices.

Bernie was busy inspecting Nyle's arm where he'd pushed up his sleeve. No doubt checking for insect bites. As Zane watched, she pulled out a small vial from her pack and smeared ointment on the bloke's skin.

"You could always throw her over your shoulder and carry her off to your cave," Elizabeth said drily.

Astonished, he swung back to gape at her.

She burst into laughter. "I was joking, Zane."

"I'm glad someone finds our situation funny," snapped Pearl, her back poker-straight as she rose to her feet. "Delroy, I believe it's high time we made a move."

Everyone gathered up blankets, spears and bags, and debated who was on stretcher duty first. Zane picked up the rope before handing each man a spear.

"You're going with them, aren't you?" Bernie marched over to his side, eyeing him as if he was a strange insect stuck on a pin.

"Yes, as far as the village perimeter. They need my help." He hesitated, the words he wanted to say drying on his tongue. *Get a grip, pal. What makes you think you know what you're doing here?* His experience with survival in the jungle might be limited, but he did know one thing for certain—if he had to, he could kill.

Her gaze slid past him. "What about the bodies we found? Are you going to tell the others?"

"I figure that's on a need-to-know basis."

"Might be one way of impressing the necessity for quiet."

"True. But we don't want a full-scale panic on our hands either."

She swallowed. He watched the movement of her throat, remembering how satiny soft her skin had felt beneath his mouth. Desire nipped hot and savage in the ball of his gut. Curling his hands into fists, he shifted his stance and made to move away, denying the need to beg her to remain with them and not take off on her own. His mother's words about tossing her over his shoulder held a lot of merit.

"I'll come with you. But only as far as the village. If we hurry, we can be there by midday," she said. "Then I'll track down the other group. I'll have the remainder of the afternoon to cover ground."

"You won't be alone. I'll be with you." He leaned closer, his lips a hair's breadth from her face and whispered, "I made a promise."

Her eyes were the deepest of blue sapphires, sparkling with a relief she couldn't mask until she ducked her head. That intriguing curve to her mouth played havoc with his imagination. He wanted to taste it. His chest expanded. He stepped forward, raising his hand, the temptation to touch her too strong to ignore.

"*Stop.* Get away from my pack," roared Colin.

For fuck's sake! Zane whirled around.

Colin and Ricky were playing a tug-o'-war over Colin's brown, waterproof pack while the others stopped and gaped with startled expressions. No one moved to pull the men apart.

"I bet you've got a secret stash of food. Give over, man. I'm hungry." Ricky's easy smile had vanished. His eyes were narrowed, his lips pulled back over his teeth.

"You don't know what you're doing. You'll ruin my samples." The tic near his eye pulsing fast, Colin slammed his open palm against Ricky's left ear making the boy splutter a curse.

A flock of parrots perched in the canopy, joined in a loud chorus of high-pitched squabbling. Three brown woolly monkeys with their long tails, watching from a nearby branch, scampered higher into the canopy and began emitting hoarse barks. The racket was bound to capture the attention of any nearby mercenary. Even a deaf person would investigate.

Two long strides and Zane solved the issue by kicking Ricky's legs out from under him then reefed the pack from Colin's clutch. Ricky fell to the ground, spitting out curses. Colin fell to his knees, his hands falling slackly to his sides as he stared with pleading eyes up at Zane.

In a heartbeat, Melanie was on the ground beside Colin. She wrapped her arms around his waist, leaning close. "It's okay, babe. It's okay."

Colin jerked out of her grasp, his eyes dilated and staring as he pointed at her. "I should never have listened to you. What was I thinking?"

"Come on, pal. Get your shit together." Zane crouched down and held out the pack. "See? It's all sealed, nice and tight."

Ripping it from his hands, Colin pressed the pack to his heaving chest. "Thank you. Thank you."

"Hey, that's not fair. How come he gets to keep his food and water all to himself." Ricky bounced to his toes, about to plough into round two.

Surging to his feet, Zane blocked him. "Don't even think about it. Can't you see the man isn't well?"

"Who cares? We need water. We need food." Ricky punctuated each word with a jab of his fist in the air.

"Maybe if you had demonstrated some restraint, our situation wouldn't be this critical."

"Chill, man."

Since clocking the fool wasn't an option, Zane turned his back and concentrated instead on Colin. Bending down, he gripped the other man's shoulder. "How you doing there, Colin? All good?"

Colin flinched, as if roused from a world only he could see. "I must check." Breathing noisily, he tore at the buckles, yanked open the flap and tugged the zipper open. Reaching into the bag, he withdrew a clear, insulated cylinder with a screw-topped lid. Inside was a wad of cotton wool and some type of plant. His sigh was long and loud. His shoulders rounded.

"This, ladies and gentlemen, is our future." His high-pitched voice shook as he held the cylinder up for everyone to see.

"This guy is *loco*." Ricky sniggered.

"He isn't crazy. He's a brilliant scientist, if you must know," Melanie fired back before softening her voice and adding, "Babe, put it back. We must keep the samples safe."

Bernie approached and kneeled on the ground. "You've discovered something important, haven't you? What is it, you do exactly?"

"I'm a bio-chemist. I've devoted the past twenty-five years of my life searching for a cure for the common cold virus amongst the plants of the Amazon rainforest." Colin carefully packed the vial back inside his bag with trembling hands.

Melanie nodded, her chin lifting with pride. "I've been his assistant for the last nine years. No one can match Colin for his devotion to his work."

"You've lived here, then? In the Amazon?" Bernie asked.

"Yes. It's been tough." Melanie sighed. "Most of the time it was just us and one or two natives as guides. Finally, we'll be rewarded for our efforts."

Colin re-opened the compartment, checked the lid of the vial muttering, "My research suggests I've found a plant extract that will surpass all others.

Have you any idea what this will mean to the world? One inoculation and a person will be cured for life—of all viruses, even cancers. Less sickness, stronger immune systems, and with further research, I'm hoping life-spans will increase. This could be a new era for all of humanity."

"That's wonderful." Bernie smiled.

Ricky snorted. "Say again? All that from bits of grass?"

"You're an idiot." Melanie glared at him, a tigress protecting her mate.

In response, the boy yawned widely.

Melanie boasted, "This discovery will prove to the world Colin's genius."

"Dosh is the only thing that matters," sneered Ricky with a disparaging glance at Colin's backpack. "You can't tell me that weed is worth anything."

"You'd be surprised how much we've already been offered."

Colin stopped fussing over his bag, snapping, "Melanie! For God's sake. I've made my decision."

Melanie spread her hands wide. "We need to keep our options open, babe. There's time to change our minds."

"I refuse to discuss this further. I wish I'd never listened to you. I wish I'd never contacted that pharmaceutical company. My discoveries belong to the world. If we're not rescued soon...if my samples die..." Colin's voice became choked. He stopped speaking as he checked the pocket flaps were secure. Again. His mouth shut tighter than a poacher's trap while hot, angry blood infused Melanie's face making her look as if she might explode.

Ricky sniggered. "Sounds like trouble in paradise, *chica*."

Flicking mud from her clothes, Melanie glared at him.

Zane blew out an exasperated breath catching the amused glint in Bernie's eyes when she glanced up at him. She turned back to Colin and with a gentle smile, held out a hand to help him to his feet. He rose, hugging his pack, his gaze darting in all directions like a crazed hornet.

"Can we go now?" demanded Pearl, hands on hips, her gazed fixed on Colin.

As if sensing Zane's attention, she met his eyes with an expressionless face. For some odd reason, his blood turned icy.

Placing a hand on the trunk behind him, Nyle dug his make-shift crutch into the mud and lurched to his feet. "Please, yes. For the love of heaven, I can't take any more domestics."

Wiping sweat from his forehead, Zane couldn't agree more.

⟲ 10 ⟳

If he'd thought it was stifling in the jungle, it wasn't much better trudging down the road that wound with drunken abandon through the jungle. For the umpteenth time, Zane twisted around to check those strung out behind like a tattered ribbon, then gazed to where Bernie marched along, her pack bobbing on her back, Cody chattering away by her side.

How she managed to appear cool, crisp and cheerful despite the heat was beyond him. He felt as snarly as a caged tiger. Apart from Cody and Bernie, no one else spoke. Zane figured everyone else felt much the same as him.

The day remained overcast, the dark clouds threatening to release another deluge at any moment. The chittering and squawking jungle sounds had hushed as if even the native birds and animals were oppressed by the humidity.

He swore he could see steam rising from the puddles of mud that now emitted that still-water stench. His polo shirt stuck to his back and sweat slicked his skin, rolling into every nook and cranny on his body. His muscles burned from the strain of being the forward stretcher-bearer. His body still ached from the crash and his eyes were gritty from lack of sleep.

All in all, he felt like shit and couldn't fight the sneaky thought that maybe his mother had been right. Maybe he should have let this group of strangers find their own way to the village. If he died out here, his birth mother's murderer would go forever unpunished. And that could never happen.

Damn. But neither could he walk away from the others. Not yet, anyway. His back straightened as renewed strength flowed through his veins. He'd see his vow through to the end. Nothing would stop him.

By his reckoning, the village wasn't too far off. Soon, he'd say goodbye and head back into the jungle with his mother and Bernie.

He jerked his chin toward a bend in the road. "Around that corner is the village."

"About time." Melanie surged forward.

"Wait!" Zane hissed.

She shot him an annoyed look, her pace faltering.

"There were mercenaries there last night. Let's try a little caution first."

Melanie gave a reluctant nod. "What do you suggest, Zane?"

"We split up. The rest stay out of sight, until we give the all clear."

"Why, man? We're gonna ask these dudes for help anyway? Why we got to hide?"

"Don't be a fool, Ricky. Do what the man, says,"

Delroy growled. "Best we scope out the situation, before we make our presence known."

"A good plan. We'll find somewhere on the eastern side of the road for the others to wait." Bernie stepped off the track and pushed her way past some ferns.

Grumbling under his breath, Ricky scrambled down the muddy slope. One by one the others followed.

Zane and Tai who held the tail-end of the stretcher were second last, leaving Delroy to brush a thick palm frond over their tracks before joining them.

They kept moving until they came across a small clearing where the ground was relatively dry, if squelchy underfoot. As soon as they placed Cheryl's stretcher carefully on the ground she opened her eyes to whisper a thank you.

Her pallid face wrenched at Zane's heart as he wondered how many hours she could hold on for. She certainly didn't deserve to rot in a jungle.

None of them did.

He held a finger to his lips and the others nodded, weariness etched deep into each face. His heart rate ratcheted up a notch and sweat trickled from his forehead as a familiar *whomp-whomp* gradually became louder.

Excited smiles chased away their gloom.

"A helicopter! We're saved." Melanie grabbed Colin by the hand and tugged him after her as she raced back to the road.

"For crying out..." Zane cut his gaze around the group, dropping his duffle to the ground. "No one else move until we get back."

"I'm coming with you." Bernie placed her heavier pack onto the ground.

"And me." Delroy stepped up.

Ricky pranced forward, all swagger and piss. "Hell, man, I'm coming too."

"Why don't we take a marching band as well?" Zane gritted his teeth.

Grinning, Bernie brushed past him. "Follow me."

The hell he would. No way would he put her first in any possible firing line. He hauled hard on the straps of her backpack, jerking her to a halt then, after exchanging a long glance with this mother, forged around her.

They made it back to the road in time to see Melanie and Colin pelting along the track. The pair reached the bend. Stopped. Then vaulted into the jungle on the opposite side.

A rumbled sounded in the distance. It only took him a second to realize the noise wasn't thunder but trucks. The sound came from the direction of the village.

Bloody hell. They had company.

"Come on." Zane led the way, crossing to the other side and sprinting to the spot where he'd seen the other two disappear.

Plunging into the undergrowth, he tracked their footprints until the jungle thinned out. He found them squatting behind a clump of bamboo, Colin hunched over his pack and shaking visibly.

Melanie waved them forward. "I think you're right. That doesn't look like a rescue team."

Zane followed her pointing finger as he crouched beside them, the others huddling close. Ahead lay the primitive village he and Bernie had located last night. Daylight didn't improve its appearance. The heavy gray clouds drifting slowly overhead, accented its bleakness.

A black helicopter had landed in the clearing and a small group of men were gathered outside the largest tent. At the edge of the village, three trucks with engines idling, stood with their noses aimed in the direction of the road.

A slighter body pressed close to his side and he breathed in the faint scent of Bernie. She gasped and pressed her fingers over her mouth. He didn't blame her.

There had to be eighteen or twenty men milling about in the mud and strapping on weapons. He recognized a variety of assault rifles, AK-47's mainly, and a few Bushmaster carbines. Each man had a gun belt with a pistol in a holster hanging from his hip, a hydration pack strapped to his back and sporting an expression almost as feral as the bunch of snapping, snarling pig-dogs straining at their leashes.

A guy with lieutenant bars on his shoulders strutted about, barking out orders. Not that Zane believed for one moment any of these felons were legitimate. He squinted, focusing in on the rifle their leader clasped in his left hand. A Co2 Injection Rifle? A tranquilizer gun?

Something more serious than mercenaries intent on some hunting fun was going on here. Or drug smugglers determined to eliminate any witnesses to their operation. All of which meant, someone from the plane was their target. And whoever these clowns were hunting was wanted alive.

He refrained from turning around and examining his companions. There'd be time for questions later. For now, they needed to retreat and put a bloody lot of distance between them and the village. Fast.

"There's nothing for us here." He motioned for everyone to move.

"They could have a satellite phone." Melanie's eyes narrowed.

Zane hesitated, recalling the expression on Cheryl's face. The woman needed help badly. "There isn't one."

"How do we know you're not lying to us?"

"Why the hell would I do that?"

Melanie shrugged. "You tell me." Mouth twisted, she glanced at the others as if seeking their support, but no one met her gaze.

Zane whispered furiously, "I *am* telling you. No phone. But I admit, that was last night and these guys weren't here."

"They must have come from somewhere," Bernie said in a low voice.

"Yeah." He rubbed his chin. "I bet there's a mercenary compound or drug processing facility not far." He froze. "They look like they're moving out."

The soldiers and their dogs began piling onto the backs of the trucks. The one giving orders swung into the passenger seat of the lead truck and with a lurch, the vehicle rolled into motion.

"Quick. Take cover." Zane dropped to his belly, yanking Bernie down beside him.

Barely breathing, no one moved an inch until the trucks had rumbled past and disappeared around the bend.

"We can't leave the others too long. Those there dogs..." Delroy muttered.

"I know." Zane lifted his head and studied the terrain.

Ricky fisted his hand. "Yo, man, we could take them on. *Mano-o-mano*."

"I count five near that tent. Two in the chopper and who knows how many we can't see. They have guns. All we have are spears. But Melanie is right. We have to check for some means of communication. But we can't risk being seen, Ricky."

The boy nodded.

Zane shifted into a crouch. His gaze sought Bernie's. "Stay here..."

Three gunshots cracked, stilling his voice. Birds squawked and rose shrieking from the trees. They wheeled away heading deeper into the jungle. As the echoes faded, silence fell. His skin crawled. He knew that feeling, the same feeling that accompanied impending disaster.

He suspected they were about to meet it, head-on.

～ 11 ～

A high-pitched scream shattered the steamy air.

A woman's scream.

Could it be Kit? Too hard to tell. Either way, Bernie had no intention of ignoring that cry of terror.

"I have to go." She tore a spear from Colin's hands, ignoring his startled jerk.

With her staff in her other hand, she wriggled off her smaller pack, dumped it and took off circling around in a semi-arc, intending to approach the village from the north side. Her sole focus on helping whoever had screamed.

The route she took wound further into dense foliage, but she had to maintain cover for as long as possible. Sweat stung her eyes. Every step forward a battle against a jungle determined to impede her progress.

"Bernie, hold up. Wait," came Zane's demand from somewhere behind her.

But she couldn't stop. Couldn't wait. Kit's life could be on the line. Seconds later, she paused to listen over the drum of her frantic heartbeats. A man shouted questions, demanding answers. Too far to hear the words but nothing could disguise the menace in his harsh tones.

She pushed through a tangle of vines, pulse pounding, her fear holding her thoughts captive in a tight fist.

A woman screamed again, terror and pain resonating in the sound that sent a flock of hyacinth macaws whirling through the branches above Bernie's head. The staff and spear slipped in her sweaty hands. A sob tore from her throat and she faltered. She didn't want to look. She wanted to find the deepest hole and never emerge into the unforgiving light.

But giving up wasn't in her vocabulary. No matter what lay ahead, she would never turn back. She would save her sister or die trying. Peering from behind a wide walking palm, she saw them. Four men beside a large tent. And two fair-haired women kneeling on the ground, shoulders slumped, heads lowered. Rhoda Bloomfield and her daughter.

Not Kit. Not her sister. Air punched from her chest and Bernie swallowed her relieved gasp, immediately guilt-ridden. Kit may not be among the captured, but two innocent women were well and truly in the mercenaries' evil grasp. Somehow, Bernie had to help.

Surrounding an open fire where a cooking pot was suspended from a crude, wooden tripod, were several villagers. Every one of them had their backs turned on the drama unfolding several yards away, unwilling to look and likely unwilling to give any aid either.

Leaves rustled as Zane joined her. Bernie shushed him before he could speak and pointed. One of the men, a stocky guy wearing white cowboy boots and waving a pistol that gleamed like gold, leaned over Rhoda. A torrent of hoarse Spanish words burst from his mouth. But he was too far away for Bernie to make them out.

He shouted again.

Rhoda shook her head violently.

Cowboy Boots viciously yanked Rhoda's hair, raising her head. Then shot her point-blank in the forehead.

He released his hold.

Rhoda crumpled—a blood soaked, motionless figure. Tatum erupted into scream after scream. Cowboy Boots pistol-whipped her across the face and Tatum subsided into heaving sobs.

"Oh...my...God..." whispered Bernie through numb lips, hardly daring to believe her eyes.

"Fuck." Zane gripped her shoulder.

Still with his back toward where they lay hidden, Cowboy Boots stalked toward the chopper, making whirling motions in the air with his left fore-finger. The two guys leaning against it, jumped inside.

A second later, the engine screamed into life as Cowboy Boots climbed on board. The chopper soared into the clouds and disappeared from view.

Bernie cut her gaze to Rhoda. The puddle of blood weeping from her head had widened. No way could she have survived a shot to the head. Two men held the arms of a squirming, sobbing Tatum. Another soldier paced back and forth, waving a knife and barking more Spanish.

Anger surged through Bernie, blinding her to danger. All she could see and all she could hear was Tatum; an innocent young girl, alone, terrified and defenseless—about to be tortured. She charged forward, holding the spear like a gladiator in an arena.

The fury of her attack forced the tip deep into the pacing soldier's waist. His shriek raised the hair on the back on her neck. Swearing and crying, he fell onto his side with his hands groping around his back as he attempted to reach the spear lodged in his flesh.

Ignoring him, she whirled her stick, knocking the pistol from another soldier's hand as he drew the weapon from his holster. Dimly, she heard an ominous click and braced herself for a bullet to rip into her body.

The shot went wild just as the man in front tackled her to the ground. In her peripheral vision, she saw a flash of movement and recognized Zane as he fought the remaining soldier, his fist smashing into the other man's chin. The next second, she was fighting for her life.

The soldier planted his hands around her neck, squeezing the air from her lungs. She bucked, hammered him with her fists, struggled to breathe. Darkness crushed her.

Her searching fingers found the soft spot at the base of her assailant's neck. Summoning her strength, she jabbed as hard as she could. He grunted. His hold slackened enough for her to drag in oxygen. With re-fueled desperation, she levelled a knee to his crotch. He squealed, rearing back, his weight easing off her prone body, so she could wriggle sideways.

Snarling, he loomed over her. Sunlight glinted off the knife he held. His gaze dropped to her neck.

Her hand closed over a stone on the ground and she raised it, slamming it against his fingers, causing him to drop the knife.

Zane appeared in her vision wearing a fierce, warlike face she hardly recognized. He locked his arms around the mercenary's neck and dragged him backwards. A choking noise gargled from the thug's throat.

Not wanting to watch, she used her elbows to pull herself over the muddy ground until she was well clear. Then, rolling onto her stomach, pushed to her hands and knees, before crawling to Tatum who'd curled into a ball.

The young girl let out a scream when Bernie gently touched her, then she flung her arms around Bernie's neck and sobbed. When those horrible, choking noises ceased, Bernie looked over her shoulder and met Zane's gaze.

"It's done," he said.

She shuddered at the terrible finality in those words, but didn't flinch from the question in his eyes. When she nodded, the lines of tension in his face faded. His dark eyes glowed with an emotion that thrilled her to her core and curled her toes. He'd killed a man, probably more than one, to save her. The thought should repulse her. But to save her own life and that of a relative stranger, she'd also been prepared to kill. Perhaps under the skin, Zane and she were more alike than she'd believed possible.

He allowed the man to slump to the ground and rose to his feet. His dark mahogany hair glowed like a fiery halo around his head. His shoulders were straight and strong enough to carry any burden. His body radiated power like a warrior of old. Like an avenging angel. And the tiny crack he'd splintered in her heart eleven months ago, spread a little wider, inviting him inside. Her belly quivered as he held her stare.

"Mom. Is Mom okay?" Tatum pulled out of her arms and went to scramble to her knees.

Breaking the connection, Bernie clasped the girl's hands, staying her movement. "No. Don't Tatum. Don't look. I'm so sorry. Your mother didn't make it."

Distant rifle shots rat-a-tatted deep in the jungle. Tiny hairs on her nape frizzled. Her gaze swept the village. Nothing. The villagers had scattered, no doubt hiding in their huts. Frowning, she looked toward the northern wall of impenetrable jungle. Squinted. Saw nothing, no one. Still the impression remained someone watched. But no one stepped forward to greet them. Or accost them. Probably another villager, too terrified to move.

Zane seized her in his arms and growled close to her ear. "What the hell were you thinking? You could have been killed."

"Ever heard of the element of surprise? Besides, we saw the other soldiers leave in the trucks."

"You mean you hoped they'd all left." Tilting her face toward him, he branded her lips in a hard, ruthless kiss. Easing back, he said through gritted teeth, "Time to go."

Shaking off her unease over the notion of an unseen observer, she allowed herself a few seconds to wallow in the comfort of his warmth before stepping aside and assisting Tatum. She wrapped an arm around the girl and led her away, leaving Zane to retrieve the weapons from the dead.

"But what about Mom? We can't leave her here. Not like that."

Zane busy tucking a long-bladed knife into a sheath, looked up. "Only bright spot is, we've now got weapons. Three rifles, a pistol, a spare round of ammo for each and a hunting knife. I'll carry them for now, if you can see to Tatum. But before we go, let's see what we can do for Mrs Bloomfield."

Giving the teenager's hands a quick squeeze, Bernie nodded. "I'll check the tents for a blanket to wrap her mother in. Tatum, wait over near the edge of the clearing for us, okay?"

After a cautious peep around the flap, although logic dictated anyone inside would have emerged by now to see what was going on, Bernie entered the largest tent. Two narrow camp beds. A few upended crates and nothing else.

No radio. No satellite phone.

But there were blankets on the beds.

Together she and Zane wrapped Rhoda Bloomfield as securely as possible within a woolen blanket. Fighting cramping nausea, her finger shook as she tucked the edges securely around the lifeless body. They both hoped the villagers would see to her burial. If they had time, Bernie knew Zane would have ensured the poor woman was buried with respect. But at any moment, a truck load of soldiers could return.

It was time to go.

They needed to re-join the others and leave what had happened here behind. But she'd never forget

113

witnessing Rhoda's death or seeing her brains splattered over the ground. The knowledge Bernie hadn't hesitated to kill another human being sat as sour as decay in her soul.

No. She could never forget.

~ 12 ~

Leading the way to where they'd left the injured under Tai and his mother's care, Zane fought the roil in his gut as he recalled those last few moments. It had been a long time since he'd experienced such a rush of sheer terror. Terror that a woman he cared for, would be cut down before his eyes and he'd be unable to save her.

But Bernie had a warrior's soul, she was no push-over. And he was no longer a scared child, but a man molded by his past and honed by his career to kick ass. This time, they'd prevailed against death. Next time, they might not be so lucky. Every instinct he possessed warned that next time wasn't far away.

Tension squeezed his chest as he checked his compass readings. He murmured to Bernie, who trudged at his side, "The road should be about thirty yards to our right. I reckon we're about parallel with the clearing. It's time we broke cover."

Ashen-faced, she nodded silently.

Turning, he motioned for everyone to follow. The

foliage thinned, allowing him to pick up the pace, and soon he could see the muddy track ahead. A quick check in both directions revealed the road to be empty, but he hesitated. In the distance came the unmistakable grind of gears and low rumble of a single truck approaching.

"We can't wait. They could cut us off from the others," Bernie pointed out quietly.

Zane nodded. "Come on. Get your asses across this road, fast." Gripping Bernie by the elbow, he headed for the concealment offered by the jungle on the other side.

The noise of the engine grew louder, now accompanied by the splash of tires through water and the creak of old springs.

"Sounds like one truck. Probably returning to the village." Or the mercenaries could well be fanning out all along the road, cutting off any possibility of Zane and his group heading west. His heart rate ratcheted up a notch and sweat trickled from his forehead as he wound further into the jungle.

With a loud grunt the engine stopped.

"Oh shit. They've seen us," Melanie said, eyes wide and staring over the hand she'd pressed to her mouth.

He held a finger to his lips and the others nodded. Fear was etched into each face as they followed his example when he sank to a crouch. No one moved. No one spoke as they waited and listened for the rush of pounding footsteps.

A door opened with a rusty squeal. Slammed shut. The faint tang of cigarette smoke drifted through the bushes. No indication of the hunting dogs, thank God.

Some guy laughed. A little of the tension cramping Zane's muscles eased.

He shifted, whispering in Bernie's ear, "Didn't see us."

"Then what are they doing?" she murmured back.

Good question. One he'd thought he'd already figured out.

His gaze met her wide eyes. "I have to see what's happening. Stay here. Don't make a sound."

Tatum drew a deep breath, her eyes glazed, like she was about to burst into tears. Moving quickly, Bernie slung an arm around the girl's shoulders, pulling her close and rubbing her back.

Delroy muttered, "You'll need back up, man."

"Exactly." Bernie's fierce gaze zeroed in on Zane. She eased the shaking teenager from her arms. "Tatum. You mustn't make a sound. Ricky will look after you until I get back. Okay?"

The girl managed a nod.

Mouth opening as if about to argue, Ricky closed it again when Zane shook his head, saying, "Wait ten minutes. If we're not back or you hear the mercenaries coming, get back to the others."

"Will do, Zane." Ricky gave Tatum's shoulder an awkward pat.

"You two." Zane looked at Melanie and Colin. "Stay with them."

As quietly as possible, he eased forward, taking care not make too much noise as he led the way to the road.

A man shouted in Spanish. Through the thinned-out foliage, Zane could see the press of men sitting on the hard seats of the open truck. Leaning against the

117

front grill, a mercenary dragged hard on a cigarette then exhaled a plume of smoke into the air.

Zane judged that the distance between their scouting party and the mercenaries to be no more than fifteen yards.

The smoker tossed his butt into the mud and snapped an order in Spanish. From around the side of the nearest truck, four men carrying rifles harried three natives in front of them. One was grabbed roughly and pushed off to the side. The soldiers forced the other two to their knees. The smoker took his pistol from his holster, walked up to the nearest captive, pressed the barrel to the side of his head.

Fired. The native fell to the ground, blood flowing into the puddles.

Fucking hell! Jaw clenched, Zane raised his rifle.

Delroy pushed the muzzle down, roughly. "No way, man. There be too many of them."

Too late. The mercenary dealt the same treatment to the other kneeling native.

"May the good Lord have mercy," Delroy said, the shock in his quiet words echoing Zane's thoughts.

Beside him, Bernie hugged her belly, struggling to hold in her distress.

The asshole walked up to the sole remaining captive, wailing and beating his chest. The soldier waved his pistol about and snarled a mish-mash of Spanish and local dialect. The guards stepped away and the captive took to his heels, disappearing into the jungle. The soldiers climbed into the truck. With a jolt, the truck started and trundled further down the road back toward the village.

Breathing hard, Zane glared into the distance. He

should have killed the bastard. Should have done something to help those poor natives.

Bernie whispered in his ear, "You did the right thing. We were outnumbered, and they would have easily found the others. We would all have died."

Maybe, maybe not. Those assholes were after a specific person. He'd stake his life on it.

After a second, Bernie added, "He killed those poor men to show what will happen if anyone helps us."

"Yeah, that's what I figured. You speak Spanish?"

"Enough to get by."

Sick to his gut, Zane indicated for everyone to retreat. They melted back the way they'd come. When they joined the others, he retailed what had happened as well as what Bernie had heard.

Hand to her mouth, Tatum turned away and retched onto the ground. Bernie went to her side, offering her water and the comfort of her embrace. Something he wouldn't mind receiving himself.

Clearing his throat, he said, "We need to get out of this area. If we use the streams, we may throw the dogs off our scent."

Bernie looked over her shoulder at him. "We can use monkey urine to disguise our trail."

"Nice one." He grimaced.

"Why is this happening?" Colin clutched his hair, tugging until the thin strands stood straight up from his scalp. "They'll never get my samples. Never."

"Easy, babe," soothed his girlfriend. "They're not after us."

"We couldn't help them, Zane." Pinning him with a flat stare, Delroy re-positioned his rifle.

The sight of the dead natives too raw in his mind to discuss, Zane muttered, "Let's get moving. I have a feeling those bastards will try and herd us back to the runway. Easier for them to pick us off, one-by-one." Or capture the person they were looking for. He studied the shell-shocked faces surrounding him. "We've got to find another way out of the jungle."

～ 13 ～

They'd been hacking their way through the thick undergrowth for over four hours, the muffled barking of dogs driving them forward, a reminder of what lay behind if they were caught.

After re-grouping, Zane had brought the others up to speed, keeping details short and to the point. But nothing could dilate the horror that had taken place. In silence, they'd set a cracking pace, given the restriction of hauling a stretcher. No complaints. No arguments. And no one had offered a logical reason for the mercenaries' actions.

Grimacing, Bernie pushed a lock of limp hair from her eyes. If she lived to be a hundred, she doubted her mind would ever be rid of the terror-filled eyes of the native before his face was blown away.

Tears of exhaustion hovered one blink away. It wouldn't take much, and she'd fold into a shaking mess, huddling in the mud, begging for this nightmare to cease.

To think, only three days ago, she'd been on her

way to São Paulo de Olivença, excited at the possibility of unearthing the ancient lost city of the were-jaguar. She'd been eager to be in the presence of her mentor and friend, Professor Kowalski. When she'd received his email, the lure of a legend had her ditching her plans of visiting her father in the States. Instead, she'd caught the next flight out of foggy London to Rio. How could she resist?

Her mouth had watered at the prospect of searching for an ancient civilization and bringing lost history to light. The professor had refrained from giving the exact location of the dig, advising he'd have guides waiting for her at the hotel. But she'd immediately sensed the barely restrained anticipation in his brief message. The find would be ground-breaking in their small field of archaeology, and the careers of the team involved would be made.

"They're steering us in the direction they want us to go." A few long strides and Zane was beside her, taking a break from being one of the stretcher-bearers.

She checked the small compass on her watch. "I know. We've been moving uphill the past hour. What are we going to do? Once we're out in the open on that runway...at least the jungle offers places to hide."

"Yeah." Zane sighed. "It'll be night soon and we need to find shelter and food."

A quick glance revealed the lines of fatigue bracketing the mouth she'd dreamed of kissing, over and over. A flood of what-ifs and might-have-beens tumbled through her mind. "I haven't heard any planes. Why aren't they searching for us?"

"It's a large area to cover."

She frowned, probing that quiver of uneasiness prickling her flesh. "All planes carry tracking devices, don't they?"

"Transponders. Plus, there's radar. But here's the thing, Bernie." Zane lowered his voice before continuing. "Before we landed? I believe you were right and we were flying way too low. And if that's the case, the plane would *not* have registered on any radar."

"But...surely..." she paused, her mind whirling. Swallowing, she began again. "Are you saying we were deliberately flying too low?"

"The thought crossed my mind." He jerked his thumb in the direction behind them. "These guys are hunting a particular person. I'd stake my life on it."

"I...I don't believe it."

"You know what, Bernie? You can damn well believe what you like about me, and that bloody amulet. But you need to get it through that stubborn head of yours that you, me, and everyone else here, is in deep shit. One of those assholes carried a tranquilizer rifle."

"Maybe he's hunting a jaguar or something." *Jaguar.* Her father's words echoed inside her head and she shivered, despite the heat. *Oh God.* She could be the reason they were being hunted and picked off one by one.

Her stomach rolled over. Nausea rose to the base of her throat, hot and sour. If she hadn't invited her sister to join the dig, Kit wouldn't be lost in the jungle, at risk of capture or death. And Bernie could do nothing to save her.

Zane muttered a vicious curse beneath his breath

and something about pig-headed women who thought they knew everything.

Her face flamed, the heat blooming over her cheeks and down her neck. Maybe he was right. Maybe she needed to rid herself of her prejudice borne mostly, from a childhood where her father's career had taken him away from her. It wouldn't be easy though, when Zane's charming smile and quiet confidence reminded her so much of her father.

And there was still that matter of the stolen artifact and Zane's disappearance at the same time.

"I doubt he's hunting an animal trophy to put on his wall," he sniped.

"Okay. Okay, I get it, alright? I realize our situation is precarious. But I still think you're jumping to conclusions." She shook her head, inwardly cursing the hurt he'd inflicted with his sarcasm.

Mouth clamped shut, he lengthened his stride as if keen to rid himself of her company leaving her staring at his back and wishing they'd met in another place, another time.

If she could only pretend those brief, wonderful moments in his arms had never happened, moments she couldn't risk re-living. Because although he'd stepped up and risked his life for strangers, doubts still flooded her.

His survival skills were impressive but more than that, his effortless manner in shouldering responsibility had won her reluctant respect. He'd said he was on holidays, but remained silent about what he did for living. Really, she knew next to nothing about him. Whatever secret he hid must be bloody dark and scary.

Sighing, she rubbed her fingers against her aching temple remembering how, for one crazy moment, she'd wondered if he was the Jaguar. That lingering suspicion kept her from sharing her worst nightmare—that she was responsible for their terrifying predicament. That she agreed with Zane, totally. Those cartel soldiers had been at the runway for a reason. Which meant, the plane had been expected to land there. Ergo, either the pilot or co-pilot—or even both—were involved.

But it made no sense for her to be the reason. She had no enemies. She was an archaeologist, devoted to her career. She had no criminal connections. Unless she counted the man walking by her side.

Her gentle sister certainly had no enemies. Their parents were wealthy, sure, their mother coming from old English money. Their father had risen from a much poorer background. Since his tenure as governor though, he'd received his fair share of threats and security challenges.

This man-hunt through the jungle could be with the intention of demanding a ransom. But by executing their captives, the mercenaries eliminated their bargaining chips. So much for that idea then.

Which only left the passengers.

If the mercenaries had gotten wind of Colin's discovery, they could be after it themselves. A rogue pharmaceutical company could have hired them. Or if one of the passengers *was* the Jaguar, it could be him or her they were after—especially, if he'd double-crossed them.

Round and round her thoughts spun. Pain stabbed behind her right eye so savagely, she could have wept.

She really needed to talk, to share, with someone.

Zane. His name whispered in her mind, threading its way through her senses and tugging hard on her heart. Longing to bury her face in her hands and hide from his too-discerning eyes, her footsteps slowed. Then she recalled the scrap of paper she'd found on the runway. She'd stuffed it inside her pack at the time and with all that had happened, had forgotten about it. Her fingers itched to zip open her pocket and reef the damn thing out and read it.

Zane swung around and marched back to her side, pinning her with sharp eyes. "What is it? Are you hurt? Have you thought of something?"

Startled he'd sensed her distraction so easily, she flung him a glance. Her hands trembled, and she raised them to grip the straps of her pack to steady herself. *Go on, what have you got to lose?* She opened her mouth.

A muffled gunshot echoed through the jungle. Monkeys squealed and shook branches. Birds squawked and fluttered through leaves. Lizards and who-knew-what rustled through the undergrowth.

Bernie jumped, her heart racing. Everyone halted in their tracks, heads turning in all directions to see where the danger threatened.

"Relax. That gunshot came from quite a distance away." Zane touched Bernie's arm, all trace of his former irritation gone from his face as he sent her a reassuring smile.

How he remained so calm, boggled her mind. Her first instinct was to run and keep running.

Delroy, who was forward stretcher-bearer, glanced over his shoulder and scowled. His dark face shiny with sweat. "I ain't stopping. We should keep moving, put as many miles between us and those animals as possible."

"I think we should circle back and make for the runway," Melanie said with a defiant toss of her head.

Tai spoke through his teeth. "We discussed this, Melanie. It's too dangerous. Bernie and Zane believe our best bet is finding a river and following it east."

"The natives live by the river. It's their life blood and once we find a village, there will be boats we can use to travel downstream," Bernie patiently repeated what she'd said earlier.

These facts were something Melanie should be well aware of, as she'd been living in the Amazon for some time now with Colin. Frowning, Bernie shifted the weight of her pack, hoping to ease that niggling feeling in her shoulders.

"A river?" Colin blinked as if just awakening from a sleep. "I rather thought we were travelling uphill."

Zane sighed. "It's the soldiers. They're attempting to force us back toward the crash site while we're trying to head east."

"So, we're heading to the runway after all." Melanie sounded triumphant as if she'd scored a point.

Zane checked his compass. "No, we're still moving north-east. But we must be walking over the lower slopes of where the land rises to form the plateau where the runway is situated."

Bernie eyed Melanie. The other woman had made that weird comment after the natives had been killed, indicating the mercenaries weren't after her or Colin. How could she have known that?

"I don't understand anything that's going on here."

Colin fiddled with his glasses, his hand shaking.

"I want to go home. Mommy, Mommy, wake up. Take me home." Cody began to sob.

"Will someone keep that kid quiet?" snapped Melanie. "They'll hear us."

Elizabeth moved to where Cody bawled beside the stretcher, his father unable to help as he was holding the rear poles. "There, there, love. Look what I've got for you. It's a special treat, but you have to be a good boy and stop crying," she said softly and held out a small chocolate bar.

"Chocolate!" Cody's tears evaporated. He hiccupped, glancing first to his mother's still form and then his father who nodded and smiled.

"It's okay, mate. Say, thank you to the nice lady."

"Thank you." Cody took the chocolate and unwrapped it. "Yummy."

"Why don't I get a chocolate? I'm a good boy." A smiling Ricky winked at Elizabeth.

She gazed back at him, deadpan. "I don't think so."

Bernie recoiled a little at the flatness of the elderly woman's stare when she turned around. It held a surprising coldness that disappeared quickly as Elizabeth met her gaze and smiled.

Despite the crash and the rigors of their journey, the older woman's back was straight, her demeanor determined and her vigor undiminished. She carried an aura of alertness about her, like she was braced and ready to meet any danger head-on. She bore little resemblance to the soft-looking lady in her pristine pants suit, Bernie had met on the plane. It was if she'd morphed into a different person.

Bernie slapped at a mosquito and shivered.

"Now that's settled, let's get going," Delroy said.

Faces grimly resigned, heads lowered, everyone followed Zane as he led them deeper and deeper into the jungle.

~ 14 ~

With nightfall a heartbeat away, the jungle darkened into a well of shadow where danger lurked behind every leaf and bush. They'd continued their trek leaving only an hour to organize shelter before total darkness shrank their world to the width of a flashlight beam. Thunder rumbled in the distance, threatening another storm could bear down on them at any moment.

Hating the stickiness of her sweat-coated body, Bernie scratched at her itchy scalp. This blasted humidity was murder. Her legs felt filled with concrete, each step harder than the one before with rest still some hours away. She stared thoughtfully at the proposed camp site, studying the contours of the terrain, before turning to Zane.

"Are we at the base of the ridge?"

He drew the back of his hand over the beads of moisture shining on his forehead. "Yeah, I think the runway isn't too far away. But the good news is, we've worked our way around to the opposite side to where the plane came down."

"I guess that's something." Bernie pressed a hand to her forehead as Elizabeth wrapped Tatum in her soft shawl drawing her away from the others.

"We'll need to keep a watch." Zane patted the rifle he carried. "Tai can take the first four hours. Delroy, you'll be up next. I'll take the last four."

Both men nodded. Lines of fatigue dragged at their faces.

"Excellent. Tai, you take one of the rifles and hand it over to the next man on watch. Bernie and I will take a rifle each. That leaves the pistol." Zane crossed over to hand the revolver with its gun holster and a box of ammo to Nyle. "Here you go, pal. Just in case you fall behind, you may need it."

"Thanks." Nyle strapped on the holster and pocketed the ammo.

"I can take a watch," offered Ricky.

After a moment's reflection, Zane nodded. "Okay. That makes it four on for three hours each. You can be up first, Ricky."

The young man beamed and looked over at Tatum as if checking to see if she watched, but the young girl sat on a log with her face hidden in the shawl.

Knowing if she didn't move she'd fall asleep where she stood, Bernie picked up her staff and dug out her flashlight.

"I'll see if I can find anything to eat." She looked skywards, although no stars twinkled through the canopy. "Let's set up any containers we have and all our empty bottles to catch rain water."

"Not another storm. More mud. More mosquitoes."

Nyle scratched at the bite marks marring his bare arms.

"There's insect repellent in my big pack. Even better use my jar of petroleum jelly. Smear it over the bites and it will suffocate any larva that may have hatched."

Nyle glanced up, eyes wide. "Shit, that sounds God-awful."

"It isn't pleasant." She made a mental note to check him out tomorrow. It was possible it wasn't mosquitoes at all. Her heart sank at the notion he could have been infected by botflies. The horrible insects laid their eggs beneath the skin and their larva had spines making it extremely painful for anyone infected. While she was at it, maybe she should check every member of the group. "Don't forget, Nyle."

"Thanks, Bernie. I won't." Nyle's smile held more grimace than acceptance.

The way his gaze drifted from hers like he feared he'd reveal too much, had her re-hashing her earlier thoughts. Perhaps he *had* been involved in some complicated plot to bring the plane down. It had to be either him or the dead pilot. He could be the Jaguar. Being a co-pilot with a regional airline would make a pretty good cover. A low-grade headache pounded behind her eyelids. No, he hardly fitted in with her mental image of a master criminal.

She coughed. The dryness of her throat made her remember it had been some time since she'd had any water. She knew it was important to stay hydrated in this climate, but their supplies were low. Hopefully, if it rained tonight, they'd have sufficient water for the next couple of days. If they were careful.

"Do you want company?" Zane's dark eyes captured her gaze.

"No thanks. I'll leave this lot to you."

"Don't forget the rifle." He handed over the weapon and dropped a spare clip of ammo onto her palm. "Do you know how to use a gun?"

"Yes."

His eyebrows lifted, but she didn't elaborate. She could barely move her lips she was so tired. Not that this was the time to share life histories, even if she trusted him.

"Don't stray too far."

"I'll whisper a password when I return, so I don't get shot." She jerked her chin to indicate Ricky running his hands in obvious admiration over the rifle he held.

"What? You can't whistle? This from the woman I thought could do everything."

"My father's the one with that talent." She laughed as she recalled his expertise with imitating bird calls. "Nor do you want to hear me sing."

His slow, sexy smile sizzled over her skin. "Then password it is. How about...Casablanca."

"That'll do. Catch you later." She turned away then was swung around by his hands on her waist.

"First, I need this." Slowly, he drew her closer until her body pressed against his.

She raised her face, eyes fluttering half-shut and focused on the quizzical smile curling his lips. One hand slid up to caress the nape of her neck, his thumb gently stroking her skin, the other trailed fingers down her spine. His mouth a breath away from hers. He held that position for one long minute, heightening the awareness zapping between them, causing her skin to frisson with delicious sensation.

Then he kissed her.

The jungle fell away. Nothing existed but the warmth of his body, the touch of his hands and the ache of need coursing through her.

His lips were a sensual glide across hers as he broke away to rest his forehead on hers, breathing deeply. "Take care out there."

"I will." Feeling like she floated above the clouds, she stepped back and walked off, the force of his gaze boring into hers.

It took longer than she'd hoped, but when she returned, her backpack was full of fruit. She'd even found the hard kernel of an old brazil nut tree amidst a thicket of ferns the monkeys had missed. Thankfully, Ricky didn't shoot her when she returned, seemingly more interested in talking to Tatum who had left the campsite apparently to keep him company. He seemed to be the one doing all the talking though. Tatum sat hunched on the ground beside him, a lost expression haunting her eyes.

Bernie raised a hand in greeting, flashlight pointing at the ground and walked past. It seemed the girl was in good hands for the moment.

Zane emerged from the shelter they'd constructed beside an emergent tree and took her heavy pack from her.

"Thanks," she muttered. A wall of fatigue crashed into her, she could barely stand upright.

"Bloody hell. You're knackered," Zane growled, slinging his arm around her waist.

She sagged against him, allowing him to lead her

to their hide, where she crawled inside and lowered her weary, aching body onto a bed of bracken and fern.

"Here, drink this, child." Elizabeth pressed a bottle and a salt tablet into her hand.

Popping the tablet on her tongue, she tilted the bottle and drank until it was empty. Some of her light-headedness vanished. "I found fruit, and tomorrow we can have a go at opening a brazil nut kernel."

"You best have something to eat yourself." Elizabeth tutted as she and Zane rationed out the fruit and handed around the knife.

"I've eaten." If one *goaiba* and one *cupuazu* constituted a meal. She gazed around at the others. "How is everyone? Cody? What about Nyle and Cheryl?"

"Everyone is as well as can be expected." Elizabeth's tone was final.

Obviously, it would do no good to enquire any further. In the morning, Bernie would assess everyone's health for herself.

Zane pressed a piece of *maracuya* against her lips. Obediently, she opened her mouth and ate. She yawned as he snugged a jacket around her shoulders, tucking it in at the sides. She sniffed, breathing in the faint masculine scent that lingered in the material. A mixture of saffron, sea-salt and sandalwood—and Zane.

Rain pattered onto their ceiling of palms fronds, branches and a space blanket. The pattering quickly changed to drumming as another storm erupted overhead.

"Here we go again," drawled Nyle.

At the sound of his voice, her earlier suspicions sprang foremost to her mind. She made an effort to clear her foggy head. "We should learn a little more about each other. It'll help us to work together as a team."

Beside her, Zane shifted position then tucked her against his hard body.

She should protest, move away. But she didn't, instead sinking into his warmth and strength—a comfort she hungered for and was too damn tired to deny.

When no one spoke, she said, "Okay, I'll go first. I'm an archaeologist and I'm in South America at the request of my old professor." No need to mention, she'd been on the flight because she'd been fleeing Brazil. Not yet. And definitely not the time to accuse one of them of being the Jaguar.

"I'm Zane MacIntosh and holidaying with my mother, Elizabeth. Our home is in London. My sister, Amelia, dropped out at the last minute. Something to do with her work. We were coming back after a river cruise along the Solimões River. Right about now, we should be lolling on the beach in Rio waiting for Mom's flight to Heathrow. Next stop for me would be Mexico City."

No mention of his job. Bernie chewed that realization over in silence.

"Cher and I are on our honeymoon. We delayed it to place a deposit on our house. This was our dream to honeymoon in the Amazon, eight years in the making, and look where it got us." Tai stopped when his voice choked up.

After a few minutes of heavy silence, Delroy cleared

his throat. "Pearl and I have a little restaurant business happening back home, Stateside. We travel to out-of-the-way villages to pick up local recipes and source different foods. Been good for our business. Ain't that right, Pearl?"

"Yes." Her voice clipped.

Delroy rambled on, "We been all over the world several times now. One of our favourite places is the South Americas. Why, we been to Mexico three times now. Or is it four?"

"Are you a chef, Delroy?" asked Bernie.

"Hell no, sweet girl. Not no more, anyways. I'm more like a manager these days. But I've still got a nose for good food. I'm like a blood hound when I git going." He gave several exaggerated sniffs.

Everyone laughed.

Delroy continued, "Ricky told me he's from Puerto Rico. Got no family. Kid's an orphan."

"And what about you, Nyle?" Bernie asked.

"Divorced and from the sunny State of California."

Short and sweet. Like a man with something to hide. Bernie wracked her brain for ideas on how to make him divulge more details, but her thoughts moved sluggishly, the only thing she needed was sleep. Glorious sleep.

The vague thought shifted through her mind that Melanie and Colin had failed to respond. Colin had already mentioned his research work and told everyone Melanie was his lover. But where were they from? Perhaps the mercenaries *were* after Colin's cure of the century.

Something important flitted around the edges of her mind. She tried to catch the thought but her eyes drifted shut. She should stay awake, question them, learn more about who they really were, where they were from and why they were on that plane. The more people talked, the easier it was to trip them in a lie.

"Sweet mother, Bernie, get some rest." Zane's lips brushed over her forehead.

She snuggled closer. Her body grew heavier as each muscle slackened then finally with a sigh, she surrendered.

⟸ 15 ⟹

Zane was dreaming. The best possible wet dream ever. He dreamed Bernie was covering him like a silken blanket, her soft hands gliding over his body, her sweet lips following their journey lower.

Lower to where he ached like he'd never ached before, to feel the tender love of a special woman. Someone's fingers dug into his shoulder and shook him roughly.

Still half-asleep, he frowned as someone thumped him. Hard.

"Zane! For heaven's sake, son, wake up."

His mother's voice. *His mother?* Peeling open gritty eyes, he beat back the sleep trying to drag him under. It was pitch black, for which he was eternally grateful considering the excited state of his body. Overhead, thunder growled across the sky, rain drummed onto their flimsy shelter and several drops of cold water plopped onto his face in quick succession.

"I'm awake," he rasped as he reluctantly inched

away from Bernie's tempting softness nestled by his side and wiped his wet face with his hand.

His mother whispered, "It's Delroy. He hasn't returned from his watch and it'll be dawn in an hour. I think something has happened."

He rubbed his bristly jaw, instant guilt clawing at his gut. *Shit.* He'd slept through his internal alarm clock. That had to be the first time ever he'd done such as thing. His job relied on his ability to spring into action in a split second. And yet here he was, lost in a sexual fantasy. No other woman had that effect on him.

He pulled his jacket up over Bernie's shoulders, tucking it in around her. After fumbling through his duffle for his baseball cap, in the hope it would keep some of the rain out of his eyes, he clapped it on his head and crawled from the shelter. He flicked on his flashlight.

His mother stood, open umbrella held over her head, wearing a pink raincoat over her clothes and a frown on her face. Despite the heat cloying the night, he shivered a little, taking a few seconds to enjoy the rain washing the stickiness off his body. Bloody hell, he could do with a shower. He could only imagine what he must smell like after two days trekking through a jungle and evading gun-toting hunters.

"Zane!" Impatience sharpened his mother's voice.

"Coming." He motioned for his mother to follow behind. They pushed through foliage, making for the area they'd set up the watch.

Apart from the steady rain, a hushed quiet cloaked the jungle. Any noises from the animals and birds no doubt drowned out by the constant stream of moisture that continued to pour through the canopy. As he held back a large prickly palm for his mother, Zane wondered what they'd do once their flashlight batteries ran out.

He emitted a low whistle. But heard nothing in return. Delroy should have responded. Gesturing for his mother to wait, he crouched down and crab-walked beneath a tree's root stilts. The narrow light revealed Delroy's prone figure. A gentle shove on the guy's legs received no movement in return.

"Bloody hell." Zane scrambled closer and bending down, scrutinized Delroy's face.

White foam bubbled from the big guy's lips. His brown eyes were wide and staring, his entire body rigid. The rifle stood propped against the tree trunk.

"What is it?" whispered his mother.

Zane shook his head, not bothering to waste his breath remonstrating with her. He should have known she'd follow him. He sniffed, but couldn't detect any odor on Delroy's breath or body.

"Delroy, can you hear me? What's wrong, pal?'

Delroy didn't respond. Didn't even betray a flicker of his eyelids.

Frustrated and tamping down his dread, Zane muttered, "I have no idea. Maybe he ate something poisonous. He could have had an allergic reaction to one of the fruits Bernie found for us."

"Did I hear my name? Move over, Zane, and let me through." Bernie's breathless voice interrupted him.

He glared as she wriggled her way through the root stilts to the other side of Delroy. "I thought you were asleep."

"I was, until I heard you stomping about like a

jolly, great elephant." She placed her hand on Delroy's chest and leaned close. "His breathing sounds all right, but this rigidness is worrisome. I wonder..." Sweeping the flashlight over the ground around Delroy, she shifted grass and leaves.

"What are you looking for? Perhaps we could help," Elizabeth said.

"An insect, maybe a tiny, brightly colored frog. I think he's been bitten or has touched something that causes paralysis."

"Sweet mother," Zane exploded.

Bernie smacked his wrist. "Shush."

"Will he...?"

Bernie looked at him. Shadows hid most of her face from him. But he distinctly saw her mouth wobble momentarily before she regained control. "I don't know. If we can work out what caused it, I may have a better idea. But I'll only be guessing. Poisonous insects and reptiles are not my strong suit."

"What about Colin? He might know."

She nodded. "It's possible. Either way, Delroy can't stay here. We'll need help getting him to camp. He's a big guy."

"I'll go and fetch Tai." Elizabeth patted Zane's arm and added, "Don't touch anything while I'm gone."

He handed over his flashlight. Mud squelched underfoot as she moved away.

Bernie continued her poking and peering, while he examined Delroy's hands and face.

After a few minutes Zane said, "I can't see any bite marks although there's a cut near his right thumb. Looks like he's had it a couple of days."

"Really? Well, sometimes you don't need to be actually bitten. If the insect poison came into contact with a raw wound, you can be infected that way."

"This place..." He stopped, jaw clenched.

In silence, Bernie lifted her gaze to meet his. The flashlight struggled to beat back the blackness. Beneath the hood of her plastic poncho, her face was a patchwork of black and gray shadows. The soul-eating weariness in her eyes shredded his heart. What he wouldn't do to whisk her away from this hell. His throat tightened savagely.

"We can't give up," she said simply. "Besides, I haven't experienced the best sex of my life yet." She grinned.

Memories of his erotic dreams slammed into him and his mouth dried as all his blood rushed to one particular member of his body. He refrained from happy-punching the air and instead said, "Remind me to book us a room when we reach Manaus."

She snorted. "Give over. Who said I meant with you?" At the sound of footsteps approaching, she added, "Come on. Let's get Delroy back to camp."

It made for an awkward journey hauling Delroy back to camp, and Zane's back itched from sweat by the time they set the big guy down under a thick clump of palm leaves.

A gloomy dawn struggled past the rain and mist as night limped back to its cave. The remainder of their group, roused by the activity, shuffled out from beneath the tree, yawning, rubbing their dull eyes and looking down-right depressed.

He couldn't blame them. Few were achieving sufficient sleep let alone rest. If bugs weren't biting, then it was the bloody rain and humidity making their lives a total misery. He, personally, felt a hundred years old.

Pearl pressed back against the tree trunk like she was terrified whatever had struck Delroy would leap on her next.

Even the little chatterbox was quiet. The kid curled into his mother's side on the stretcher and damn, if he wasn't sucking his thumb. The teenager took one look at Delroy then yanked a space blanket over her head, hiding from the sight.

Colin and Melanie kneeled beside Delroy who had yet to make a sound and spoke in low voices as they examined the black man's still form. Standing stiffly nearby Bernie appeared to watch their every move with sharp eyes. What did she think they would do to the bloke?

After a moment, Colin leaned back on his haunches then adjusted his glasses over his nose. "This is only my opinion, of course, but Delroy's condition may be caused by a species of dart frog. I have no idea if its fatal or a temporary reaction."

Biting back a curse, Zane stretched his back, working out the kinks then stood under the shelter of a nearby palm. The rain kept pissing out of the sky.

Bernie, his mother, Colin, Melanie, Tai and Ricky joined him in a huddle.

"We've got a problem." Zane shoved his hands into his pants pocket as water dripped down his back. He shivered.

Ricky cracked a sarcastic laugh that Zane suspected covered the boy's lack of confidence.

Melanie scowled. "You think?"

Ignoring their jabs, Zane continued, "We don't have time to build another stretcher before those scumbags find our camp."

"Bearing two people will slow us down. The thugs will be on us before we can get very far," his mother pointed out. She stood a little beyond their circle, her brolly held over her head.

Zane met her inscrutable gaze. "We can't leave him behind. There's a good chance he'll recover."

His mother set her jaw and averted her eyes. He knew without asking that she wouldn't be the only one who'd harbored the opinion that Delroy wouldn't survive. "Our problem is, we've no idea how long before we know either way. There's only one thing for it. Someone has to draw the soldiers away while the others build another stretcher."

"I agree." Bernie pushed back her hood with an impatient hand. "And we have to move fast before they pick up our trail again. Wading through ankle-deep water yesterday afternoon will have thrown them off for a while, but their dogs could still pick up our scent if they keep moving in this direction."

"Exactly." Zane met Bernie's resolute gaze and shook his head. *Damn. I know she's planning something risky.*

Melanie rolled her eyes. "What a surprise–not."

Zane flicked Melanie a quick glance, taking in the possessive hand on Colin's arm. The woman never seemed to let the bloke out of her sight. As for Colin, he appeared to have forgotten his drama-queen act of yesterday. In fact, for the first time since Zane had laid eyes on him, the guy acting like he was giving their situation careful thought.

Colin lifted his head. "Why are they still chasing us? With this weather, shouldn't they have given up by now?"

"No idea, Colin. The point is they're hot on our tail. I don't believe we should wait around to ask."

"I'll do it." Bernie raised her chin.

"Absolutely out of the question. I'll divert those bastards' attention while you organize things here." His gut muscles cramped. If he was caught, he'd be saying goodbye to his last chance at nailing his mother's killer. Saying goodbye to his Mom and sister. Saying goodbye to Bernie.

His hands fisted. "Strap both Delroy and Cheryl onto the stretchers using the rope I made. I know it's going to be hard not taking a break, but we have to move faster than yesterday. It's imperative we push through their net."

"And go where?" Melanie flung a hand sideways.

"East," said Bernie in her no-nonsense voice. She squatted and cleared aside leaves then, picking up a stick, began to draw in the mud.

Intrigued, Zane dropped down beside her.

"This is us." Bernie marked an 'x' then drew a hut roughly south-west of that position. "Let's say this is the village and over here, is where we landed on the plateau. I asked Nyle again this morning for a rough estimate of the location, and I figure it has to be around this area."

She drew another hut about a foot away. "Now here is São Paulo de Olivença. I've no idea how far away it is, but you can see the relative position of the landing area compared with the town." She stabbed the stick into the mud well to the north-west and close to the border.

Zane nodded slowly. "Meaning we travel east to south-east to get back there." He looked up at the faces surrounding him and Bernie. "Any questions?"

"I vote we leave the injured behind. Send help back for them when we reach civilization." Melanie planted her hands on her hips.

"No way." Tai's furious gaze shot to Zane. "I'm not leaving my wife."

"Then stay here," spat Melanie.

Zane straightened and glared around the circle. "No one is leaving anyone. We all stick together. Safety in numbers, got it?"

Melanie's mouth twisted, but she jerked a nod.

The light drizzle changed to a sudden downpour and Bernie pulled her hood over her head. "I've got another idea. The archaeological dig may be closer than São Paulo de Olivença. They'll have a satellite phone where we can call in help."

Zane rubbed his jaw. "That's assuming your guess is correct about our exact location."

"I know it's a gamble. But what choice do we have? West, we walk right into the soldiers' territory. If we head south or south-east to where I think the river is, the lower the terrain. It's the end of the wet season, remember? We'll be hauling stretchers through what may well be thigh-high water crawling with snakes and caiman. Not a good idea."

Zane frowned as his mind conjured up a vague mental map of the region. "Are you talking about the Solimões River?"

She shook her head. "I think we landed further

north. I think the Putumayo River lies south of our position."

"Sweet mother." He swore softly.

"Or we could be caught between where the Putumayo winds almost back on itself before it reaches the border. If that's the case, then we have quite a trek through the jungle to reach either the Solimões River or São Paulo de Olivença. I believe both are too far away. We won't make it."

Zane's lips thinned. "Sounds like the dig is the best option."

"Aw, man. This is fucked up." Ricky pulled a pack of smokes from his jacket pocket then lit up, sucking down hard on the in-hale like he needed the nicotine fix.

"If you're wrong...if you're wrong..." Tai's voice cracked. Pressing his hands to his face, he turned his back.

Tears glistened in Bernie's eyes as she whispered, "I know the stakes."

Zane slung an arm around her shoulders, pulling her close. "This isn't on you, Bernie. It's on all of us, as a team." Smiling wryly, he nudged her chin to gaze into her eyes. "We can..."

The crack of wood and rustle of leaves caught his attention. "What the...?" Releasing Bernie, Zane swung around.

A small wild pig burst out of the undergrowth on the opposite side of the clearing. Snorting, it stopped, quivering and sniffing the air.

"Man, oh man. Dinner!" Ricky charged forward, scooping up a rifle that lay near the shelter.

"Wait," yelled Zane, taking off after him.

Too late. Ricky aimed. Fired. The shot echoed through the jungle, setting off an explosion of noise—monkeys, birds, God knew what else. And the fool had missed.

The animal bolted with a terrified squeal. Its friends—a herd of larger females and their young—rushed out of the bushes, snorting and charged in a wild-eyed mass toward the group.

"*Shit.* I didn't think." Ricky's mouth fell open, the rifle dangled from his hand.

"Quick, into the trees." Zane waited a beat to ensure his mother and Bernie were scrambling up a tree then sprinted across the clearing to the shelter.

Women screamed, competing with the high-pitched squeals of the terrified pigs. Branches snapped and leaves crunched while hooves thudded through the mud. Instead of climbing a tree, Tai joined him and handed over a spear. Sweeping the spears in front of them, they succeeded in blocking the pigs away from Delroy and from entering the shelter. Seconds later, the last pig trotted into the jungle.

Zane cast his glance around their camp. His mother and Bernie were climbing down from their perch, as were the others. Unfortunately, someone had carried out a couple of bags from the shelter earlier, including the duffle containing their food supplies. The contents were now trampled into the mud. Several water bottles had been gored by the pigs' tusks and were now empty and useless. The remaining spears were little more than broken twigs scattered over the clearing.

"What a fucking disaster," he muttered, jaw clenched.

Panting, Tai wiped a shaky hand over his wet face. "Ricky is a moron. The bloke is out of control."

"Just thoughtless, I think." Mouth tight, Zane began gathering undamaged water bottles.

He heard Tai reassuring his wife and kid and settling the terrified sobs of the teenager. Bernie touched his arm. He met her concerned gaze as she shook her head.

"Let me do this. You need to go. All that noise..." She clamped her mouth shut.

Time was their enemy. At any second, those thugs could discover their camp. He pushed back his sleeve and took a reading off his compass watch then agreed with her on the co-ordinates where they'd meet up.

"About that room..." He raised his eyebrows.

"Don't you ever give up?"

"Not where you're concerned."

Her eyes glowed like blue fire as her soft lips twitched then deepened into a tender smile. "I'll expect a spa bath, champagne and chocolate."

"Consider it a given."

"And please heaven, a back rub." A gentle sigh escaped from her then she leaned forward. Her mouth brushed against his in a kiss as evocative as butterfly wings. She whispered, "If you promise *not* to behave, I may even let you share my bed."

He chuckled, sliding his hand beneath her hood to cup the back of her neck, drawing her in as he claimed her lips. Her skin butter smooth and warm, stirred his blood, igniting his hunger for more of her touch.

Allowing himself another moment of bitter-sweet pleasure, he nibbled his way along the line of her jaw before resting his forehead on hers. "Stay safe."

"Don't be late." Then she twisted out of his hold and walked away.

~ 16 ~

With one thing and another, it was fifty minutes before midday before they moved out. Zane had left camp several hours ago, taking with him one of the rifles and the hunting knife.

After he departed, Bernie swung into action, ordering another stretcher to be made and hounding the others to salvage what they could of their supplies. She would have liked a few minutes alone to pray for her sister and for Zane. But she had work to do. And certainly no time to waste mooning over a man full of charm and probably low on commitment. A man far too similar to her father—glib, a smooth operator and with a core of rock-hard stubbornness.

Bernie had always thought it was her father's ruthless, driven nature that had alienated her more social-loving butterfly mother. His focus on climbing the political ladder had overridden his desire to be with his family. No woman wanted a man like that, but she couldn't deny that a man who didn't give up easily was exactly what was needed here and now. Zane sure displayed all those qualities—and more.

Sighing, she rummaged in her pack for her first aid kit looking for her insect repellant and bottle of iodine. Not only did mosquitoes carry the threat of tropical fevers but some carried human botfly eggs. When bitten by a mosquito, body heat triggered the eggs to hatch into maggots that would then enter the host via the bite. If anyone ended up infected, the larvae would need to be cut out carefully so it didn't rupture and release its bodily fluid. Another possible disaster as the person could experience anaphylactic shock. And they were fast running out of able-bodied stretcher-bearers.

Glum silence had fallen over the others while Bernie, and Melanie under protest, performed medical checks. A wave of resignation weighed down Bernie's spirits when she discovered Nyle, Tatum and Delroy were infected to varying degrees. More time slipped past while they were treated with petroleum jelly and iodine.

She'd been packing her depleted supplies in her pack when the heavy quiet had been broken by the distant rat-a-tat of machine gun fire and the returning crack of a rifle.

Exchanging a horrified glance with Elizabeth, she'd harried the others to finish building the other stretcher. It was a more primitive affair than the previous one, made from vine rope and a couple of donated jackets. Being not as structurally sound, they'd decided this one would accommodate Cheryl and not the heavier Delroy. They were both strapped on with rope made from vines to ensure they didn't slide off while being carried. Covered with space blankets, they looked like dead bodies being hauled to a morgue.

Bernie shivered at the thought and ensured she kept her eyes averted as they finally left camp. An act that proved easy to do since she had to maintain constant vigilance as well as marking a trail for Zane to follow.

Colin and Tai were the bearers for Delroy, while Bernie and Ricky pulled Cheryl's as they trudged through slush and mud. Cody alternatively clung to his father's back or walked beside the stretcher. Sometimes Tatum carried him in her arms. Rain beat consistently onto their weary bodies forming a gloomy mist that made vision a challenge.

Every so often, Bernie called a halt to check her compass and the passage of time, her emotions a minefield of pain and numbing fear. She'd spurned her last opportunity to search for her sister. Zane may have signed his own death warrant by volunteering to divert the mercenaries. There were no guarantees any of them would survive the day. But they had to keep pushing on. One step. Just one step more.

Wearing a narrow-brimmed cloth hat on her head, Elizabeth walked beside Bernie, a rifle held in steady hands. Her eyes were alert as she constantly scanned the area in front or behind them, appearing to listen for sounds only she could hear. She gave off the aura that she'd done this before. Who was this woman?

Suddenly, Elizabeth halted. Bernie and Ricky followed suit, as did the others stumbling along behind. Through the pattering rain, a low droning noise became gradually louder.

"A plane. They're searching for us." One-handed, Bernie fumbled in her pack for her flashlight. Then hesitated. It could be the mercenaries. Or the Jaguar.

Quickly, Elizabeth snatched it from her and flicked it on and off, aiming its beam skyward. But with the dark, purplish-gray clouds blanketing the sky and the dense jungle canopy, it was a futile hope the pitiful light would be seen.

The engine noise faded. The plane turning south. Away from them. Pearl burst into quiet sobs while Bernie retrieved her phone and checked for a signal. No bands.

Ricky pulled a crumpled pack of cigarettes and a lighter from his pocket and using one hand, lit a cigarette with a shaking hand. "Fuck. Anyone want one?"

"Me." A weeping Tatum sloshed over and took the proffered cigarette from him.

Ricky flicked the lighter and Tatum took a drag, coughed, before blowing out a thin stream of smoke.

Frowning, Pearl emerged from blowing her nose. "That looks like my lighter. I had it packed in my suitcase. How did you get it? What else did you steal from me?"

"You'd be surprised by what I found." A cocky grin smeared over his face as Ricky patted his waistband. "I was looking for anything we could use...like a gun."

Pearl's lips twisted. "You...!"

"A gun?" Bernie studied Pearl closely, recalling that moment when she'd thought she'd heard the click of a pistol.

Pearl radiated conservative, middle-class suburbia, hardly the type to carry a weapon. But Bernie knew little about these people apart from what they'd divulged. They could be hiding any manner of secrets. She glanced from Pearl to Ricky then back again.

"Sure thing, *chica*." His white smile didn't diminish.

"My name is Bernie," she said narrowing her eyes. "Pearl, did you really have a gun in your bags?"

"Absolutely." Pearl looked down her nose. "It's all legal-like. When we travel to these primitive places, Delroy always makes sure that his woman is protected."

"But how did you get it into the country?"

Pearl didn't blink as she adjusted the shoulder strap of her handbag. "Got it first thing once we arrived in Brazil. My man knows how to take care of me. He made sure we'd not be robbed again, like we were last year in Mexico."

She stepped forward, hand held out and after several long seconds, Ricky gave her the gun. Pearl tucked the weapon inside her handbag.

"Anything else the rest of us need to know?" Bernie glared at each person.

No one spoke. Not by a flicker of an eyelid did anyone indicate they hid other secrets. But tension settled over the group as smothering as a wet blanket. One of them was lying.

"Right then. Time to go." Stone-walled, she stashed her flashlight and phone back in her pack and waved everyone into motion again.

Melanie grumbled and whined about needing a rest.

Ignoring her, Bernie lowered her voice and looked at Elizabeth. "Not that I believe a word out of that boy's mouth."

"Yes, its possible Ricky was looking for money or items he could sell or trade."

"That sounds more like him," she said, thinking at least they had another weapon on hand.

The terrain became more difficult to traverse. A group of white-face monkeys jabbered at them from where they hung from branches then pelted them with hard seeds. Water often lapped as high as their knees adding extra stress on the bearers as they struggled to keep the stretchers above water. There'd been one hideous moment when everyone had collectively frozen as a terrifyingly long anaconda swam lazily past.

Arms feeling like they were being pulled from their sockets, her legs wooden, Bernie eventually called a halt. Night was setting in, rain still hammered from the sky while the jungle merged into deep pools of shadow.

Bidding the others to remain where they'd stopped, she scouted ahead until she found a relatively clear area suitable to make camp. Unable to locate an aerial root tree, they cut down palm branches and weaved them together to form shelters. Over the largest one, they threw a couple of space blankets to protect the injured and Cody.

By the time they'd finished, night had fallen, and they were exhausted. Conversation deteriorated to short, terse sentences. Bernie carefully rationed the food and, beyond a resentful glance at her portion, not even Melanie whined.

After dinner, Bernie poked her head into the shelter where the injured—together with Pearl, Elizabeth, Tai and Cody—were squished together.

Keeping her flashlight beam directed at the ground, she asked, "How is everyone? Any change in Delroy or Cheryl's condition?"

"Cher wouldn't eat anything, but I managed to dribble some water into her mouth." Tai soothed hair from his wife's forehead. Her eyelashes fluttered at his touch.

"My man's sleeping, and I do believe his body isn't so stiff. Here, see for yourself." Pearl wriggled over to make room for Bernie.

Bernie squatted beside the prone man, felt the muscles in his arm and upper thigh. Instead of tight cords, they felt slack to the touch. Hoping that was a good sign, she smiled at Pearl. "Let me know if he wakes."

"Any sign of Zane?" Tai asked.

"Not yet." Bernie kept her smile pinned in place.

"How far you reckon we've travelled?"

She'd already calculated the distance but, out of habit, she checked her watch. "All up, seven and a half miles, Tai. We really pushed hard today."

The tense lines in his face faded and he flashed a quick grin. "That's good then, hey? We should be outta those buggers' reach by now."

"I hope so."

"How far from here is your dig?" Pearl folded her arms over her ample chest.

Although, this wasn't the first time she'd been asked, Bernie answered patiently, "If we're lucky, another nine miles should see us close to the mark."

Tai snorted softly. "Lucky!"

"I know. Well, try and get some sleep. See you in the morning." On hands and knees, she shuffled backwards out of the shelter then straightened. Pulling her hood over her head, she squelched her way through the dismal drizzle to check on the rest of their group.

In the other shelter, Melanie, Colin, Ricky and Tatum huddled like bundles of wet laundry on a pile of bracken and palm leaves. Since no one was inclined to talk, Bernie made herself scarce and headed to an emergent tree with a wide trunk and low spreading branches.

She climbed onto a branch wide enough where it joined the trunk to form a shallow cradle of around three and a half feet wide by four feet long before it tapered out with numerous smaller branches sprouting on both sides. The area made a reasonable bed and a nice change from sleeping on the sodden ground. Earlier, she'd draped her space blanket over the branch above to form a crude tent as well as capture water. With the thick canopy overhead, it was relatively dry beneath. Hopefully, it would also prove a barrier to curious snakes and lizards.

She checked her rifle still lay where she'd slipped it into a long crack in the bark. Using her smaller pack as a cushion between her back and the hard trunk, she settled onto the picnic rug she'd had in her pack then hugged her knees. Squeezing her eyes shut and locking her throat against the anguish tearing her heart, she allowed her thoughts to escape.

That plane they'd heard, could Kit be on it, safe and well? If so, the authorities would have realized how many passengers had survived the plane's forced landing. They'd keep up the search. Hot emotion surged through her chest and she smiled.

Her sister would never allow them to do otherwise.

Her body grew slack as she relaxed. The arduous day finally taking its toll as exhaustion weighed heavy. Muscles she hadn't known existed, throbbed and ached. Where was Zane and that bed he'd promised her?

The bastard. He'd better not renege on his offer or... Dry, heaving sobs welled from the depths of her soul. Shoulders shaking, she covered her face and cried silently into her hands.

Zane. She wanted him back. Here. Alive. With her. She needed to see his crinkly smile. She longed to hear the teasing notes playing in his smooth-as-whiskey voice. God, she just wanted the reassurance of his warm body wrapped around hers and his steady heartbeat against her cheek.

But night had well and truly settled in and he hadn't returned.

~ 17 ~

From somewhere to the right of the camp, a twig snapped. She stilled, held her breath. Listened. Her tears dried cold on her cheeks.

A low whistle. Zane.

Moving with great care, she bent at the waist then lifted the edges of the blanket and stared into the blackness.

A faint light blinked on then off as whoever it was crept through the bushes. The light grew dimmer, as if moving away from them. If it was Zane, then he'd missed the signs she'd left him. If it was someone else...she allowed the thought to sit in her mind for a few seconds while she pondered the implications.

Following might not be a good idea. But she couldn't chance losing Zane. Slipping the rifle's strap over her shoulder, she swung out of the tree. She didn't dare switch on her flashlight and give away her position. Relying on her mental mind-map, she took a cautious step forward.

Feeling her way, hands outstretched as she

ducked beneath dripping foliage and did her best to make as little noise as possible, she stepped over the soggy ground. Her heartbeats roared like breaking waves in her ears, her eyes watered from the strain of attempting to locate a reference point in the darkness.

The light had disappeared. *Blast.* She'd missed him, gone in the wrong direction. She stopped, swallowing hard as the night seemed to press in on her. She should go back. The thought of being lost and alone, had the strength in her knees dissolving.

About to turn and retrace her steps, she gasped when an arm locked about her chest and a hand clapped over her mouth. Desperately, she clawed at her assailant's skin and kicked backwards, her shoe smacking against a shin.

"Ouch. Let off, Bernie. It's me," whispered Zane furiously near her ear.

Panting, she stopped struggling. Zane released her. She straightened and whipped around to answer just as furiously, "Why the blue blazes did you scare me like that?"

"We don't need you screeching like a peacock and waking the jungle."

"I don't screech. And it's a peahen." She trembled where she stood, curling her hands into fists so she wouldn't fling them around his neck and collapse onto his solid chest.

Oh, and wouldn't he just lap that up? It didn't matter that she'd been mourning his absence all day and worrying herself sick over him. She had no intention of sharing that tit-bit. Not yet, anyway.

"You're late."

He gave a soft snort. "I've wasted the better part of the last two hours fumbling about in the dark. Why did you stop leaving me signs?"

"I didn't." As if she'd ever do such a thing. She swallowed her outrage and lowered her voice. "You obviously didn't look hard enough."

He scoffed. "Hey, I'm getting quite good at this commando stuff. I swear they weren't there."

"Maybe the monkeys took them."

"What? And now I suppose they're decorating their trees with them."

And to think I missed him! Teeth gritted, she snapped, "Come on. This way."

Taking his hand, she guided him one step at a time, to their camp.

"Where's Mom?" he asked when she stopped near the tree she'd claimed for the night.

Switching on her flashlight, she swept the beam toward the smaller shelter. "She's sharing with Colin and co."

"I'll let her know I'm back." He hesitated, then added, "Where are you sleeping?"

Wordlessly, she indicated her tree.

"We need to talk."

The grimness in his voice stilled any objection she might have made. "Don't take all night. I'm tired."

"Sweetheart, wild horses couldn't keep me from your side."

Rolling her eyes, she dimmed her flashlight, trudged off to her tree then climbed into the branches. Zane swore softly as he stumbled over something on the ground. Smiling, she made herself as comfortable as possible. She'd lied. She may have been tired earlier, but now she was wired and edgy. And sleep was the furthest thing from her mind.

It wasn't long before the crunch of leaves and the rustle of the blanket being moved signaled Zane was in her tree. She switched on her flashlight then had to shake it a few times before a wobbly thin beam illuminated her cubby hole. The battery was dying.

Zane had braced himself against the branch and his teeth gleamed in the gloom. His face an artwork of shadows. "Ah, nothing like five-star accommodation."

"And it comes with water." She waggled her half-empty bottle. "We're all out of chocolate, but there's fruit."

"Any room for me?"

Pulse kicking up a gear, she hesitated. The idea of another person's solid form close to her was a comfort she had no intention of refusing. Especially when it was Zane on offer. But the only way he'd fit without falling out of the tree, was if they curled up, spooned together. Her body heated at the very thought of being up close and personal with him.

"Quite cozy," he murmured.

She licked her dry lips. "This isn't going to be easy," she said, inwardly pulling a face at her husky tones.

"The important stuff in life never is." He paused for a few seconds, his voice deepening when he added, "I can sleep elsewhere, if you prefer. We can talk in the morning."

She whispered, "No. I want you here. With me."

After some maneuvering, she found herself nestled over his lap, facing him and inwardly debating whether to lean closer. His body felt tense and she swallowed over a suddenly parched throat. "Water?" she croaked.

"Thanks, but I've not long had a drink. Save it for yourself."

"What happened out there?"

"Wait for it...you will be impressed. I used animal dung, mainly monkey. I scooped a pile into a plastic bag, backtracked sprinkling it over our trail. Then I headed west for a while and began to circle back using more dung to cover my tracks."

"Monkey poo? With your bare hands? Yuck!" Smiling, she reared backwards. "To think I invited a smelly man to share my tree."

He sniffed his fingers and winked. "See? All good. I washed in a stream not far from here, every single inch of me. I'm down to my last two shirts and boxers now though. I could sure use a laundromat."

"Do you think they'll find us again?" She worried her lower lip with her teeth.

"Yeah. They're a determined bunch. I got as close as I dared to a couple of thugs who'd wandered off to answer nature's call. But it was worth the risk. I overheard them talking about other survivors being sighted. Bernie, there's a good chance your sister is amongst them."

"Of course, she is. She's clever and smart." She blinked rapidly warding off tears.

"I'm sorry, I didn't mean to worry you, but I thought it might comfort you to know."

She nodded, unable to speak for the moment.

After a few seconds, Zane continued. "I reckon that by morning they could pick up our trail again. If I was in charge, I'd split them into three groups; one going west, one east and one north. Fan them out and have them move in a curved pattern, meeting up at a specific point." He gestured to show his meaning.

"That sounds like a military tactic."

"I must have read about it somewhere." He shrugged. "The point is, they won't stop chasing us. One of those guys boasted about what he'd do with the reward money. A lucrative cash incentive to capture us will spur them on."

"Blast. And who knows what they've been threatened with if they fail." They both fell silent, Bernie recalling the executed natives and poor Rhoda.

Zane shifted his legs beneath her bottom. The movement of his strong thigh muscles caused a tiny quiver in her abdomen.

"Do you remember Mexico?" His voice rich and deep, he placed his hand on her hip. His long fingers rested lightly on her belly.

Liquid fire turned her bones molten and her blood sizzling. "I may have one or two vague recollections."

"I've dreamed about you often," he admitted slowly, as if the words were being dragged from the depths of his soul. "I did my best to forget you."

She said tartly, "Other women? Seeking oblivion in a bottle?"

"I'm not much of a drinker and I haven't wanted another woman since we last met." He applied a light pressure, pulling her toward him.

An invitation to continue where they'd left off all those months ago. If she pulled away, he'd let her go. But he hadn't forgotten her, and his admission thrilled her. Sent a dizzying sensation of power coursing through her, headier than French Champagne.

"I want more than a few kisses." She sighed, indicating their surroundings.

He grinned, his eyes glinting mischievously. "Sweetheart, I believe we can manage more than a little snogging."

"Really?" *God, I sound so eager.* But he was just as eager. His erection already hardening beneath her. And to show him her eagerness, she rubbed against him.

"You missed me. I knew it." He planted a loud kiss on her nose.

"Get over yourself." She moved forward to place a soft kiss against the fading bruises on his face. Then smiling, laid her palms on his chest, enjoying the feel of him through the thin shirt fabric. "I've got condoms."

"Ah, a lady who knows how to pack. We should save your batteries." He switched off her flashlight and she heard the soft clatter as he laid it down.

Pitch black rushed in to surround them, but in the cozy hide Bernie didn't feel any fear. She could have been blindfolded. The thought was highly erotic.

He deftly fed the edges of her tunic up through his fingers, then glided his hands over her back. "Your skin is so soft," he murmured before dipping his head lower.

She stretched up to meet his searching lips, moaning softly as he nibbled over the contours of her mouth before snatching her breath in a hungry kiss. *Flash point.* Her senses ignited.

He handled her body with a fierce possessiveness that exhilarated, and made her eager for more. His mouth explored hers thoroughly, his hands sliding between them, filling his palms with her breasts. Her nipples peaked stiffly, as his thumbs flicked over them. Sighing, he nipped along her neckline. "Not wearing a bra?"

"I took it off earlier and washed it." She arched to give him better access. "I couldn't stand not being clean any longer. Used the last of my water, hoping I'll get a re-fill tonight when it rains." Leaning forward, she swirled her tongue around his earlobe.

"I like a woman who can think ahead."

They both laughed softly before he claimed her mouth again. Heart pounding, she broke off the kiss to tug off his shirt, stashing it next to them. His hands remained under her tunic, fondling her breasts while she lowered her head to nip and tease his left nipple. She drew it deep into her mouth, bit down gently on the tip, smiling when he groaned.

His fingers tightened over her breasts. She wriggled, her eyes closing as she relished the sensation of his rigid penis pushing at the seam of her leggings against her sensitive crotch. Heat blazed over her skin. "I need to get my clothes off."

"Yes, ma'am." He went to remove his hands to help.

"No. Leave them where they are," she panted.

While he planted deep tongue kisses on her mouth, she toed off her shoes, then pulled off her leggings. She hesitated, her hands on the edge of her bikini pants.

"Leave it," he ground out before pushing her slightly backwards to take her right breast into his hot, moist mouth.

She mewled as he lathed her breast with his tongue. He sucked hard, eased off, swirled his tongue over her tip before sucking hard again.

Raising herself a little, she worked open his fly, her hands molding the length of his penis before tracing her fingers lightly over his swelling balls.

"Bloody hell, Bernie. You're killing me," he muttered.

She grinned. "Good. Because that's what you do to me."

"Glad I'm not the only one suffering." He dragged his open mouth over the tip of her breast then nibbled the sensitive underside before feasting on the other one.

Panting, almost crying with the need raging in her body, she pulled down his boxers so his cock and balls were thrust forward by the elastic band. Her hands were swift as she stroked and fondled him while he nipped sharp biting kisses over her breastbone and along the line of her neck. Wriggling one hand between their bodies, then under her bikini pants he began to rub her sensitive nub.

A shudder rocked through her.

Busy nipping and blowing over her skin behind her ear, he slid his other hand down her back, his gliding fingers blazing a passage of fire over her skin to her bottom. He kneaded first one cheek, then the other, then his fingers slid under her bikini pants to torment her throbbing pussy.

He swept his lips up to nuzzle the sensitive line of her throat. "Bernie, sweetheart. I think this is going to be quick. I want you so much."

"That's okay. I'm with you all the way." She rose

more fully onto her knees to reach around him to her pack. The bark of the tree branch was hard beneath her knees although the blanket softened the sensation. Her breasts brushed against his hard-packed chest and she pushed herself closer while she fumbled in one of the zippered pockets.

He took full advantage while she was distracted, whipping both hands under her bikini pants and spreading her thighs wider. He stroked her faster, rubbing his thumb harder and harder, faster and faster over her aching nub.

"Oh God!" She almost collapsed onto his chest, trembling as she hovered on the cusp. "I've got it!"

Wriggling backwards on her knees until she sat on his thighs, she ripped open the packet then found his straining cock in the dark. She placed the condom in her mouth with the reservoir tip facing inward, gently holding the edges with her lips and opening her mouth. Edging back, she wrapped one hand around the base of his penis, she placed the condom on his tip before carefully rolling it down with her lips. Then she ran her lips over his length to press out any air.

He moaned as stiff as a board by the time she raised her head. "Sweet mother! Bernie, where the hell did you learn to do that?"

"You're not the only one who likes to google." She giggled as she wound her arms around his neck. "Not bad for a first time."

"You'll be the death of me." He caught her mouth with his, his kiss hotter than a furnace as his hands lifted her up, roughly pushed aside her bikini, then positioned her before driving her home.

His cock filled her. Moaning, she met him kiss for kiss as he drove up and she came down. Their pace turned frantic. Her skin slick with sweat as his hands and lips moved everywhere, demanding, owning, possessing as she raced to the edge. A scream welled which he swallowed with a kiss that went on and on while she splintered into a million sizzling pieces of ecstasy.

He kept pounding into her until with a guttural groan he stiffened, spilled his seed. Mouth bruised, body shaking, she sagged against him.

His arms tightened around her as if he'd never let her go. His chest still heaving, he wove his fingers through her hair, tenderly massaging her scalp. Sighing, she nestled closer, panting and listening as his rapid heartbeat gradually steadied.

She felt limp and deliciously sated. He'd been everything she'd dreamed of, a considerate lover who with the touch of his hands or glide of his lips over her skin raised her internal temperature to boiling point.

He yawned then nibbled along one ear. "I told you we'd be good together."

She snorted. "No one likes a know-all."

"Except you, Bernie-babe."

"I hate that term."

"How about sweetheart?"

"We're not that close."

He chuckled, sliding his hand down to cup her breast, his thumb soothing over her taut nipple. "I beg to differ, sweetheart."

"Hah!" Smiling, her fingers sought her pack and withdrew a pack of wet-wipes. "I need to clean up a little."

He shifted to lie on his side allowing her sufficient room to kneel beside him while she made good use of the wipes. Finished, she adjusted her clothing.

"My turn."

She felt his body move against hers, as he removed the used condom and placed it into the plastic bag she handed him.

After handing back packet of wipes, he waited until she'd stowed them away then pulled her back to snuggle against his chest, curled into his side.

"Will you be able to sleep? I know it's a bit cramped."

"I'll be fine sweetheart. It's been a long day." He yawned then chuckled. "As long as I remember not to stretch out my legs."

With a little sigh, she rested her palm over his heart. Reality snuck back into her mind. Was Kit safe from the dangers of the night?

"Tell me about her." Zane shifted to rest his hand on her waist.

The companionable action brought tears to her eyes. "Kit's gorgeous. She's sweet and gentle, and fascinated by anything to do with plants. It's my fault she's here, lost in the jungle. I invited her to join the dig."

"You sound close."

"We are. When Dad left the army, he embarked on a political career that soon swallowed him whole. t was like we were no longer important. At first, Mom was ecstatic, she always loved mingling with society. I guess that comes from my English grandparents' side of things. Always hobnobbing with the rich and famous. Personally, I hate that kind of life. I once fell asleep in an armchair when we had visiting governors and their wives to dinner."

"I can imagine that went over well."

She giggled. "I soon convinced Mom I wasn't cut out to be her protégé and had no interest in making what she considered a suitable marriage. With Dad coming home less and less, Mom became lonely, bored. They divorced when I was fifteen. Mom took off for London, dragging Kit and me with her."

"Parents, huh?"

"They're okay really, just focused on their own lives. I always knew what I wanted to do as a career. They didn't stand in my way once they realized I'd never change my mind."

"That sounds like you. Pig-headed."

"What a charmer."

"What can I say? I'm a sweet-talker." Raising her hand to his lips, he planted a kiss on her knuckles making her laugh again. "You can't blame yourself for your sister being in this situation. We're all here by chance."

Amusement died. "That's where you're wrong. We were never meant to be on the plane. We should be at the dig by now. But Dad phoned us at São Paulo de Olivença, ordering us to head for the US Consulate Agency in Manaus."

Zane stiffened. "Why?"

"He'd received a warning that I was in danger. But the connection was dreadful, probably due to the storm rolling in, so we couldn't make out a lot of what he was saying. I was the one who insisted we change our plans and take the next flight out of there. And here we are. Me with you, and Kit...missing."

173

He whistled low. "I can see why you're blaming yourself, but sweetheart, there is no way you'd know our plane would crash land. Or that we'd be lost in the jungle."

"I guess, but it looked like the soldiers were coming to meet the plane."

He sighed. "Drugs, I suspect. This region is remote. There's always the chance they were in the area, heard the plane and decided to investigate. But I don't buy it."

"Me neither."

"And, it doesn't explain that tranquilizer rifle."

"Then they're after someone specific." Her voice turned hoarse as she whispered, "Zane, it *could* be me."

"Don't beat yourself up over this, Bernie. There's no blood on your hands. You're not the one giving orders."

The Jaguar...the name curled through her mind like the cold fingers of death searching for its next victim and she shivered.

Desperately wanting to think about something else, she wriggled closer, her eyes drifting closed. "What about you? Who is Zane MacIntosh? When he's not smuggling stolen artefacts out of the country."

"Talk about a party-pooper. And just when I was beginning to like you."

"Come on. Don't be shy."

He was silent for so long she began to think he'd fallen asleep, bored by the conversation, or devising some dumb story to fob her off with.

"Amelia and I are foster kids. Mom adopted me

when I was twelve. A year later, she adopted Amelia and the three of us have been a family ever since."

"I never expected that," Bernie mused as images of a gangly youth with dark auburn hair and wary eyes took root in her mind. "What were you like as a child?"

"Terrible. I always acted out, made it difficult for foster carers to connect with me on any level. I hated the world."

"Because you were an orphan?" She raised her head, attempting to discern his expression, but foiled by the darkness.

He drew a sharp breath. "No. Because when I was five, I witnessed my father murder my mother."

"Oh my God!" She sat up, stunned. Then leaning forward, kissed him tenderly on the lips. "How terrible for you."

"Afterwards, he disappeared like he'd never existed. But I'll find him. One day I'll find the bastard then I'll watch him rot in jail for the rest of his life."

~ 18 ~

The thin glow of dawn began its daily battle with the darkness of night. With humidity high, a thin veneer of moisture already coated Bernie's body. Intermittent drips splattering onto the foil blanket indicated the rain had stopped. Frogs were in full swing with their morning chorus backed up by the chirping of crickets and the ear-ringing cicadas that sounded like deranged maracas.

Zane roused her by nibbling along the edges of her left ear then dipping his tongue in and around her sensitive lobe. His hand slipped deftly under her top to caress her right breast and flick over her nipple which stiffened in response.

Passion awoke in the pit of her belly. Emitting a deep sigh, she wriggled, enjoying the hardening of his penis under her bottom. Inside their make-shift tent, the air was scented with sex and a faint undertone of damp clothes.

Her heart rate kicked up several notches. Raising her head, she sought his mouth and found it. His lips were warm and supple. His tongue languidly dueled with hers in a teasing manner that fanned the flames of her simmering desire. What she wouldn't give to laze the day away in his arms.

She eased her mouth aside, trailing a blunt fingernail down the strong column of his neck. "What's for breakfast?"

"Me," he growled low in his throat, then captured her lips in a body-blistering kiss that seared tingles over every inch of her skin.

She squirmed closer, loving his muffled groan and sneaked her hand in between them to gently stroke his hard length.

Breathing hard, he slid his tongue over her lower lip, muttering, "Sweet mother, Bernie. You going to put me out of my misery anytime soon?"

"Depends on your sins. How naughty are you?" She had to force the words out of her thick throat.

"Oh, I'm very good at being naughty."

Her breath caught as his hand sneaked beneath her leggings and squeezed her bottom. Her simmering passion ignited.

"Why the hell did we keep our clothes on?" he growled as he tugged the waistband of her panties. "Going naked has its perks. We should give it some serious consideration."

Half laughing, half gasping, she giggled. "I am *not* going naked in front of Colin."

Zane snorted. "If we're here much longer, none of us will have a choice."

"Not an image I want to have in my head." Her palm nestled over the bulge in his pants and gently she dragged a fingertip over his contours loving his swift, indrawn breath and how he hardened beneath her touch.

"Zane! Bernadette! Where are you?" called Elizabeth.

Bernie froze.

"Bloody hell!" moaned Zane. "Talk about bad timing."

Fallen leaves crunched as Elizabeth approached. "We need to leave."

"Your mother's heading this way." Her libido screaming a denial, she pushed to her knees and attempted to finger comb her hand with one hand.

The events of yesterday crashed through her mind. Elizabeth was right. They needed to move fast, put more distance between them and their hunters. In a rush, Bernie reached for her pack. Missed.

And fell from the tree.

Winded, she lay on her back staring up at the canopy, while water from the soggy ground seeped into her clothes. Branches shook, and leaves rained down to flutter onto her face.

"Bernie! *Shit.* Are you all right?" roared Zane.

"Oh my. Here, let me help you up, dear. Are you hurt anywhere?" Elizabeth bent over her and slipped an arm around Bernie's shoulders.

Still dazed, she blinked into Elizabeth's anxious face and spat off a leaf.

"I'm fine, thank you, Elizabeth." She sat up, sucking in a deep lungful of stinking, steamy air. Grimacing, she pushed up her sleeves and inspected a couple of cuts on her arms. She suspected bruises would bloom on her body later. *Oh well.* More to add to her litany of woes. She'd have to use some of her fast-dwindling petroleum jelly to protect her abrasions from insect infestation.

Zane climbed out of the tree, his arms full of her packs and his duffle bag which he dropped onto the ground before crouching beside her. "That's one way to evade my advances."

She couldn't help herself. She started to laugh then found she couldn't stop. For some reason, the astonishment on Zane and his mother's face sent her off again until she wheezed and hiccupped to a stop.

"Tut. Tut. Hysteria," Zane said to his mother. "Do you think I should slap her?"

"Don't you *dare*." Bernie sent him a mock glare as she scrubbed at the mud on her leggings, flicking off small clods and a leech.

Zane soothed a few strands of hair from her face and drawled, "Back to normal, I see." He gently massaged her lower back. "Sure, you're not hurt?"

"I'm fine." She gazed into his eyes, lapping up his concerned frown.

A broad knowing grin spread over Elizabeth's face as she stared at them. "Now I know why you two are late getting up."

"I'll fetch your rifle." Grinning, Zane re-climbed the tree then returned moments later, chuckling. He showed the weapon to his mother. "Check this out."

Bernie had covered the muzzle with a condom to protect it from water.

"A most ingenious idea." Elizabeth raised her eyebrows. "I don't suppose there's any left?"

"I'm good, but not that good, Mom."

They both laughed.

"Oh, for..." Fighting a grin, Bernie launched to her feet then snatched the gun off Zane.

"Do you always travel so well prepared?" He rocked back on his heels, a teasing light glinting in his eyes. "Or were you hoping to meet up with me again?"

Not knowing whether she wanted to slap his smirk from his face or kiss it away, Bernie muttered, "Survivalist Techniques 101."

"Brilliant."

Irritation vanished in the face of the proud smile he directed at her. Ducking her head, she cleared her throat. "After everyone has eaten, we should make tracks."

"I agree." Elizabeth frowned. "Who knows how long it will be before the mercenaries realize they're chasing a ghost? There's something else." She waited until Bernie and Zane looked at her. "Pearl's pregnant."

"Pregnant? But Delroy said they couldn't have children?" Bernie frowned. "Isn't she a bit old?"

"She's forty-nine." Elizabeth gave a grim smile. "Pearl doesn't want her husband to know—which I find strange."

"Maybe she doesn't want to worry him. How is he this morning?"

"A little better. He's awake and moving about. I'll hurry everyone up." She marched off.

"Wonderful, just wonderful. This is all we need." Shaking her head, Bernie slung the rifle straps over her shoulder then retrieved her gear.

Zane reached for the bag. "Here. I'll take the heavy pack."

"It's not that heavy. I handed out the remainder of the fruit last night. My medical supplies are low, and I've given away clothes and ditched what I don't need."

"Let's shuffle things around then, so you only have one bag to carry."

"Thanks. I kept meaning to do that, but other stuff got in the way."

Together they re-packed Bernie's gear into the larger pack before she joined the others who were picking over the last pieces of fruit.

Zane touched her wrist. "I'll scout the perimeter." After pressing a lingering kiss to her cheek, he disappeared into the foliage.

Bernie's gaze swept the camp and her shoulders sagged, fatigue and despair stealing her optimism. The others were a miserable looking bunch. She doubted she looked any better.

Tatum squatted in the mud, staring down at her hands, a cigarette burning forgotten between her fingers. Her clothes were filthy and hung limp on her thin body.

Delroy, red-faced and sweating profusely, and already propped on his stretcher, managed a feeble wave. A wary-looking Pearl stood beside him, hugging her stomach. Cheryl and her small family were still inside their shelter. Tai's soft voice could be heard coaxing his wife to sip some water.

"Man, I could kill for anything but fucking fruit right now." Ricky eyed his last morsel of *maracuya* before popping it into his mouth. He continued to pace the length of the narrow clearing. "If we'd found the river, we could have fish to eat."

Bernie flexed her shoulders to ease out a tight knot then directed a dark look at him. Ricky stopped, winked at her and made kissy noises. *Little tosser.* She didn't have the energy to argue. If he hadn't attempted to shoot that pig yesterday, maybe they wouldn't be on such strict rations.

Sighing, she squinted at the level in her water bottle then decided she could afford one more mouthful. It might help to alleviate the emptiness of her belly.

"I told you I'm not changing my mind."

Colin stormed out of the bushes, zipping up his pants as he walked and causing Bernie to jump. The bottle slid from her fingers. Quickly, she scooped it up then tightened the lid.

Scowling, Melanie stalked behind him, as close as his shadow. "Please don't make any hasty decisions. The offer was fabulous. You could leave your wife. We'd be set for life." Grabbing Colin's arm, she broke off, as all eyes turned toward them.

But he shook her off. "Leave it, Melanie. It's no good."

"I can't believe you're doing this to us. What about our plans? Our dreams?" Her voice grated harshly against the backdrop of singing birds and the distant chattering of monkeys.

"Not again. Their domestics are getting really old," groaned Nyle, being helped to his feet by Elizabeth.

Colin scooped up his pack, then checked his precious specimens were carefully secured inside before shrugging on the bag. A rare beam of sunlight cut through the clouds and tree tops. The light reflected off his glasses as Colin turned to face his irate girlfriend, making it hard to read his expression.

"My discovery will be given to the world. For free."

"No!" Melanie cracked him a smack across his face so hard, the blow whipped Colin's head sideways.

He stumbled, tripped over a rotting log then landed heavily on his pack, crying out as his ankle twisted beneath his leg. "My sample! My sample!"

Instantly, Melanie fell to her knees. "Colin. Babe. I'm sorry. This humidity is making me crazy."

Breathing noisily through his mouth, Colin ripped open his pack, examined his jars then re-fastened the straps. "How could you?"

"I said I was sorry. Are you hurt?"

"My ankle's probably broken. I won't be able to walk. You'll leave me behind and I'll never get my discovery to those in need." Colin hugged his pack to his chest, his eyes darting from face to face.

Nyle sighed wearily. "Someone please shut him up before I kill him."

Bernie didn't blame him, hard pressed not to snap and snarl herself. The morning was advancing faster than an army of ants before a thunderstorm. They hadn't finished stowing their gear and had yet to move an inch from the camp site. She stashed her water bottle in her pack then headed over to Colin. Both she and Elizabeth reached him at the same time.

Melanie hovered, pulling at Colin's sock.

He slapped her hands away. "Don't touch me. I'm tired of you pretending you care."

"Excuse me," said Bernie.

Elizabeth had no such scruples. She simply snapped, "Move."

Snarling like a feral cat, Melanie scrambled out of the way.

After poking and prodding his ankle for a few seconds, Elizabeth straightened. "It's not broken. You should be able to walk fine, Colin."

"I'll help you up." Bernie wedged a hand under his armpit and steadied him while he gingerly tapped the ground with his foot.

"I suppose it's okay," he admitted in a grudging tone.

"Good." Bernie stepped back and exhaled.

Colin slid her a hunted glance. "I can't possibly be on stretcher duties. I've got weak bones and I'm not physically strong. My samples must be my priority..."

Bernie interrupted, "It's fine, Colin. I understand." But it meant more pressure on herself, Zane, Tai and Ricky who surprisingly had stopped complaining when pressed to be a bearer.

Since Rhoda's death, Ricky now spent a lot of time with Tatum, ensuring the girl had food and encouraging her to drink. As well, he often drew Nyle into conversation and sometimes just sat beside the co-pilot while the guy dozed or stared into space. Anxious for companionship or was Ricky up to something?

Scrubbing her hands over her face, Bernie stole ten precious seconds for herself and thought of her sister. *Kit. Please be safe.*

The Jaguar was close; she could sense it.

Zane reappeared and crossed swiftly to her side. "I checked for those markers you laid down and couldn't find any."

Frowning, she locked eyes with him. "There should have been piles of three white pebbles five hundred yards out, circling the camp at intervals of about ten feet."

He shook his head.

Nonplussed she stared at him. "Zane, someone must have taken them."

"The monkeys." His attempt at humor failed dismally as they stood in silence, mulling over possibilities.

"Someone didn't want you to come back," she eventually muttered. Nausea cramped her near-empty stomach. She fought down the rising bile. They had an enemy in their midst. "But it doesn't make sense. Unless its someone you've pissed off."

"Hey, I'm a regular nice guy." His quick smile turned to a grimace. Running a hand through his damp hair, he admitted, "I don't know what to think."

Her hand shaking, she fished out the crumpled page from her pocket. "I found this on the ground in the runway shelter. I only remembered to read it this morning."

He took the paper, soothing out the wrinkles with his fingers and read in a low voice, "BB, two hundred thousand will be wired upon completion of your... It's hard to make out the next bit. The water has smeared the ink. I think it says...contract? Then those last two words...?" Squinting, he held the slip of paper closer. "El...El...something."

She forced out, "*El* Jaguar." The words sounded thick and heavy on her tongue.

"Does that mean something to you?" He glanced up, his eyes narrowed.

She stepped closer, laying a hand on his arm. His scent enfolded her and for a second she leaned against his solid form. He shifted so she fitted snug against his side then slid his arm around her waist. "*El* Jaguar is the reason we were on the plane."

Zane whistled low. "Bloody hell. He or she could be anyone." He paused then added slowly, "It could be one of the passengers."

Bernie shivered. Lifting her head, she gazed around the camp. Tatum was tugging her hair into a ponytail using a piece of string. Delroy, Pearl, Ricky, Colin, Melanie, Tai and even Zane's mother appeared to be staring fixedly at the paper in Zane's hand.

Pearl and Delroy travelled with a handgun. They traipsed all over the world and had been in Mexico when Bernie had been on Professor Kowalski's last dig. Did it have any connection?

Colin was a queer stick and his girlfriend wasn't much better. Both were obsessive and had lived in Brazil for years. That whole 'miracle cure' and crazy scientist act could be a cover. But what would be the point? Unless it was a scam to defraud pharmaceutical companies.

Ricky, Bernie suspected, would probably sell his mother for a few dollars. Although, lately he showed signs of a nicer side. Like Melanie, he had links to the region through his Latin heritage.

Tai? Bernie chewed on her lower lip. If he turned out to be anything more than an anxious father and husband, she'd eat her pack. The same went for his wife, Cheryl.

Logically, Nyle—as co-pilot—had to know something. But what? He didn't radiate the aura of a criminal. Rather, he appeared to be sinking beneath the crush of despair. Although, it could be guilt.

Pulling away from Zane, she flicked a nervous glance in his mother's direction. She recalled the competent manner with which Elizabeth wielded the rifle and her unflappable attitude. The woman had to be in her sixties, yet she was as fit, if not fitter, than Bernie. A retired schoolteacher shouldn't have much recourse for handling firearms.

Who did that leave?

Zane. An artefact thief. Or so, she'd once believed. Another perfect cover. As for his reason for being in Brazil—a holiday then following a lead in his quest to find his mother's killer. Of course, he could have spouted a mouthful of lies. No, she didn't believe that. No one could have faked that lost, desolate inflection in his voice.

If he'd wanted to harm Bernie, it would have happened by now. But she couldn't rule him out. He certainly wasn't a tourist. His actions over the past few days had revealed his skill with covert surveillance. And he'd killed three soldiers. Who was he really?

"Those thugs were expecting the plane to land on that runway." Zane's voice cut through her ruminations and he flicked his finger at the paper making it snap. "This Jaguar bloke must have paid someone to...what? Land the plane? Sabotage it?"

Plucking the paper from Zane's fingers, she folded it into a neat square, letting her gaze settle on Nyle. "Either are possibilities. Those mercenaries are after us for a reason. I believe they're hunting me. And my sister."

She tucked the page into a side pocket of her pack, hating the thought that if she'd never boarded that plane these people would be going about their normal business. No one would have got hurt. No one would be dead.

The memory of Rhoda's execution flashed through her mind. A fifteen-year-old girl had been robbed of her mother. It didn't matter that Tatum had placed both herself and her mother in danger by running off. By boarding the plane, Bernie had started a chain of events and it would take a miracle for any of them to survive.

Zane's brows knitted together. "If you're right, then the mercenaries could be working for the jaguar. But why?"

She inhaled sharply. The other passengers had stepped closer, so she lowered her voice. "The warning was given to my father. He's the governor of Florida."

Zane's eyebrows rose. "So, this *El* Jaguar person must want you and your sister alive. That would explain the tranquilizer gun. One major possibility comes to mind; ransom."

She raised her chin. "Whatever their reasons, I have no intention of being taken alive."

~ 19 ~

They'd been on the move for several hours and making better time, now that Delroy was able to walk. Judging by the drier ground, Zane reckoned they'd been moving steadily away from the river. Hunger gnawed at his belly making his muscles cramp. The distant barking of dogs indicated the mercenaries were back on their trail and gaining ground.

"We need to pick up the pace," Zane said, slashing his way through a tangle of vines blocking their passage.

Sweat stung his eyes and he flicked his head in annoyance. *Damn this humidity.* He cast his gaze over the bedraggled group, noting how the space between each person lengthened by the minute. They were exhausted. Defeat was a black cloud swirling mere inches from their bodies. It wouldn't take much for hope to be entirely smothered. Then, they'd be easy pickings.

Those bloody dogs were too close to stop. They

had to keep pushing forward. A hand touched his arm. Glancing around, he met Bernie's eyes. Something inside loosened at the sharpness of her cheekbones and the slackness of her threadbare tunic. It had only been a couple of days and yet, she'd lost weight. Like the rest of them. They needed something more sustaining to eat than fruit and berries. He suspected sheer determination was the only thing keeping Bernie on her feet. His respect for her rose another notch.

"Delroy has collapsed," she said.

So much for not stopping. He swallowed his curse and fought the nagging frustration biting at the edges of his mind. Every second delayed them further from their objective. Food. Medical help. Safety. For Bernie and his mother. Everyone was aware of the stakes. No one wanted to die in this fucking jungle.

Dropping his pack, he and Bernie headed to where Delroy was on his knees, head bowed. Pearl stood with her hands at her throat and doing absolutely nothing to assist her husband. The others stumbled to a halt, no doubt grateful for the break.

From the rear, Colin called out, "Gotta use the john."

Hand clamped over his belly, like he had gut pains, he pushed through some palms and disappeared out of sight. Melanie, with a sour expression on her face, sagged against a tree trunk then began to dig in her pack.

"Hey, man. How are you doing?" Zane crouched beside Delroy who smiled weakly.

"Sorry about this, Zane. I ain't doing so good," Delroy rasped, his dark skin had a gray hue beneath and his body stank of sweat. "But I wont be carried on a stretcher no more."

"It's okay, pal. Time we had a rest anyway." Zane gave a tight smile, then rising to his feet indicated for Bernie to follow him. Stopping a few feet from the others, he ground out, "They're slowing us down."

Bernie nodded. "I know."

"There's only one alternative. We find somewhere they can hide while you and I make a run for the dig. If it's just the two of us, we'll cover the distance faster. It's our only chance."

"I don't like leaving them." Her mouth shook. Tears glistened in her eyes.

"We haven't got a choice." He turned to face her fully then placed his free hand on her shoulder, feeling her tremble at his touch. "We both know if we continue on like this, none of us will make it out alive."

"I'm not going anywhere unless we find them somewhere safe. But searching for a suitable spot will also delay us."

"Damn." His hand fell from her shoulder and he stared glumly at where his mother, bless her, carried young Cody in her arms.

She'd passed her rifle over to Ricky. With her lank hair, tired face and dirty clothes, she resembled a refugee from a war-torn country. He couldn't bear the thought that he might lose another mother. But the pace he and Bernie would have to set to reach the dig and return with help would be too grueling for a woman her age, no matter how fit she was. He'd have to leave her behind with the others.

His mother reached their side and smiled. "What have you decided?"

He'd never had to spell out anything to her. She'd always seemed to know his thoughts and feelings, usually before he was aware of them himself. He gave her a quick update then asked, "What's your opinion of Delroy?"

Elizabeth sighed. "I doubt he can walk much further today. Although, I'm certain he'll insist on trying."

"We shouldn't have given into his insistence on ditching the stretcher."

"He was right though. We've made better time with only one stretcher, even with his weakness."

Zane scratched his chin. "I can't hear the dogs, but I suspect those bastards don't intend to give up. I'll attempt to lead them away from the group while Bernie scouts for a hiding place."

"There's something else."

"Yes, Mom?"

His mother shifted Cody into a different position in her arms. The kid sucked gustily away on his thumb. Zane frowned. Wasn't he too old for that?

"I believe someone is following us."

Bernie gasped. "You too?" She turned to Zane, saying, "Ever since we discovered Rhoda's body, I've sensed someone watching."

"And you never said anything?" Frustration and fear sizzled to the surface. Zane planted a hand on his hip and glared into Bernie's beautiful eyes.

"I wasn't certain if it was my imagination. It can't be a mercenary. Otherwise we would have been captured. It could be curious natives."

Zane stroked his jaw thoughtfully. "We could ask for help. They might guide us to a village. Or town."

Bernie shook her head. "There're still a lot of tribes in Brazil that have little to no contact with the outside world. We can't risk spreading disease. It would wipe out their entire population. At best, we could attempt to approach within speaking distance to judge whether that's the case."

"The markers that disappeared."

Bernie nodded. "That's my understanding, too. Taken or moved out of curiosity."

"Which leads us right back to where we started. I'll tell the others to move out." He inspected the compass on his watch. "Where shall we meet up?"

"No way, Zane. You really think it will work a second time?" Bernie scoffed.

"Shit." He yanked out a water bottle and unscrewed the lid with a savage twist. "Drink?"

Bernie accepted with a word of thanks and took a mouthful before offering the bottle to Elizabeth and Cody. "Zane, you stay here, while I do a little recon. With luck, I may stumble across our shadow."

"We'll cover more ground and we'll finish faster if we both go. You one way, me the other. We'll meet back here in fifteen."

"Someone needs to keep these guys toeing the line."

"You sound like a soldier."

She shrugged, a tiny smile tugged at her lips. "My father is an ex-Marine. Plus, I like adventure movies."

"Same." Warmth spread through him when her smile bloomed into a wide grin.

"Movie night then. After that five-star hotel room."

"Deal. Be careful out there." He took back the water bottle, watching as Bernie shrugged off her pack then picked up a rifle. If he cupped her sweet face in his hands and kissed her, would she return the kiss or push him away? Before he could decide, she pushed into the undergrowth and was gone.

He stared at the spot where she'd been, his eyes burning. If the fates decreed it, he might never see her again. The knowledge just about sent him to his knees.

"Zane, we need to talk." His mother's firm voice shattered his disturbing thoughts.

"Sure thing, Mom."

"Don't worry about Bernadette. She's a very resourceful young woman who doesn't take chances." She gently nudged his arm with hers and they fell into step, walking back to where the others were resting.

Flexing his taut shoulders, Zane tracked their positions. His jaw clenched when he realized several members were missing. Now where the devil had they gone? Hopefully they hadn't wandered too far off in search of privacy.

"What was that paper you and Bernadette were reading?"

"Huh?" Pre-occupied, her words didn't penetrate for a few seconds. Frowning, he glanced sideways at her. His skin prickled at her set expression. "Just a note Bernie found near the runway. We both believe it has a lot to do with our current situation. Mentioned the name of some person Bernie knows."

"Oh? Like who?"

He shrugged. "Some clown calling himself a jaguar."

Elizabeth drew a sharp breath. "And Bernadette has met this man?"

"Hell, Mom. I doubt it. She seemed more frightened than anything. We think this guy may have paid someone to arrange for the plane to land on that bloody runway."

"An interesting scenario." Elizabeth looked down at the little boy asleep in her arms. "I'll lay Cody down next to Cheryl. He's getting quite heavy. I'd like to see that letter if possible."

"Bernie has it. Here, let me carry Cody over to the stretcher." Smiling, he took the kid and strode to where Cheryl lay, then set the child down.

Cheryl didn't stir. Her breathing seemed shallow, her chest rose and fell slowly. She appeared smaller, as if shrinking inside her skin. How much longer could the poor woman hold out? She needed a doctor. If it wasn't already too late.

He heaved off his duffle, sank onto a nearby log then rested his head on his arms. He looked up as Melanie and Tatum returned. Melanie tossed him the much-depleted toilet roll which he took with a brief 'thanks'. Delroy remained scrunched on his haunches as if even the effort of moving onto his butt was beyond him. Clearly, he couldn't travel any further for the moment. Damn, that bloody frog.

Zane rose stiffly to his feet, roll in hand, intending to seek a little privacy himself. And maybe round up the missing while he was at it. Including Bernie. Whether or not she'd found somewhere for the others to hole up, the two of them had to make that dig. If not, they were all going to die.

To his right, branches cracked and palm leaves rustled. He swooped for the rifle he'd lain on the ground, his finger tightening on the trigger, ready to fire, when Bernie crashed into view.

Sweat shone on her ashen face. Her eyes were wide, her chest heaved as she gasped for breath.

He bounded to her side and took her cold hand in his. "Steady on. Take a long, slow breath".

Bernie blurted, "Colin. Oh my God! It's Colin. Someone's killed him."

~ 20 ~

Tremors shuddering through her, Bernie led Zane to where Colin's body sprawled face-down in the mud, his arms and legs splayed.

"There." Ensuring she stood a good few feet away, she pointed at the body. Panic clawed at her throat, her gaze transfixed on the broken spear protruding from Colin's back. Blood stained his tattered shirt and puddled beside his torso.

Face grim, Zane crouched down and examined the wound. Then gently turned Colin's face out of the mud and checked for signs of life. After a few moments, he glanced over his shoulder. "You're right. The poor guy is dead."

Zane looked up and carefully studied the surrounding foliage. Not a leaf stirred in the breathless air.

Bernie quickly averted her head. No way did she ever want to see the terrified expression frozen on Colin's face again. Heart heavy, she recalled her impression someone followed them. It could be *El*

Jaguar haunting their footsteps. This could be a warning. Colin might have stumbled across him then the bastard had murdered him.

Melanie came running through the palms, skidding to a halt beside Colin's prone figure. "Babe! Talk to me. Is he...please tell me, he isn't dead?" Melanie turned imploring eyes to Zane.

"What is it? What's going on?" called Tai, appearing out of the jungle.

Ricky with Nyle limping beside him, brushed through a knot of hanging vines. They all stopped and stared at the motionless figure.

"What is this shit?" Ricky muttered.

Zane stood slowly, bringing his weapon around to the front. Although the muzzle pointed to the ground, Bernie gained the impression any wrong move by one of them and he'd press the trigger. "Colin was murdered."

"The spear," gasped Melanie, whirling around, her hands curled into claws, as if about to charge into the jungle and tear it apart, leaf by leaf. "Some shit native has killed my babe."

"Melanie, lower your voice," Zane snapped. "You're mistaken. That spear was made by me. Someone in our group is a killer."

"Look," Melanie's voice rose.

Bernie jerked her gaze to a sapling fig tree, spying the small brown figure watching them.

Melanie plunged forward, her face a battleground of fury and grief. Bernie intercepted her a few feet from where the native girl still stood. Wrapping her arms around Melanie, Bernie struggled to contain the enraged woman.

"Let me go. Let me go! I'm going to kill her."

"Quiet, Melanie. You're giving away our location." Scowling, Zane pushed in front of them and protecting the native who peered around his body. "You're mistaken. That's definitely one of our spears."

"I don't believe you."

"See for yourself," Zane said.

"All right. You can let go of me, queen bee," Melanie spat, turning her head to glare at Bernie.

Eyebrows raised, Bernie released her stranglehold and stepped away, hands in the air, ready to grab Melanie if she attempted to attack the girl. Thankfully, the kid hadn't turned tail and run.

Meeting Melanie's gaze, Bernie pointed at Colin. "He wasn't killed by her or any other native."

Head bowed, Melanie stumbled back to Colin's body. She kneeled and, after pressing a kiss to his forehead, began to wriggle his pack from under his slack body. It looked like he'd torn the bag from his shoulders then hunched over it as if fearing his discovery would be stolen.

Tai joined Zane and Bernie, saying, "Are you sure about this, mate?"

Zane nodded. "I'm positive. One of us killed Colin."

"One of us," repeated Nyle in a dazed voice. He limped forward. "This is all my fault. I'm responsible. It wasn't the Captain who brought the plane down. It was me."

"What?" roared Tai. He lunged forward, fists bunched and slammed a punch into Nyle's face. "My wife is dying, you bastard." He swung again, slogging another into Nyle's gut.

"Umph!" Gasping, Nyle staggered, lost his grip on his staff and fell heavily to the ground.

"Get up. Get up!" Tai balanced on his toes, eyes blazing with retribution.

Zane moved fast, positioning himself between Tai and the fallen Nyle. Stunned, Bernie's met Zane's grim gaze.

Nyle was the culprit. He was responsible for the danger they all faced. He was responsible for Kit lost in the jungle. Because of his actions, people had died.

Bernie squeezed her eyes shut for a few seconds, battling her rage. She longed to kick and punch Nyle until he was nothing but a pile of broken bones. She longed to scream blue murder and rant until her lungs gave out. She longed for this living nightmare to be over. Her anger drained away. Fatigue took its place.

"Why?" Bernie whispered, dully. She needed to know.

"Gambling debts I couldn't pay. My nickname around the casinos was Bad-luck Beau. Gives you an idea of how much in debt I owed." Holding his stomach, Nyle crawled to his knees. No one moved to help. "An hour before we were due to take off for Manaus, I was offered two hundred thousand to land the plane on the runway. No idea who pay-rolled me. No idea why. I took the money and asked no questions."

"Bastard." Tai spat onto the ground, then turned away as if unable to even look at the co-pilot any longer. He raised his knuckles to his eyes.

Zane gripped Tai's shoulder. For once, Ricky had no crude or sarcastic comments, merely goggling at Nyle like the man had grown another head.

"Did you kill Colin?" Zane asked, tension holding him so tight, the muscles in his neck corded like thin ropes.

"I'm no killer. I've got no reason to see him or anyone else dead." Nyle dug his stick into the mud, heaved to his feet. Blood dripping from the side of his mouth. He didn't wipe it away, his expression that of a beaten dog.

Bernie's instinct told her, he spoke the truth. No way either could Nyle be the Jaguar.

Allowing his hand to drop from Tai's shoulder, Zane shook his head and turned his back on Nyle. "Shit."

"What are we going to do with him?" asked Bernie.

"Nothing for the moment. Someone take that handgun off him." Zane wiped sweat from his forehead.

Ricky darted forward and wrenched Nyle's gun from his holster then tucked the weapon into the back of his pants.

Bernie crossed to Zane and laid a hand on his arm. His muscles bunched at her touch. His bleak expression wrenched her heart. "I don't think Nyle killed Colin."

"My gut agrees, but it doesn't negate the fact we have a murderer in our midst."

Tai's hands fell to his sides and he said in weary tones, "It wasn't me, but I guess we're all going to say the same thing. I'll be with my wife and son."

"We can't stay here," Bernie warned.

Tai's throat worked then he said, "You need to think about saving those you can. Leave Cher and me behind. But, please, take Cody. Promise me, you'll save our son."

Grief and despair stung her eyes. Blinking back tears, Bernie managed a nod and watched as Tai walked away. Keeping a respectful distance, Nyle stumbled after him.

Was it a good idea giving Ricky another gun? Troubled, Bernie gazed at Zane and the native girl who were eying each other warily. The girl was not from some long-lost tribe. No more than fifteen or sixteen, small-boned with wide shoulders she wore a green tank top, faded jeans and had a wide, multi-colored beaded choker around her neck. Her blue-black hair hung straight and thick to her shoulders and tiny brown tattoos adorned her forehead and cheeks.

"Soldiers come." She jerked her head backwards.

"You speak English," said Bernie with relief.

The girl nodded. "Missionaries live in village for much time. Why you here?"

"We're lost. We need help. Can you take us to your village?"

"Soldiers have guns." Her eyes drifted to Zane's rifle and she took a step backwards.

Bernie studied the girl, noticing she wore no shoes. "They're after us."

"Why?"

Bernie hesitated and exchanged a glance with Zane. She may be able to communicate with them, but the odds were that she'd received little education living in such a remote area. And if they revealed too much, the girl could decide to leave them to their fate and not risk harm to herself or her people. "We're not sure but we need help. Some of our group are injured."

202

"Is your village far?" Zane pushed his rifle strap over his shoulder.

The wariness returned to the girl's face. She slid an uncertain look at Colin's body. "Soldiers not kill him."

Bernie turned cold. Had the girl seen Colin's killer? *One of us.* How to ask? The question blocked her throat.

"Did you see who did it?" Zane asked in a low voice.

All her muscles tightened, as Bernie waited for the native girl to respond. Her fingers inched toward the rifle over her shoulder. The killer could be behind her. A weapon aimed. Ready to blow her or Zane on a one-way journey to death.

The girl shrugged. "No."

Air wheezed from Bernie's lungs as she exhaled, her shoulders slumping. "Can you show us the way to your village? Do you have a phone?"

The girl shook her head, her mouth turning mutinous. "Soldiers follow. Have guns," she repeated.

"Damn," muttered Zane, looking at Bernie. "She's right. We can't risk her people's lives."

"This is bullshit. Make her talk. Can't you hear those fucking dogs?" Melanie snarled.

Bernie tilted her head. Melanie was right. While they'd been caught up in the horror of Colin's murder, their hunters were gaining ground. The loud barking rang with a viciousness that made her skin crawl. The soldiers shouted, baiting the dogs to stay on the scent. Should they keep running? Or was it time to stand and fight?

～ 21 ～

Bernie crossed to the Indian girl. "I'm Bernie and this is Zane. We need somewhere safe to hide. Will you help us, please?"

"I am Piku." The girl nodded. "I know good place. Come." She beckoned as if about to melt instantly into the leaves behind her.

"Wait. We need to get the others."

"Must go. Soldiers here." Turning, Piku plunged into the jungle.

"If we don't hurry, we could lose her." Bernie grimaced at Zane.

"Let's get everyone back here as fast as possible. Hopefully, we'll be able to pick up her trail."

"Colin...?" Bernie's voice cracked.

"We can't do anything for him." Zane took her hand in his and they ran past Colin's body.

In a few hours, little would remain of him. In the jungle, anything and everything was food. When they reached the camp, they found Tai had been busy rounding everyone up, ready to leave. They all looked up when Zane marched over to him.

"No one will be left behind. This is our last chance to escape..." His steely gaze swept their faces. "Tai and I will take Cheryl's stretcher. Ricky, you and Pearl help Delroy. Nyle..."

Everyone turned to look at the co-pilot.

But he shook his head. "Don't worry about me. I can manage alone."

Which was probably a good thing. Judging by the hostile faces surrounding him, Bernie reckoned no one would lift a finger to help him.

"I'll take scout position." Bernie strapped her pack on then positioned her rifle at the ready.

Melanie lifted her chin defiantly, hugging Colin's pack close to her chest. "Colin's samples are my priority. I'm not going to let his legacy die with him."

"I'll bring up the rear. Tatum, you carry Cody on your back. Wake him up," ordered Elizabeth in a firm voice.

Wiping tears from her face, Tatum rushed to obey. In seconds, they were on the run. Bernie jogged ahead, favoring her injured knee. A swift glance over her shoulder revealed Zane and Tai were half-running, half-walking, the stretcher jostling behind them. The others bobbed along behind. A raggedy bunch of people desperate to survive.

Passing Colin, she apologized under her breath, forcing aside the grief and guilt. Another companion dead. Jaw clenched, she plunged through the foliage, her focus on the Indian girl's faint tracks.

Her lungs soon ached from the desperate pace she set, the hot, humid air and the need to continually duck under branches and push through tangles of vines and palms. God knew how Zane and Tai were coping. Sweat dripped from her hairline and under her armpits. Her thin clothes felt tacky against her sticky skin. She knew the others were on her heels, their labored breathing and thudding footsteps hard to miss.

A dog bayed in a terrifying howl. The hair on her nape stood on end. Knees trembling, heart pounding, she paused to listen. The soldiers were too close. Bernie scanned the ground. Nothing. No footprints. No leaves. Had she lost the trail?

Zane whispered, "Bernie, what's up?"

She shook her head unable to voice her fear. Eyes straining, she took a cautious step forward, scanning the ground around her. Which direction should they take?

Palm leaves rustled and Piku's face appeared. "Come."

"Thank heavens," Bernie half sobbed and shoved through the fronds to join the girl.

The underbrush crackled. A huge, snarling dog leaped out of the bushes, jaws agape, frothing from its mouth. It lunged. Piku screamed, turning to run. The dog rammed into her. She fell, tumbling down in a flail of arms, legs and maddened animal. The growling dog locked its jaws onto her arm.

Bernie paused mid-charge. Too close to fire her gun and terror held her fast, in case she missed and hit the girl. Exhaling, Bernie shifted her grip to the barrel, stepped forward and brought the heavy butt crashing down onto the dog's head. It yelped, releasing its grip. Bernie swung again, this time aiming for the dog's gut. She made contact, propelling the beast off Piku, who scrambled away on her hands and knees.

"Move, Bernie," roared Zane.

Bernie flung herself sideways, landing heavily. Zane fired and the dog shuddered, dropping dead in a bloody heap in the mud.

"Bernie, Bernie, are you all right?" Zane dropped on his knees at her side, his hands patting her down, checking for injury.

"I'm fine."

He helped her to her feet and they hurried to where Piku huddled under a palm. Murmuring soft words of encouragement, Zane quieted the terrified girl while Bernie worked off her pack then pulled out the first aid kit. Her medical supplies were almost all gone, but she washed away the blood with clean water then disinfected the wound.

"Let's hope she doesn't need a tetanus or rabies shot." Bernie wrapped the last clean bandage around Piku's arm. She sank onto her haunches, exhausted and shaking inside now that the rush of adrenaline had passed. She looked at Zane. "That was some shot. What exactly do you do for a living?"

He touched the side of his nose and winked. "Artefact thief?" But his tone was teasing rather than serious.

"I don't believe that any more."

"I know." The fleeting amusement died from his eyes, replaced with something tender that curled around her heart. Leaning forward, he placed a soft kiss on her forehead. "No rest for the beautiful. Up you get, my girl."

Placing a hand under her elbow, he assisted her to her feet before helping the Indian girl upright.

Shouting came from behind them. Dogs barked. Everyone turned to look. Zane handed Bernie her pack.

Piku gasped. "Must go." She ducked around a walking palm and set off in a stumbling jog.

Zane took up his post beside Tai on the stretcher and, after a quick glance to ensure no one was missing, Bernie followed Piku. The girl seemed to follow no discernible trail that Bernie could see, snaking around logs, clumps of palms and impenetrable vines. The yells and barking echoed perilously close.

Heart in her throat, Bernie stumbled over a pile of pebbles, water sloshed over her feet. Mud sucked at her shoes. Ahead, Piku looked over her shoulder and beckoned.

Quickening her pace, Bernie followed. Ducking beneath a huge palm frond, she spied Piku scrambling down the side of a cliff. At the bottom of the narrow ravine, a winding snake of a stream glittered through the foliage. Panting, she waited for Zane and Tai.

Zane peered down the ravine and sighed. "Shit."

"You sure we can trust her?" Sweat glistened on Tai's face as he pushed forward to look.

"We've got little choice. I can take the rear stretcher posts while you two take the front poles. That way we should stop the stretcher from tipping over or being caught on rocks." Bernie slipped the rifle strap over her shoulder.

Zane frowned, but he couldn't debate her logic, and they had no time to find an alternate solution.

Tatum—with Cody clinging to her back—

appeared with Pearl and Ricky, supporting Delroy between them. Nyle and Elizabeth trailed at the end of the line.

"Where we going, *chica*?" asked Ricky.

"Down. Don't wait for us, keep following Piku."

"Sure thing."

Grabbing the rear poles, Bernie called, "Ready."

They began the tortuous climb down the cliff-face. Bernie stumbled several times on loose pebbles and skidded a couple of heart-pounding feet when she slipped on wet moss. Up front, Zane or Tai muttered a soft curse every so often.

Her biceps screamed for mercy. Just when she thought she couldn't hold on any longer, they reached the bottom. Gulping in lungsful of thick, steamy air, she lowered her end to the ground. Zane and Tai kept on going. It took a few seconds before Bernie could flex her stiff fingers from where she'd gripped the poles.

Her arms ached, as did her wrists and her shoulders. Her thighs shook so much, she slumped against a boulder for a moment, longing to flop onto the ground. She felt like she'd been pummeled with stones. She wanted to close her eyes and never move again. Where the hell was that bed Zane had promised her?

Tatum sat Cody onto a patch of grass and arched her back, groaning loudly, but Melanie brushed past them, her gaze concentrated on where Piku sloshed through the stream several yards ahead. Delroy, hanging like a side of beef between his wife and Ricky, swayed on his feet, hung his head then vomited into the grass.

"Fuck!" Ricky skipped sideways as the big guy retched for a second time.

Halfway down the ravine, Elizabeth turned her head constantly, searching for danger, rifle held in steady hands. Reaching the bottom, Nyle stumbled toward them.

"Don't stop." Bernie waved them on.

Tatum wailed, "Cody is getting really heavy. I can't carry him anymore."

"Get on your feet. All of you." Zane ordered. "Bernie, I need you. Get up and keep moving, damn it."

With difficulty, Bernie raised her head. It could have been made of stone. The fierce determination blazing in Zane's eyes as he looked at her over his shoulder, fired the last of her reserves. Dizziness clouded her thoughts, reminding her she was badly dehydrated. She swallowed several mouthfuls of water then offered the rest of the bottle to Cody, who sat cross-legged on the ground. He looked so woebegone that Bernie pushed aside her own distress. While he took a drink, she passed her nearly empty pack to Tatum.

"You carry my bag. I'll take Cody."

Tatum murmured, "Thank you."

Her red-rimmed eyes had sunk in her thin face, reminding Bernie that it hadn't been that long since the girl had witnessed her mother's execution. Bernie patted the teenager's arm and received a wobbly smile in return.

"Hold my rifle while I pick him up," Bernie said. As soon as Cody clung monkey-fashion to her back, she retrieved her weapon and waved Tatum forward. "Hurry."

Bernie set off after the others who hadn't stopped. Her eyes fixed on Zane who kept throwing her ferocious glares, ensuring she was following.

Smiling to show him she was fine, she said, "Hang on tight, Cody."

"Are we going home?" he asked, sniffing.

"Yeah, sweetie. We're on the way." *I won't fail you. Somehow, I'll save you. I won't let you die out here like Colin and Rhoda.* Her heart ached. *Where are you Kit?* If only she knew her sister was safe. She'd give anything—her life if she had to—if it meant Kit survived.

She could attempt to bargain with their hunters. Her life in exchange for the lives of the others. For Kit.

Her steps slowed. Head bowed and silent, Tatum trudged past her. She could allow the distance between her and the others to widen. Then she would wait, hands held in the air, for the soldiers to arrive. Ask to speak to whoever was in charge.

Pearl and Ricky lurched around her, almost dragging Delroy, sweat marking his shirt and dripping from his chin. If the soldiers wanted her, surely they'd abandon the hunt, if she surrendered? The others would have a chance to escape, especially with Zane and his formidable mother looking out for them.

A small hand patted her cheek. "Choccie?" asked Cody.

A sob ripped from Bernie's chest. She'd need to foist this cherub onto someone else so she could go through with her plan. She shook her head, becoming aware Elizabeth walked beside her.

"You're falling behind and that will never do,

dear." Zane's mother spoke casually. "Let's not have any sacrifices. The drug lord will honor no promise and you will have thrown your life away for nothing."

Startled, Bernie stared. "Why did you mention sacrifice?"

Elizabeth shrugged. "Isn't that what you were just contemplating?"

"I'm the one they're after."

"They could be seeking any one of us. Some people call me Betty, by the way." A note of warning rang cold in Elizabeth's voice.

Unnerved by the woman's perceptive comments, Bernie stepped into the fast-moving stream, picking her way as quickly as possible over boulders and twisting tree roots.

Massive fig trees, tall palms and thick undergrowth grew to the water's edge on both sides of the stream making wading through the water the easiest way to traverse the narrow ravine. The thick canopy above their heads revealed only tiny patches of gray sky giving the area a gloomy atmosphere. No wind stirred the heavy air.

A deadened hush sent unease scurrying along Bernie's spine like the cold feet of a startled insect. Apart from their breathing and the splash of feet through water, nothing else stirred. Where were the hunters and their dogs?

Maybe the mercenaries had given up the chase and they were finally safe.

～ 22 ～

Elizabeth nudged her elbow and Bernie tracked the direction of her gaze. Resting in the V of two tree roots, lay a caiman. The reptile had to be a least six feet long. As Bernie stared, its tail swished to the side. Amazing how the caiman's black scaly skin blended with the deep shadows beneath the tree.

"There's a caiman," Bernie called out softly.

"Yeah, we see them. Keep moving," came Zane's grim voice in response.

Them? There was more than one? Bernie peered into the dark tree bases, shuddering when she caught the glint of several pairs of eyes.

A group of mercenaries burst from the bushes ahead, firing into the sky. Everyone scattered, shouting, screaming, scrambling over the rocks to reach shelter among the trees.

Adrenaline pumping, Bernie struggled out of the water, dimly aware of Elizabeth following. A bullet whizzed past her ear. Bent over, trying to present as small a target as possible, she reached the bank and ran through the sticky mud. Gasping, she made the cover of the trees as a bullet drilled into the trunk beside her. She dived for cover, branches imploded all around her.

"Take Cody," Bernie shouted attempting to wrestle the screaming boy off her back, but he clung like a limpet.

"No. You see to the boy. I'll see if I can circle around them." Then Elizabeth bounded up the incline, disappearing behind a clump of palms.

Bernie pressed behind the tree to protect Cody, heart slamming against her chest as her gaze zeroed in on Zane.

Unable to return fire or drop the stretcher, he and Tai sank into a crouch, crab-walking as fast as possible out of the stream.

Tatum scrambled to reach a rock and huddled there, sobbing. Melanie and Piku raced for the opposite side of the stream. The Indian girl leapt over a large tree root, landing in a roll before crawling into a thick tangle of vines. Melanie tripped and fell to her knees in the water. Nyle crawled through the shallows toward the bank. Ricky, Delroy and Pearl—being closer to the edge of the stream—had also reached the trees, but were several yards distant from Bernie. Ricky flung off Delroy's arm, leaving him to Pearl, then fired off a shot as he dropped to one knee.

One of the soldiers fell, clutching at his chest. His compatriots took one look at their mate, then cursing in Spanish, ducked behind a pile of boulders. The next instant, they popped up and unleashed a spray of bullets.

Bernie hesitated, her hands trembled, the rifle slipping in her damp grip.

Ricky continued to fire like he was on a battlefield. The explosion of sound deafening. Melanie splashed her way to the opposite bank of the stream. Piku called encouragement. Zane yelled for everyone to stay down and kept firing his revolver. Both he and Tai were in the open, using their bodies as shields for Cheryl strapped to the stretcher. Any second now, a bullet could find its mark and Zane would fall.

Heart in her throat, Bernie raised her rifle, aimed at the widest-looking soldier and squeezed the trigger. He flew backwards with a hoarse shout. She lined up another shot.

Two mercenaries broke cover, firing as they waded across the stream, heading to where Melanie kneeled in the shallows. Blood ran down her left arm.

From a clump of bamboo, Pearl screamed, "Melanie, look out."

"Get down," roared Zane.

Melanie glanced toward the approaching soldiers, dragged Colin's pack from her back, hunched over it and staggered back into the stream.

What is she doing? Bernie aimed at one of Mel's pursuers, squeezed the trigger. Her rifle jammed. "Go back," she screamed, gesturing frantically.

Two thugs bounded toward Melanie. One of them fired, hitting Melanie in the leg. She flailed sideways, lurched forward another step, then twisted at the waist and half-swung around. In her hand was Pearl's revolver. Melanie fired at the closest soldier. His face disintegrated into a mess of blood, gore and bone.

Snarling, his companion let loose with his semi-automatic weapon. Drilling into Melanie. Her back arched, her hands lifted, her face a caricature of agony and disbelief as blood spurted from her torso. Colin's pack dropped into the stream. She fell face-first into the water.

The soldier who'd shot her landed beside her, his shirt drenched with bright blood. Shot in the back. The water surrounding them rapidly turned red. Shots continued to blast the air. Another soldier screamed. Shouting and barking echoed from the cliff tops.

"Caiman, caiman," shouted Piku, pointing upstream.

"Everyone, out of the water," yelled Zane.

Bernie looked up to see dark, log-like shapes slithering down the banks. Heading to the bodies. She thought of Colin and the passionate zeal in his eyes when he spoke about his miracle cure. She couldn't let it die with him and Melanie. But more importantly, she needed to be certain the other woman was beyond help.

"Stay here, honey. I'll be right back."

She urged Cody onto the ground, held a finger to her lips and bade him to be quiet. She waved Pearl over. Without waiting to see if the woman had moved, Bernie rushed across the sand and splashed into the water, slinging her rifle onto her back.

Her heart pounded in slow thuds. Her skin felt like it was shrinking over her bones. At any moment a bullet could shred her flesh. Blackness encroached on her peripherals, but she surged forward to where Melanie floated in the knee-deep stream. The current swirled, tugging Melanie in a semi-circle.

A quick glance to the left revealed a caiman

approaching fast. She had less than a minute before the reptile reached them. Gripping Melanie by the shoulders, Bernie turned her over. Melanie's eyelids flickered. She was alive.

"Come on!" Bernie gripped Mel under her armpits and dragged her backwards.

The water rippled, tiny waves broke over the surface. Within seconds, the caiman would be upon them.

"No...no...samples," wheezed Melanie. Black blood bubbled from her mouth, staining her chin.

"I'll come back for them."

"Col...I...killed...h..."

"What?" Bernie stumbled, going down on one knee. Had she heard correctly?

"Samp...promise...safe..." Melanie emitted a bone-rattling gurgle.

Oh my God! Shaking, Bernie pressed her fingers to Mel's throat. No beat. No pulse. Nothing. Her eyes already beginning to glaze over as she stared sightlessly at the sky.

"Bernie, Bernie!"

Ignoring Zane's frantic shouts, she checked again for breathing, for a heartbeat. But Melanie was dead. Three bullets zinged into the water close to Bernie's right leg.

"I'll keep them safe, Mel. I promise."

Crying softly, Bernie picked up Colin's pack from where it had lodged next to a boulder and waded to the opposite shore. Like Melanie, she hunched over the precious pack. Several heart-stopping seconds later, she reached the shelter of the trees and leaned against a trunk. She pressed an arm against her eyes, silent sobs shaking her body.

Pebbles rattled. She refocused, lowered her hand. Halfway up the side of a ravine, stood a black jaguar, its elongated yellow eyes unblinking as they traded stares. For a long three seconds, neither moved. A dog howled. The jaguar bounded gracefully up the incline.

Bernie exhaled loudly. Clasping Colin's pack in one hand, the rifle in the other, she crept around the tree. Thrashing and splashing came from the stream. Melanie. The slain soldier. Shuddering, she hiccupped over a sob. No way would she look. Bending over, she dry-retched into the reeds.

Shaking uncontrollably, she straightened, wiped her mouth then realized the shooting had stopped.

Strong arms pulled her close. With a sigh, she rested her head on Zane's chest, allowing his warmth and strength to wash over her. She squeezed her eyes shut, wishing herself anywhere but in this nightmare.

"Never do that again." His voice lacked bite. It resonated with relief and fear.

She gulped, unable to answer apart from a nod. His hands moved soothingly up and down her spine, while tears dripped from her chin.

"We can't stay here," he muttered.

"How...is anyone else hurt?" Fishing for her handkerchief, she eased out of his arms and rummaged in her pocket. After blowing her nose, she stuffed the damp rag away.

"No, but those murdering bastards are all dead." He didn't need to mention Melanie.

"What? All of them?" Bernie shuffled Colin's pack over her shoulders.

Zane's brows knitted together. "I got one and both

you and Ricky wounded another. The rest were shot from behind."

"Who could have done that?"

"No idea. The bad news is we've used up a lot of ammo." Zane sighed. "Let's go, before more reinforcements arrive. Piku is waiting for us. She wants us to cross over further downstream."

Zane slipped his arm around Bernie's waist and they shuffled to where the others were sprawled in the mud behind a large boulder.

Longing to sit, but fearing she'd never get up again, Bernie sagged against a rock. Delroy lay on his back, tear tracks stained his haggard face. A dishevelled Elizabeth squatted beside the stretcher, holding Cheryl's hand. A leaf hung from Elizabeth's tangled hair, like she'd been crawling through bushes. Bernie recalled how someone had bush-whacked their assailants. Whoever had performed such a feat would have to be an expert marksman. Or woman.

Zane's mother? Impossible. The retired schoolteacher had to be sixty if she was a day. But then Zane also displayed a surprising familiarity with weapons. Maybe their idea of family bonding was a day spent at the gun range.

Not so hard to believe. Bernie's father had taught her how to shoot by lining up tin cans on a fence railing. But she'd never understood the lure of hunting. How ironic then, that here she was, the one being hunted.

A gray-faced Pearl handed Bernie a partially filled water bottle. "Mel took the gun from me, last night. Saying she didn't feel safe now that Colin was dead. Perhaps if she hadn't fired at those men, they wouldn't have shot her."

"It's hard to say, Pearl. These guys mean business." With dizziness assailing her, Bernie sucked down a few mouthfuls of water.

Dogs barked again. About to give back the bottle, Bernie stilled, holding her breath. Everyone swung around to stare along the ravine, but with the mass of jungle, it was impossible to determine how close their pursuers were.

"Bloody wankers. They just won't give up." Tai cuddled his son close.

Zane counted the number of bullets he had, before shoving the pistol in his waistband. "Time for us to go."

"My rifle jammed," Bernie said, remembering that terrible moment. If she'd taken the shot, Melanie might have survived.

Shaking his head, Zane held out his hand. "Wasn't your fault, sweetheart. Let me take a look." He cracked the barrel and peered inside. "A piece of spent cartridge. This gun hasn't been maintained. We should check and clean our weapons the next chance we get." After removing the blockage, he handed the gun back to her.

"Thanks."

"We can't outrun them." Zane looked at Bernie, his expression bleak. "I need you to take my place on the stretcher."

Denial gave a vicious kick to her belly. She knew what he proposed to do. She could see it in his eyes and in the determined set of his jaw.

"No." One word. So simple. So innocent. So devoid of the agony bleaching her heart of all color, all life.

Zane touched her lower lip with this thumb. Deep lines of fatigue bracketed his mouth. His dark mocha eyes were eloquent with the words he hadn't said.

She'd do as he asked. She'd leave him behind. And die inside if they never met again.

"I'll hold them off as long as possible." Zane kept his gaze locked on hers for another few seconds as if implanting her image in his memory, before he turned away.

No last kiss. No last touch. No time. She fisted her hands to stop reaching out to him.

"Hell, you won't be alone, Zane, my man. I'll be staying with you," growled Delroy, rolling onto this side and pushing to his knees.

"We need someone who can shoot. Not sway." Ricky snorted, stubbing out his cigarette. "I'll do it."

"Make your shots count, then." Zane sent him a pointed look. "Standing upright presents a larger target. If you can't find cover, kiss the dirt. Bernie, it's up to you to keep these people safe."

He glanced over at his mother. They exchanged a nod full of understanding. Then he and Ricky were gone.

⌁ 23 ⌁

Mouth trembling, Bernie jogged after the Indian girl determination as hard as a rock in her soul. A headache throbbed behind her eyes. Her legs and shoulders ached, her right leg in particular. Her knees shook. But none of that really mattered—not when Melanie was dead. Cut down like she was as insubstantial as a rag doll. Melanie, who with her shoulder-length dark hair and similar age, could have been mistaken for her.

Bernie hoped the mercenaries would give up the hunt once they discovered Melanie's body. Disperse and run off, thinking they'd killed the one person they were supposed to take alive, if they *were* on *El* Jaguar's payroll.

But if they didn't throw in the towel, the mercenaries would be on the hunt again with a vengeance; given several of their compatriots had fallen victim to the hunted's bullets. The distant sound of gunfire echoed along the ravine. Bernie choked back a sob. Those devils had no intention of giving up.

They crossed the stream further up from where they'd been ambushed. Here, the ravine had widened with thick jungle growing right to the water's edge, hiding the other side from view. They'd gained ground with Zane and Ricky holding the soldiers at bay. But with limited ammunition, it wouldn't be long before the two men were out-gunned, fell to bleed out in the mud, or captured then tortured to death.

Bernie glanced at her companions, gauging the limits of their strength. Pretty low. They were at the end of their endurance. Strain etched deep in their bleak faces, bowed shoulders and stumbling steps. Frowning, she realized that at some point, Elizabeth had disappeared.

Maybe she'd retreated to help Zane. They couldn't turn back and search. Bernie had to save those she could.

The day bled rapidly into night, increasing the difficulty of moving through the dense jungle. But their hunters had no need of stealth now. They'd use flashlights and keep hounding their quarry until they all dropped in their tracks.

About to call out to Piku they needed to rest, Bernie changed her mind when the Indian girl waved her to a halt. Swaying, Bernie placed a hand on a nearby palm trunk while Piku shoved aside a curtain of lianas. Crouching down, she scrabbled about in the mud between the roots of an immense emergent tree. Eventually, Piku turned around, her teeth gleaming in a wide smile.

"Follow."

She patted a twisted tree root then pushed aside a thick blanket of fern and bracken. The next instant she lowered herself into a hole in the earth. Blinking, it took a few seconds for Bernie to register what had just happened. Elation hit her, her fatigue falling from her shoulders. This could be the perfect place to hide. She and Tai lowered the stretcher to the ground.

"Wait here."

She bounded forward, digging her flashlight out of her pack. Impatiently, she slapped it a couple of times until a thin beam flickered into life. She swept it over the area where Piku had disappeared and located the hole. Sinking to her knees, she poked her head and shoulders through the aperture then emerged, grinning broadly. Their prayers had been answered.

"I'll go first. Pearl, you're next. Tai, you and Delroy lower Cheryl down to us. Once we have the stretcher inside, everyone else can follow."

"What is it?" Tai frowned.

"A cave."

Tatum backed away, shaking her head. "There could be spiders. Snakes."

"Like there ain't no snakes out here. I'm for it." Pearl stepped forward.

Bernie wriggled off the pack then re-placed it with her rifle. Turning around, she swung her legs into the hole and looked at the others.

"I believe this is the ruins of an ancient city. Come on. This is our chance to lay low, somewhere the mercenaries won't find us." Taking a breath, she disappeared into the crypt-like darkness.

It took some maneuvering, but eventually everyone was safely below the surface. Sweat beaded Bernie's forehead. The dry air with dusty overtones scratched the back of her throat. She coughed as she clambered up a tree root to the opening where she pulled the bracken over to cover the entrance, before jumping to the floor of the cave.

Pearl handed back her flashlight and Bernie moved the beam about until she found Piku's smiling face.

Piku nodded. "Good hiding place."

"Yes, it's perfect. Thank you." Bernie glanced around.

Earthen walls surrounded the small space with tree roots dangling from the dirt above their heads. Sand and small pebbles covered the floor. Behind where Piku stood yawned a tunnel where carved rock steps led down into pitch darkness.

Piku beckoned for the flashlight and Bernie handed it over.

"This way."

Bernie turned to the others. "We're going to need all the light we have. If anyone has any battery life in their cell phones, please turn them on."

A general shuffling ensued and soon light flooded the area. Cell phone in one hand, Bernie took one stretcher pole while Tai took the other. They lifted the stretcher, the other end dragging along the ground and moved off after Piku. The others brought up the rear whispering in excited voices.

The steps were wide and shallow and covered with brown lichen. Bernie and Tai picked their way carefully to avoid as much discomfit to Cheryl as possible. At the bottom of the stairs lay another tunnel, which they followed for some time before it flowed into a large, almost level area.

Intriguingly shaped stone fragments littered the

sandy surface. Crumbling mud-brick walls outlined what had been a settlement before the people who had once lived here vanished and the jungle reclaimed the land.

The dim light made it hard to see how far the intricate maze of broken walls spread. A search within the shadows might reveal nothing but solid walls of mud, stone and tree roots. Or it could reveal a settlement of great significance. Tunnels, complete dwellings, old wells or springs. Even places of ritual sacrifice, altars, tombs, ceremonial centers...

Anticipation buzzed as Bernie pondered the possibilities. Her heart pounded. If she'd stumbled across the lost city of the were-jaguar her career would be made—but more importantly, once unearthed, the history buried in the clay and mud would be amazing. She could prove the link between the Olmec civilization and the ancient tribes of Brazil.

After Bernie and Tai lowered the stretcher, she moved over to examine the closest wall and traced her fingers over the outline of a brick. She followed the line of wall to where a good portion had succumbed to age and time, turning to rubble. A family of six finger monkeys capered along a wall several feet away and she smiled.

Stepping over the mess, her gaze fell on a partly buried ceramic pot. She kneeled and using her sleeve, carefully brushed the earth from its sides. Squinting, she examined the pot under the light from her cell phone. Faded images appeared before her eyes. A couple looked familiar. Frowning, she went to peer closer when Tatum emitted a squeal.

This wasn't the time to indulge her fascination

with lost civilizations. She placed the pot closer to a wall, then made her way back to where the others had collapsed on the soft sand.

"We should conserve our phones for later."

"I don't want to sit here in the dark," wailed Tatum.

Bernie didn't blame her. They had no idea of how far beneath the earth the ruins stretched and what creatures inhabited them. "Tai? How about you and I look around? There might be something we can burn for light."

Tai tucked a space blanket around his wife. "I need to see to Cher first."

He sounded weary beyond comprehension and Bernie's heart went out to him. His wife's chances of surviving were pitifully slim.

"Of course." Bernie retrieved her last bottle of water and offered it to him.

"Thanks." He pulled out a plastic self-sealing bag from his pocket and tipped some of the brown powder it contained, into the bottle before assisting his wife to drink.

Curious, Bernie peered at the powder. "What is that?"

"Colin gave it to me. Said it should help slow the rate of Cher's internal bleeding."

Another miracle cure Colin had discovered? Bernie remembered how the scientist had continually scribbled in a notepad. It was highly probable his notes would be just as important as his find.

Quickly, she inspected every pocket in his pack, giving a thankful sigh when she opened the last zipped compartment and spied a yellow dry-pouch.

She snapped open the buckle and unraveled the neck over the plastic fastener. Upon opening it, she found a small book, thankfully intact. A rifle through the pages revealed the pad to be crammed full of Colin's crabbed writing. She resealed the bag, stowing the pouch carefully inside his pack.

Bright light flared. Swinging around, she discovered Piku had a burning torch made from bracken and twigs in one hand. The girl handed a lighter to Pearl.

Smiling, Bernie said, "Piku, you amaze me. Where did you find that torch?"

The Indian girl wedged the torch into a crack in the earth wall. "You come." She trotted across the cave to the far side and melted into the shadows.

Depositing her pack and Colin's bag on the ground, Bernie followed, cell phone in one hand, her rifle in the other. Piku led her through what appeared to be a hand-dug tunnel so low, Bernie had to bend over almost double, shuffling forward.

Piku must have eyes like a cat, thought Bernie, groaning over the pull in her already sore muscles.

When they emerged into another cave, she straightened slowly, rubbing her aching back. Curious, she swept her cell phone about to illuminate their surroundings. Crouched near the opposite wall, Piku gathered up a pile of torches. A pile of fresh palm fronds stood as high as her knees. They'd certainly come in handy as make-shift mattresses.

Smooth stone covered the surface underfoot. Bernie ventured a few more steps, gasping as her gaze alighted on a rectangular stone bench in the center of the chamber. Waist high, the bench was sufficiently long and wide enough for a person to stretch out on the top. A sacrificial stone?

Images were carved into the sides.

This could be an altar or metate, a stone ceremonial seat. Bernie kneeled and holding her phone closer, examined the carvings of the same motif repeated over and over. A cleft head with slanting almond-shaped eyes, open down-turned mouth filled with pointed teeth. Linking the heads together were carvings of double-headed snakes with forked tongues.

"A were-jaguar. Although they're usually depicted with no teeth." Adrenaline fizzed as heady as champagne in her veins. She'd found the lost city. Grinning, she looked up to find Piku standing beside her.

"Our god watches over my people. Provides us with water and food."

"Your god?"

Piku must be an actual descendent of the tribe that had once inhabited this settlement. An off-shoot of the Olmec civilization who'd originated in the south-eastern coast of Mexico. That ancient tribe had revered the jaguar, reflecting their belief in stone carvings. They'd also developed an extensive trading network with other parts of Mesoamerica and possibly they'd traded with Piku's ancestors.

Her head whirling, Bernie stood. For the first time, she realized the tattoos on Piku's face resembled miniature were-jaguar heads.

No smile lit the younger girl's face. In the gloom, Piku loomed taller, her expression serious and a cold shiver pricked Bernie's skin. Perhaps the girl had brought them here for her own nefarious reasons.

Bernie's gaze dropped to the lit torch held in Piku's hands, then tracked over to the remaining pile. Beside them, a were-jaguar effigy carved from rock lay half-buried in the sand. Like a warning not to touch.

"My father's father is shaman. He trains me to be shaman. Many seasons we have watched over the god's sacred house."

"Your English has improved," Bernie pointed out drily.

Piku shrugged. "I did not know if you my friend or friend of *El* Jaguar."

Bernie started, the cell phone fell from her nerveless fingers with a loud smash.

"You know him?" Eyes narrowed, Piku stepped backwards.

"No," Bernie's voice cracked. "I've heard of him. I think he's the one chasing us. You saved our lives by offering us sanctuary."

"Why would he hunt you?"

"I don't know."

"How do you know of our were-jaguar god?" Piku's soft tones had hardened.

"I'm an archaeologist. I was supposed to join a dig to search for this very city."

"This is not your god. Or your history. It belongs to my people." Piku took another step backward as if about to run.

Bernie lifted her hands, like a plea. "The city would be excavated by professionals. The artefacts preserved in a museum and the world would learn of this wonderful, lost culture. That way, your history would never die."

Piku turned her head and stared into the deepest shadows as if listening. A low purr rumbled from somewhere behind Bernie. An animal. No—a wild cat. She froze, not daring to breathe. All moisture dried from her mouth.

The animal growled, a low rattling gargle from the back of its throat. *Shit!* Moving stealthily, she slid her finger towards her rifle's trigger. Her heart pounded like a taiko drum.

Silence.

Lordy! She froze. The slightest movement on her part could antagonize the jaguar to attack.

⌒ 24 ⌒

Piku expelled a loud breath, then smiled. "He accepts you. We go now."

As if unconcerned about the prospect of being eaten alive, she trotted towards the tunnel leading back to the other chamber. Before following, Bernie swept an anxious glance behind. Yellow slits peered at her through the darkness.

She blinked, and they were gone. Whatever she'd seen or thought she'd seen had vanished. Knees shaking, she picked up her cell phone then several torches from the pile, and hurried after Piku. With every step she took, she expected to be knocked to the ground as sharp teeth ripped into her flesh. The distance widened between herself and the sacrificial chamber. Nothing happened, and she began to relax, no longer sensing the animal's presence.

With five torches burning bright and banishing the shadows to the furthest reaches of the cave, a more light-hearted mood settled over Bernie and her group. Although her body begged for rest, she kept busy; dispensing what little food and water remained, checking on Delroy and making up a nest using her woolen pullover for Cody to sleep on.

Piku perched on a nearby slab of stone, watching her every move. Tai saw to his wife's needs, then sat beside her holding her hand. A chatty Tatum shared her water with Ricky and Cody. Pearl, rambling on about a new menu they'd draw up the instant they arrived home, tucked a space blanket over Delroy's recumbent form.

Bernie, her much-diminished first-aid bag in hand, approached Nyle where he sat slumped against the wall, away from the others. "How are you feeling?"

"Like hell." Nyle swallowed, glancing away as if ashamed to meet her eyes.

"Come on. Roll up your sleeve and let me check those bites." She helped him expose his skin, frowning as she saw the extent of the infestation. Inflamed and swollen, the flesh below his right elbow rippled and moved from the hatching larvae.

Blast. She'd hoped she'd dug out all the maggots yesterday morning. Obviously, she'd missed as few or he'd been bitten again. Biting back her repulsion, she began to lance each bite. Using a disinfected needle which had a tiny hook on its tip, she moved it about beneath his skin until she made contact with a larva. Each time she located one, she carefully eased the wriggling blob out then squashed it with a rock. Not a pleasant process and quite painful, but Nyle didn't utter a word of complaint.

"I'm a gambling addict," he muttered.

About to pierce the last bite, Bernie paused. Looking up, she met the resigned sadness in his eyes.

"You mentioned you gambled."

"That's why my wife left me and took our daughter. I haven't seen either of them in five years."

"I'm sorry." And she did feel bad for him. Addiction to anything was a terrible illness, its impact hard on both the addict and their family. "Did you seek help?"

He gave a harsh laugh. "Nah, I was too full of myself, too caught up in the excitement of the game." His gaze wandered over the others, then settled on Tai gently stroking his wife's face. "Because of my arrogance, I lost the most important thing in the world, my family. And now it's too late."

"Don't say that. When we get home, you can call them. Tell your wife you'll do whatever it takes to beat your addiction."

"I don't deserve forgiveness. I slipped a micky into the captain's coffee just after takeoff. It's my fault he suffered a heart attack." Nyle shook his head. "I'm done for. I took a hit."

"What?" Shaken by his admission, Bernie leaned closer when he eased forward, jerking his chin toward his shoulder.

Bernie peered at his lower back, biting back an exclamation at the blood soaking his shirt near the waistband of his chinos. He'd been shot. "Let's get this shirt off you, so I can take a closer look."

"Bloody hell," Tai said as he approached and kneeled beside them. "That looks bad. Can't say I'm sorry though. It's your fault we're in this mess."

"I know. And I'll never forgive myself." Nyle glanced at Bernie. "Elizabeth took a look earlier. The bullet is lodged deep, possibly near my kidneys." He pulled away, sagging against the earthen wall. "You can't do anything for me, Bernie."

"I'll find something to use as a bandage to stem the bleeding."

Nyle said, "No need. Elizabeth slapped a WoundClot bandage over the hole. She also gave me a shot of morphine so I could keep up. She's gone after Zane. Said you weren't to follow her."

"I don't know what to say." Shaking her head, Bernie flopped back on her ankles. Elizabeth had her own stash of morphine plus a military-issue bandage Bernie had only heard rumors about. Elizabeth had a skillset that boggled the mind—an instinct for sensing danger, the ability to track, ambush and kill. And she'd mentioned how some people called her Betty. *Betty.* That blasted note had been addressed to a person with the initials *BB*.

Zane's mother could be in league with *El* Jaguar. Of course, the note could belong to the co-pilot. His nickname was Bad-luck Beau. *BB*. And he'd admitted to bringing the plane down.

Time she discovered the truth. Grimly, Bernie marched over to her pack and retrieving the note, marched back to Nyle. She held the paper out. "Read it."

Nyle took the page and Tai shuffled closer so he could read it too. Nyle frowned. "Sorry, this means nothing to me. I told you, I don't know who paid me to divert the plane."

"I've got no idea either." Tai looked at her. "I don't understand what a note from some wanker with an animal fetish has to do with us."

"I believe he's a local drug lord and he could be after me."

"Why?" Tai stared at her, a rich flush of anger beginning to mount in his face. "Are you working for him? A drug smuggler who stole from him?"

"*No*, I'd never do anything like that." Bernie pressed her fingers to her throbbing forehead. How to explain what she didn't understand herself? "It could have something to do with my father being the governor of Florida."

Avoiding Tai's suspicious eyes, she took the note off Nyle and rose to her feet. "I think we're safe for now. I'm going outside to search for food. And fill some bottles with water from the stream while I'm at it."

"You want some company?" Tai asked, but the offer sounded reluctant.

"I'm okay." Bernie doubted he wanted to be in her vicinity right now, seeing as she could be the reason they were fighting for their lives.

Raising her chin, she dusted sand off her butt then began to gather up empty water bottles. She informed the others of her plan while she stashed bottles inside her pack. "Piku, will you stay here with everyone?"

The girl nodded.

Everyone watched in silence as Bernie shrugged on her pack, inserted her last battery into her flashlight before walking off. They'd all heard her admission and by their set expressions, they didn't know whether to believe her or blame her. In their shoes, she'd probably feel the same. If she *was* the reason, she had to do everything possible to ensure no one else died.

Instead of re-tracing their footsteps to where they'd climbed down the tree roots into the cave, she crept along the tunnel she'd travelled earlier with Piku. If a wild animal could get in, then there must be another way out.

Once in the sacrificial chamber, she began a careful sweep of the ground with her flashlight until she found proof of her suspicions. Paw prints of a large cat. And the only big jungle cat that came to mind was a jaguar.

She swallowed hard when she calculated the distance between the prints and herself. Less than three yards between her and certain death. Yet the creature hadn't attacked. Perplexed, she kept the beam trained on the ground, following the tracks.

Every so often she left a marker for herself; three small pebbles that she'd taken earlier from the stream. The jaguar wound a tortuous path down low-ceilinged tunnels, twisting through three immense chambers of crumbling stone and half-buried mud walls.

In these lower levels, the air was cool and dry, a balm after the heat and humidity above ground. The faint drip of water echoed eerie and lonely through a silence punctuated only by her harsh breathing and stumbling footsteps. Occasionally she heard the soft scrabble of tiny feet in the sand and her belly cramped. Lizards? Large insects? Whatever shared the darkness with her, she had no time or desire to investigate.

Finally, the paw prints led upwards through another tunnel where she spied the faint gleam of daylight trickling through a wall of leaves. She breathed in fresh, moist air. Near the exit, she paused, performing one last sweep of the cramped space around her.

Crystal glittered in the mud-coated tree root dangling from the roof. Bernie placed the flashlight between her teeth and dug away the dirt with her fingers until a stone dropped near her feet. She picked it up, holding it close to a patch of daylight. Her breath caught. *How beautiful.* An emerald pendant bigger than her thumb.

Carved in the stone was an image of a snarling were-jaguar and on the back of the jewel, tiny markings were etched in the flat smooth surface. Squinting, she held it closer. An inscription or possibly even an incantation.

What a find! She quickly pulled out a thin silver chain she usually wore around her neck but had removed after she'd boarded the plane. Threading the pendant onto the chain, she popped the necklace over her head, tucking it under her tunic. The stone felt cold against her skin.

She stashed away her flashlight before pushing aside a branch and wriggling through hanging vines until she stood beside an enormous boulder. An intricate carving, most of the grooves worn down by centuries of wind and rain, indicated that here was indeed the entrance to a settlement of great importance. One that she hoped to re-visit and explore.

Thunder rolled across the darkening sky. Another storm that could wash away their tracks and possibly the markers she'd left for Zane. She shivered, cold despite the waning heat. She'd search for food on the way to the stream, then wait for the two men to return. Dipping her hand into her pocket, she brought out the last magazine for her rifle then counted the remaining bullets. Four.

No matter. She had a much more powerful weapon. She had love.

~ 25 ~

With Ricky breathing loudly near his ear, Zane waited behind a clump of bamboo for a sign their hunters were still on their trail. After drawing the soldiers' fire and wounding a few, they'd zigzagged across the stream several times before charging into the jungle.

The ruse had worked. The bastards had followed, making enough noise for an entire army as they jeered, tramped and slashed through the foliage. But gradually even the baying of the dogs had faded. Now Zane worried the mercenaries had decided to return to the ravine.

Perhaps the single muffled shots he'd heard had caused them to fall back. The shots had been intermittent, nothing like the erratic fire of the men chasing him and Ricky.

Someone else could be out there. Picking off the mercenaries one by one. He recalled how the soldier who'd murdered Melanie had been shot in the back of the head. Quite an expert shot. A feat he couldn't imagine anyone in their group being capable of, but then, what did he know about any of them? Only what he'd been told. And good liars were hard to detect.

He should know. He excelled at assuming different identities.

A swarm of mosquitoes buzzed around his head, despite the mud they'd smeared over their faces and necks. Bloody blood-suckers. He squashed one where it landed on his hand.

He checked the time, calculating they had an hour before it became too dark to press forward. Either he or Ricky needed to break cover and check the mercenaries' position. But it was possible the bastards were holed up, waiting for someone to do exactly that. In that case, whoever revealed himself would be cut down.

Damn! He and Ricky couldn't remain here forever. He jerked his thumb to the left. "We've got to split up."

Alarm sprang wide-eyed in Ricky's face. "No way, man."

Ignoring the younger man's agitated jiggling of his feet, Zane continued. "Wait here. I'll backtrack around and check where those bastards have got to."

"I don't want to stay here alone."

Zane gripped Ricky's shoulder, keeping his gaze steady and his expression calm. "You're doing a great job, Ricky. I know you can handle it."

"Yeah?" Ricky ceased his fidgeting. Sweat still tricked from his forehead, but the cocky tilt to his head had returned. "You're not shitting me, man? You think I did okay?"

"Yes. You're solid." Zane smiled at the grin

spreading over Ricky's face. "Stay low and don't shoot me when I get back. No smoking either. It'll give away your position."

"Sure thing, Zane."

Reasonably confident the boy would do as directed, Zane slipped away. He followed the path they'd cut through the jungle then turned off, angling to the left. The thinner undergrowth made it easier to traverse but it meant less cover. About to grab a vine swaying gently in front of him, he froze.

White eyes with vertical pupils stared unblinking at him from the large, flat head of an emerald tree boa. He recognized the breed courtesy of a school friend with a passion for keeping pet snakes.

The reptile hung by its tail, coiled around a branch above Zane's head. The snake hissed, opening its mouth, revealing enormous fangs. While Zane knew its bite wouldn't kill him, he suspected it might induce a serious reaction. He also knew the deep pits in the scales around its yellow mouth could detect the body heat of its prey. Remaining perfectly still, hand still out-stretched, knee lifted, he waited as perspiration trickled down his sticky back.

Finally, the boa ascended then wrapped itself around the branch. Wiping his damp upper lip with his sleeve, Zane cautiously backed away before skirting a wide berth around the tree. He slashed his way through a prickly thicket, the thorns tearing through his thin shirt, scratching his skin. If Bernie was here, she'd be all over him with her ointment. He filed Bernie away with his other special memories.

He pushed on then diverted off course when he spied a length of beige material on the ground. Closer inspection revealed the body of a fallen mercenary. Shot in the back of the head. Beside him lay a dead dog, also shot.

A stick cracked to his right. Swiftly sinking into a crouch, he spun around, rifle at the ready, finger on the trigger. Nothing moved, but he didn't shift his gaze from the direction of that sound. Something or someone watched him.

"Zane?"

"Mom?" Incredulous, he rose to his feet and strode over to where his mother emerged from behind a palm. "What are you doing here?"

"Looking for you." His mother shouldered her rifle before embracing him. After a quick hug, she slid a hand beneath his elbow, steering him away from the dead.

"Hold on." Zane ran his hand along the muzzle of her rifle. Warm, like it had been fired recently. *"Mom?"*

"I never wanted it to come to this." She sighed, her usual straight-backed posture rounding. Fatigue looked out from her eyes along with dull resignation. After scrutinizing their surrounds carefully, she made for a nearby log and sat, resting the rifle in her lap. Looking up, she patted the seat beside her. "I'll make it quick as we have to intercept five mercenaries before they reach Ricky."

"Five more..." Zane gulped. "How do you know all this?" He flopped onto the log.

"Because it's my job. I'm a hit woman. I only worked part-time as a teacher. The rest of the time..." His mother spoke coolly, as if discussing the weather. "Didn't you ever wonder where the money came from to send you and your sister to those posh schools and later, to Cambridge?"

"I thought..."

Bloody hell. What had he thought? Probably nothing. He'd never questioned anything about his adoptive mother. He'd been too damn grateful to be done with foster homes, the neglect, the loneliness. He'd been so eager and ready to open his heart to the woman who had given him stability, safety, a sense of family. And an education that had set him firmly in a career on the right side of the law.

He snuck a sideways glance, noting the sereneness of her gaze. His mother. Someone who killed people for a living. A killer like his father.

His world turned on its axis. Since the age of twelve, this woman had been the foundation upon which he'd built his life. And with a few words, she'd destroyed everything.

So much for family. His gut rolled over. He forced down the shuddering heaves, attempting to make sense of his dazed thoughts.

"I'd hoped to spare you this knowledge. But it's done now." She raised her gaze from where she'd been staring at her hands and met his. "That letter Bernadette found. I'm afraid it belongs to me. In this line of business, I'm known as Black Betty."

He finally remembered to close his mouth then ground out, "I don't know what to say."

"I'm here on a job, but my contract has nothing to do with our present situation."

He reared back. "How do I know you're telling the truth?"

She shrugged. "You don't. Go with your instinct,

Zane. It's never let you down in the past." Rising to her feet, she scoped out the surrounding bushes with the rifle. "We have to move."

"Wait." Zane put a hand on her arm, noting the firm muscles. "Who is your target? And do you know the identity of *El* Jaguar?"

"I make a point of never meeting my employers in person. My target isn't anyone in our group and I don't know *El* Jaguar."

"Mom, you know what I do for a living."

"Don't worry, son. I'll ensure you won't have to choose between me and your career." After another comprehensive glance at his face, she strode off leaving Zane bewildered.

She was wrong. Her admission had entangled him in her crimes. If he did nothing and kept her secret, he'd be guilty by association. And his sister...what the hell should he tell her? If Bernie ever learned the truth, she'd recoil from him, the way he'd recoiled from his mother.

Remorse twisted a knife in his heart. Maybe he'd been too quick to judge. Maybe his mother had a good reason for her actions. Her skill with a rifle had saved their lives today. She could work for the good guys. Hell, he knew he was no saint. Only a day or so ago, he'd killed to protect an innocent teenager. Then again today he'd killed to survive. But to kill for money... There was a hell of a difference between killing for money and doing it to stay alive.

Head pounding, Zane quickened his pace to catch up with then pass his mother. In fraught silence, they made their stealthy way to where he'd left Ricky. But before they reached him, Elizabeth tapped Zane on the shoulder. She indicated her intentions of circling around and approaching from the opposite direction.

Zane nodded, half of him unable to believe he was using military tactics with his mother of all people.

From over to his right came the slight rustle of leaves. A movement. He sank slowly to his haunches, pivoting at the waist, scoping the area until he had a bead on the mercenary easing his way through the jungle.

The man appeared to be alone. Not that Zane believed that for one moment. His friends wouldn't be far behind, possibly fanning out in a semi-circle to cut off all avenues of escape. They were closing in on Ricky.

Lowering his rifle, Zane slid the knife from its sheath and palmed it. If his mother was as good as he suspected, he could trust she'd take out at least two of these bastards. That left three for him. And damn, if he wasn't in the mood for a good fight.

Slinging his rifle over his shoulder, he crept forward on hands and knees, keeping a wary eye out for snakes and stinging nettles. He did his own circling around, coming up behind the mercenary who carried a semi-automatic pistol in his hand.

Timing it perfectly, he rose in one fluid movement, clasping a hand firmly over the man's mouth while driving his knife deep into his back. A grunt. Blood gushed from the wound. The bloke arched, then his muscles slackened.

Zane bore the brunt of the man's weight, lowering him to the ground. He wiped his hand on the dead man's shirt. Then, he checked for weapons, confiscating the pistol and a box of ammo. He pulled a fallen palm frond over the body. Now for the others.

A footfall alerted him to another mercenary rushing at him from behind. Zane spun to meet him. The man lunged at him with a machete. Using his rifle butt, Zane deflected what would have been a killing thrust. A savage kick to his opponent's knee cap sent the guy staggering off-balance. But the bastard recovered quickly, driving the machete toward Zane's neck.

Ducking, Zane weaved, came up under the man's weapon and rammed his rifle butt hard into his gut. The mercenary grunted, face grimacing with pain as air whooshed from his open mouth. Tossing his rifle to his other hand, Zane swiftly powered an uppercut at the guy's chin, the full force of his body behind the blow. The mercenary's eyes rolled back in his head. Spittle flew from his mouth and he fell backward, landing with a crash on the ground.

A flock of parrots rose screeching from the branches above. Another mercenary broke cover, rifle up, aiming squarely for Zane's chest.

Time seemed to stand still.

Zane brought his rife up. *Too slow.*

A smirk spread over the man's face.

Another rifle cracked. Blood bloomed over the man's upper arm, surprise over his face, knocking his aim off even as he fired. The shot burned past Zane's thigh at the same moment he fired his own weapon. His bullet found its mark in the mercenary's throat. Gurgling and clutching at the blood spurting from his neck, the bastard went down, writhing.

"Did I get him?" Ricky pushed aside branches and appeared beside Zane.

"As good as." Zane grinned at the young man. "Keep me covered."

Zane strode over, kicking the dying man's gun away from his body before kneeling to check for hidden weapons. He moved to the unconscious mercenary. He'd have to kill him. He couldn't risk the thug coming to and following their trail.

He looked up at Ricky. "Turn your back."

After a second, the boy obeyed. Zane heaved the man's inert body against his chest, then laid his arm against his windpipe, pressing hard until he'd stopped breathing.

Now I really am a killer. Like my mother. Like my father. The memory of his birth mother's face swam into this mind. The image hazy. Her smile sad. Tight-lipped, Zane collected the weapons, sharing them with Ricky, then they left the dead behind.

His mother found them near the bushes where Zane had told Ricky to wait. Ricky's eyes almost popped from his head as he goggled at Elizabeth with her steely eyes and the dried blood stains on her clothes. "You one serious *mujer dura*," he said.

"Then you'd better do as I tell you." She swept her gaze over Zane then frowned. "You're hit."

"A scratch. I'll deal with it later. We should catch up with the others."

"We'll never find them." Elizabeth went to step forward, no doubt to check the wound on his thigh.

He waved her back. "Bernie will leave markers for us to follow. We'll make our way to the stream, check for any mercenaries before looking for the others."

Without another glance in his mother's direction, he pushed off. If they didn't pick up Bernie's trail quickly, they'd have to hunker down for the night. In the morning, this area could well be flooded with mercenaries. He suspected the bastards had retreated to wait for reinforcements.

While he'd been able to replenish their arsenal, it would be no match for the full force of a drug lord's army.

～ 26 ～

By the time they'd reached the banks of the stream, Zane felt hungry enough to eat a caiman. It had taken longer than he'd expected to re-trace their steps. He hadn't realized they'd taken such a circuitous route through the jungle.

For the past two hours, they'd had to rely on his flashlight to traverse the terrain and locate the markers he'd left so they'd be able to backtrack. With the moon hidden behind brooding clouds and his battery running so low the beam kept switching off, they'd wandered away from the trail several times. Which had been a good thing, as they'd come across a grove of banana trees and jackfruits. Hope lightened their spirits as they filled their packs with the ripe fruit.

At the tree line, Zane paused, straining eyes and ears for movement. No trace of the mercenaries could be found either near the stream nor sound from further up the ravine. A wary reconnoiter along the bank for several yards revealed even the dead had been removed—a fact Zane found highly suspicious. No way did he believe the mercenaries had abandoned the hunt.

Imbedded in the mud close to the water's edge, he found the paw prints of a large animal—a cat, possibly a jaguar. The creature wasn't known for attacking humans unless under threat, so it was unlikely to have caused the soldiers' retreat.

After an uneasy scrutiny of the impenetrable shadows, Zane returned to the others. "I can't see any caiman, but that doesn't mean they're not around. We cross in close formation and move fast. Ready?"

Upon receiving his mother and Ricky's nods, Zane stepped into the water. The current tugged at his legs causing him to stumble over the rocky bottom. With a sense of relief, he soon trudged up the opposite bank, his mother and Ricky close behind.

"Now what?" Ricky said in a low voice. "*Maldita sea*, I could do with a *buen filete*."

"Ditto." Zane sighed as his gut rumbled at the thought of a juicy steak. Even a sausage would be a feast. A handful of fruit and nuts did little to fill his empty belly. "Wait here while I scout around for Bernie's markers. Whistle if you hear anything."

Thunder growled across the sky. Another bloody storm but at least it should wash away their tracks. He lowered his pack to the ground then picked his way up stream, his gaze fixed on the ground.

He found the first set of markers half-hidden amongst river pebbles right on the water's edge. An empty brazil nut shell with one small white pebble inside. At the sight, his heart filled with elation.

Bernie, bless her. She hadn't failed him. There

wasn't a woman on Earth who could match her in integrity and courage. The one woman he could easily settle for. On this sobering thought, he stopped walking and raised his head to the sky. Raindrops splattered on his upturned face.

"What *are* you doing? Praying to the god of rain and thunder?" And there she stood, her voice warm with amusement and relief.

"Where were you?" He cast his gaze around, seeking but not finding any of the other survivors.

"Behind this boulder. I thought it wise to have something hard and solid guarding my back." She closed the gap between them swiftly, then wrapped her arms around his waist, leaning against him with a weary sigh. "You were so long. I was beginning to fear... Oh, Zane, if I'd lost you too..."

His eyes burned as he dropped the flashlight, his arms automatically closing about her as he rested his head on her tousled hair. *Yes, if I'd lost you...* When had this woman become so precious to him? His gut cramped viciously at the thought of a life lived alone, without her. Yet the truth of his parentage could bring them nothing but pain. Revulsion. Better for her to never know. His arms tightened as he savored the moment, memorizing forever the feel of her softness melding against him as if they'd been made to be one.

She shifted, raising her head, one hand sliding along his throat to tenderly massage the back of his aching head, like she'd sensed his anguish. Then her lips touched his. They tasted salty and he realized she'd been crying.

He couldn't resist. *Give me this night. One more*

night of pure bliss. Their kiss tender and sweet before a hungry desperation swept through him, stirring his blood, blinding his logic. He crushed her to him, his hands slipping beneath the shirt she wore to explore her satiny skin.

She answered his primal call, dueling her tongue with his, rubbing against his stiffening cock and eliciting a bone-shuddering groan from his throat.

"Ahem..." said his mother from behind them.

Great timing, Mom. But her voice alerted Zane to the danger they had yet to escape. Reluctantly, he drew away, pressing one last kiss to Bernie's soft lips.

"Yo, Bernie," said Ricky. For once no smart-ass comment.

"I did ask both of you to wait for my return."

"I'm not getting any younger, son," his mother said drily. "Bernadette, my dear, I'm so glad to see you're unhurt. Where are the others?"

"Just a moment, Elizabeth." Bernie scooped up the flashlight and handed it to him. "Zane, the most amazing thing has happened." She paused, practically dancing on her feet.

Amused, he drawled, "My kiss?"

She play-punched his arm then slid her flashlight from her pack. "My last battery," she muttered, shaking it into life.

Rain began to spill from the sky.

"Bernie, are you going to tell me, or do I have to make you?"

She snorted. "I'd like to see you try. Piku led us to the lost city of the were-jaguar. It's why I came to Brazil. I needed evidence to establish the ancient

253

Olmec civilization travelled this far south. Evidence that the city of the were-jaguar had existed."

He gave a low whistle, then smiled in the face of her excitement. From his own research, he knew how momentous such a discovery would be.

"I know!" She flung her arms around his neck and hugged him fiercely. "Wait until you see it, Zane. From what I've found so far, there are a huge number of artefacts to be unearthed. These ruins could date back to 1200 to 400 BC. Imagine the history we'll uncover."

"I like the sound of that *we*." He grinned, forcing back the sick denial strangling his heart. "Which way do we go?"

"Hang on." She darted off then returned a few seconds later dragging a bulging pack behind her. The faint light from the flashlight revealed her wide grin. "I've got more water. And I've caught seven fish using a bamboo pole, a super-thin vine and a safety-pin. I had to do something to pass the time while I waited for you slow-coaches."

"Oh, *chica*! Real food." Ricky snapped his fingers then, without being asked, hastened forward to stash some of the bottles spilling from Bernie's pack into his own. "We've got bananas and...what did you call them, Zane?"

"Jackfruit."

"That's great, Ricky. What happened with the mercenaries?" Bernie heaved her pack onto her back and began to walk, her flashlight directed ahead of her feet.

Zane longed to whip the damn thing off her back, but his pack was probably just as heavy if not more.

He also carried two rifles and the machete he'd confiscated. Also burdened with their finds, Ricky at least had taken some of the weight from Bernie. Zane could hardly ask his mother to carry anything more.

"We drew them into the jungle. They followed us for a while then we lost them." No need to trouble her with lurid details over the men he'd dispatched. "When we arrived back in the ravine, there was no sign of them."

"I've been here for over four hours and haven't heard them. Strange." She shivered as the drizzle became a steady shower. "I'm really over this weather. Let's hurry."

Leaving the stream behind, they wove their way through thick jungle, following the markers Bernie had left for him until they reached their goal.

Pushing aside the plant covering, Bernie illuminated the opening to the cave with her flashlight. "I'll go first. Then, Zane, you can feed me the packs before you climb down. Don't forget to conceal the opening."

Soon they were inside the ruins.

"This is unbelievable." Zane took his time, looking around.

"But wait, there is more." Bernie grinned. "This way. And mind your heads."

She led the way down a tunnel and then into a large chamber lit by burning torches wedged in the mud walls.

"Zane, Ricky. Ain't you a sight for sore eyes. Man, am I glad to you see you both," boomed Delroy. His teeth flashed in a wide grin. His wife gave a short smile.

Tatum burst into tears and clapped her hands, startling Cody and making him run over to his father. Tai cheered and swept his son into his arms, bounding forward hand outstretched. After shaking both Zane and Ricky's hands, he offered his hand to Bernie.

Zane announced, "We've got fish."

Magic words. Those who were mobile, sprang into action. Piku lit a fire and soon fresh water and fruit were being passed around, while Zane gave a brief report of the day's happenings. Ricky gutted the fish under Delroy's supervision and before long, the mouth-watering scent of food roasting in the coals filled the cave.

Gazing at his companions happily eating their first decent meal in four days, with Bernie sitting by his side, Zane wondered if just maybe, they could escape the jungle alive.

But not all of them, would be that lucky. One quick examination of Nyle, who'd fallen unconscious, had confirmed Bernie's assessment. The guy didn't have long to live and damn, if Zane didn't know whether that was a good thing or bad. All that waited for Nyle once they returned to civilization was a prison sentence—probably for life.

Across the crackling fire, Zane's eyes met his mother's. If she didn't work for a government agency, he had a major problem. As an agent of the law, he had a duty to ensure she faced the consequences of her actions. But if he did so, he'd lose another mother.

Hating the war raging inside him, he broke the contact, staring down at the morsel of fish in his fingers. He'd lost his appetite.

After the meal, most curled up and drifted off to sleep while the rest appeared content to stare into the dying fire's flames. His mother had made a bed for herself and lay with her back to the wall.

Zane doubted she slept.

With a finger to her lips, Bernie rose to her feet and held out her hand.

Zane took it, feeling the strength and purpose in her firm grip. He allowed her to lead him away from campfire, grabbing his duffle bag in passing. She plucked a burning flashlight from the wall then, dropping his hand, her own pack from the floor which she slipped over her shoulder.

Keeping her voice low, she detailed her theory of Piku and her ancestors then showed him the remains of a ceramic pot. "One day, I'll come back."

"I know you will."

In the dim light, he saw her bite her lip before she murmured, "Zane, this is the perfect place for the others to hide while we go to the dig for help."

"I've already thought of that, but if we don't make it, they may never be found. Piku won't take them to her village."

Tears glistened on her cheeks as she nodded.

He smiled wryly. "You know that saying? Damned if you do..."

"That's us."

She touched the side of his face and he turned into her hand. Her thumb gently stroked his bristly jaw and a quiver ran down his spine.

She murmured, "We'll tell them in the morning before we leave."

"We'll have to source more food before we go."

"True. It will have to be fruit. We won't have time to catch more fish. Plus, it will spoil too quickly." She sighed. "This way." She beckoned, leading him into another chamber. The torch light swept over a heavily carved stone bench then moved around the small cavern, revealing a pile of palm leaves.

She grinned wickedly, her eyes dancing in the gloom. "The makings for a fine bed."

He eagerly rammed the torch into a crack between two mud bricks and they set about making a haven for themselves. Zane took Bernie's pack from her and dropped both bags onto the sandy floor. They laid a space blanket and their jackets over the fronds. Bernie kneeled and with a thankful sigh removed her shoes and socks.

"You've got different clothes on," Zane finally realized.

She snorted. "That is so typical of a man. Never noticing anything new about a woman. I took advantage of the stream, had a lovely long wash and changed clothes." She began to release the buttons of her long-sleeved cotton shirt, one by one. Slowly.

Minx. Well, two could play that game. He gave a soulful sigh. "I could do with a bath myself."

Watching her from the corner of his eyes, he turned away and took out a bottle of water from his pack. He pulled his filthy shirt over his head and tossed it onto the ground. Wherever it landed, the damn thing could stay there. No way was he putting that on again. Tomorrow he'd wear his only remaining T-shirt. But now... Another peek.

She'd stilled her unbuttoning. Fingers poised, her

gaze seeming to burn over his torso like fire. Heating under her sparkling regard, he poured water into his cupped hand then began to smooth his hand over his chest. Those bright blue-green eyes followed his every move. She licked her lips. It was just as well he was already on his knees.

An enticing smile curing her lips, she scrambled over to sit in front of him. "Let me." She held a scrap of fabric he recognized as part of her tunic. Dampening the rag with water she leaned forward and smiled. "Bath time."

Her strokes were slow, moving over his skin, paying attention to every detail, setting his nerve ends afire. Moistening the cloth, she washed down his torso, up over his shoulders, along his arms before saying, "Turn around."

Lust and something else, hot and intense and all-consuming, swept through his veins, heating him to combustion point. His hands bunched into fists to stop himself from tossing the rag aside and pinning her beneath him.

She was enjoying this, evident by her soft, quick breaths, tiny sighs and the way her hands lingered as she stroked him. Even though the slow pace tortured him, he half-closed his eyes, enjoying every second. By the time she finished with his upper torso, he was a shaking mass of tense muscles, his arousal an aching throb he hungered to release.

Her hands drifted away. He heard the rustle of clothing then shuddered when she pressed against his back. Her breasts were soft and cushioning, her nipples stiff little peaks poking into his skin as she wrapped her arms around him, leaning in.

She teased his earlobe then whispered, "Those pants need to come off."

"Yes, ma'am."

Twisting out of her hold, he whipped off his shoes, socks, pants and boxers while she giggled. He soaked the rag with the last of the bottle then sloshed the day's grime and sweat from the rest of his body before tossing the cloth aside.

He looked up. Bernie kneeled before him. Naked. The light from the burning torch painted her creamy skin pale gold and her eyes were huge in a face framed by dark, tousled hair. She reminded him of pagan goddess, and the tender smile on her lips shook him to his core. That and the desire shining in her amazing eyes.

Her gaze travelled over him. She frowned, leaning forward. "You're hurt."

"Bullet graze."

"I'll put some antiseptic ointment on it and a plaster." Pulling her pack toward her, she retrieved the necessary items and proceeded to attend to this wound. "There, done." She sat back and beamed.

"You're beautiful." His voice hoarse as his throat swelled.

Hell, just about every part of him swelled to bursting point. Courageous and kind, she'd captured his heart, enslaved his body. He craved her like he'd never craved another woman. *I want more. I want all of her. Forever... I'd die for her.* The urge to share his shameful secret, the hurt tearing him up inside at the fear he'd lose her, had him squeezing his eyes shut to lock down the words.

Her fingers moved over his face, like she was

learning the contours of his bone structure by touch. "Let's take this moment for ourselves, Zane. Forget everything and everyone."

He took her mouth, fiercely, giving, receiving with a hunger that robbed his mind of all thought. Her skin flowed like silken water under his hands as he molded and roved every inch of her body.

Heart thumping, he laid her gently on the picnic blanket. Reaching into her pack with one hand, he found the last condom packet. Ripped the bloody thing open with his teeth and peeled it over his aching cock.

"Am I going too fast?" He drew back, searching her face now shadowed by the ruined walls.

She smiled. "You could go faster."

Grinning, he ran his hands down the back of her legs to the sensitive spots behind her knees. Finger-sketched tiny circles, enjoying her gasps and how she tensed and wriggled beneath his touch.

He shifted until he was between her widened legs. He scooped his arms beneath her legs, raising her thighs to gain better access to her sweet spots. Groaning, he nuzzled her entrance. Using his mouth and tongue, he stroked and sucked until she writhed under him, her fingers digging deep into his shoulders.

Knowing they were both on the brink, he dragged his open mouth over her flat stomach, delved into her navel with his tongue. Up to two of the plumpest, softest breasts he'd ever been privileged to kiss, to her mouth. Then drove deep into her, wanting to roar out his pleasure as her muscles contracted around him, increasing the heady sensation.

His kisses muffled her screams of release as she

met him thrust for thrust and he pumped into her until he was totally spent.

Three long, loving kisses later, he moved, shifting his weight from her body and tucking her neatly into his side, as he removed the condom. He tugged the space blanket over their bodies, smiling when she snuggled against him.

He didn't know how long they lay there, cuddled together, his hand gliding up and down her arm, but he knew he could have stayed like this for the rest of his life.

Bernie shifted, sighed then trailed her fingertips across the expanse of his chest, smiling as his skin goose-bumped beneath her touch. Her wistful smile told him her thoughts had winged elsewhere. Their brutal reality had re-appeared.

"You're thinking of your sister. I can tell." He soothed back strands of her hair.

Biting her lip, she admitted, "Yes. It's tearing me apart not knowing whether she's lost in the jungle. Whether she's been captured or rescued. I hold onto the knowledge Kit's intelligent and has been on digs with me before in the Amazon."

His voice deepened, ringing with sincerity. "We'll find her, sweetheart. We won't give up until we bring your sister home."

"Oh, Zane." Tears glistened as she gazed at him.

"I swear." He slid his thumb down the side of her face. "When this is over, we could work together. I think we make quite a team."

"What are you talking about?"

"I have a confession to make. Sweetheart, I am *not* a thief."

She rolled her eyes. "Yeah, I'd already figured that out, honey."

He grinned, loving how she always gave as good back. "I work for Interpol, currently investigating drug trafficking out of the Amazon. One line of enquiry I've been working on is a Mexican guy called Rodriguez who's now based in Colombia. We suspect some of the cargo is being smuggled in and out of countries using archaeological digs as fronts. Although I've yet to establish a link between the two."

"What?" Frowning, she reared up. "You're not suggesting Professor Kowalski is involved?"

"I've got my suspicions."

"You need more than suspicions. You need evidence. What have you got?"

"The evidence is mostly circumstantial so far. But my gut tells me, he's involved up to his neck."

She slapped his chest. "Rubbish. I don't believe it."

"Are you calling me a liar?" He tossed back the same question she'd asked of him on the plane.

Folding her arms, she rested them on his chest before laying her chin on her wrists and scowled up at him. "Very funny. Not. Professor Kowalski is one of the leading preeminent archaeologists of our time."

"He's also a total tosser."

"You've really got it in for him. And you say I'm stubborn." She shook her head, huffing a loud sigh. "Tell me about this team idea of yours."

"I've been considering working in your field. I've got degrees in Criminology, Political Science and Ancient History. May help. But being on the Mexican dig, was an eye-opener for me. I believe I've found my true passion." He searched the expression on her face, his heart banging a hectic beat as he paused. She didn't need to know *all* the truth. They could still have a life together. If they survived. "How about it, Bernie? Fancy the two of us, heading up our own archaeological dig? We could travel the world, reliving history."

A huge smile lit her face, her eyes sparkled. "That sounds suspiciously like a commitment, Zane."

Tension drained from him, as he tapped her cute nose. "You're a keeper, sweetheart. I knew that the second I laid eyes on you."

She turned serious, her eyes searching his in the gloom. "I want the full deal, Zane. The ring, the vows and children. I want a real family, the forever thing."

"If you're trying to scare me off, it isn't working."

"I always thought if I decided to have a family, I'd adopt," she mused, slowly.

He sucked in a sharp breath. "Sweetheart, that's right up my alley."

Her smile brighter than a thousand-watt lightbulb, she wound her arms around his neck and whispered close to his lips, "A boy of twelve."

He thought of his adoptive sister. "And a girl of eight. Maybe a few of our own, if we're lucky." His kiss was hard, fierce and she met it with a hunger that both thrilled and exhilarated. Breaking off, he cradled her face in his hands.

"But not before I keep my promises—find your sister and bring my mother's killer to justice."

~ 27 ~

I know he's keeping something from me. She'd heard the faint evasive tone in his voice, saw the shadows veiling his eyes when he spoke of keeping promises.

A moment earlier, he'd been laying out plans, dreams for a life together. Then, snap, he'd shut her out.

Anger and anguished disappointment rose, a whirlwind of turbulence that stripped away her newly-built trust in his integrity. It brought all her misgivings over smooth-tongued men racing back with their insidious whispers, but only for a few seconds.

After all they'd experienced together, she'd thought they were past keeping secrets from each other. But apparently, not. So, whatever it was, it must be big.

He was nothing like the shallow, self-absorbed smuggler she'd pegged him as. This man had killed to protect her.

He'd put his life on the line more than once for a

bunch of strangers. A dependable man who didn't give up, a man with many of her father's qualities and more endearing ones, like an innate kindness and courtesy to everyone he met. A man with a big heart, a man who turned her knees to putty in a heartbeat. The man she wanted and intended to spend whatever life she was blessed with, together.

Worry haunted the darkness of his eyes and she strongly suspected his secret had to do with his mother. Bernie wasn't a fool. As if that mild-looking, gun-toting woman was a retired schoolteacher. She snorted softly to herself. The woman had almost confessed as much when she revealed her nickname. That letter must belong to her. *Betty.* Which meant Zane's mother was involved in criminal activities with an infamous drug lord. A drug lord who had ordered his minions to hunt down two sisters and execute anyone who got in the way.

The concept made her head dizzy with questions. But what really tormented her was why, and whether Zane knew about Elizabeth's connection with *El* Jaguar.

Blast the man. He needed to be taught full disclosure was paramount where she was concerned. She'd accept nothing less. So, she in turn kept quiet about the other entrance to the ruins. But the decision didn't sit easy on her soul.

She lay beside him, staring into the gloomy cavern, hoping for a future while worrying over Kit and bargaining with God until fatigue finally won out.

Despite being sexually sated and physically exhausted, she slept badly. She dreamed she was alone on a raft floating in the ocean. There was a sheet of paper nailed to a plank. Snatching it up, she read, *Zane is El Jaguar.* The paper slipped from her fingers, transformed into a morpho butterfly and, with a flutter of its glorious blue wings, flew across the sea. Thunder clapped overhead. Icy rain drenched her skin as she scanned the rising swell. In the distance drifted another raft. Surrounded by a cloud of different colored butterflies, Kit sat on the planks, calling Bernie's name. Then the seas turned mountainous and she lost sight of her.

Bernie woke to find tears on her cheeks and an empty ache in her heart. She'd recognized the butterflies as being highly toxic and shuddered. Hoping the dream wasn't a portent of her sister's fate.

Zane murmured soothing words in her ear, his arms wrapped around her, holding her close. She curled into his side, listened to his breathing, relishing the moment until the alarm she'd set on her watch chimed.

Zane yawned, nuzzling her hair and mumbling, "Don't tell me its morning already. You didn't sleep well."

She met his lips with a lingering kiss. "I dreamed of Kit." *That you're my enemy. That I lost my sister forever.*

"We'll find her, I promise sweetheart. If we're correct in our calculations, we should reach the dig tonight. Tomorrow, we'll have this place swarming with search and rescue teams."

Bernie sat up, scrunching her eyes to make him out in the darkness, the torches having burnt down to embers during the night. "And that's another thing. Where are they?"

She saw the quick frown that marred his forehead. "Probably searching the route, we should have taken to Manaus. This Jaguar joker is a smart bastard. And very powerful. He could still be pulling strings in the background and delaying the teams widening the search."

Shivering, she pulled on her clothes. "I want him behind bars for this, Zane. That's another thing you have to promise me. That he'll pay for everyone who died."

"I'm working on it."

"I don't think that I'll ever forget them...Rhoda, Colin and Melanie. Plus, those poor people on the plane. Oh, Zane, promise me you'll catch him and put him away forever."

"We will." He caught her hand and raised it to his lips, kissing her knuckles. "Curious, how you're not baying for his blood."

"Hasn't there been enough death?" Her voice thickened with the grief welling inside.

"You're not after revenge then?"

She stiffened. "Justice is what we and all the people who died, need." A memory flashed through her mind. "Did you know, that's my father's major political platform? Justice for all. I never realized until now, how important impartial justice is for society."

Their bed of bracken and palm leaves rustled and creaked. He moved away from her. Why didn't he say something?

She felt it then. A coldness separating them. That blasted secret. He'd gone quiet after she declared her stance on retribution. Could *he* be contemplating revenge? He'd been the one to bring it into the conversation. He'd know how to exact vengeance too, so he'd never be caught.

What if his talk of being an Interpol agent was a pack of lies? A cover for his and his mother's criminal activities.

No, what rubbish. She was positive Zane hadn't faked that emotion when talking about his birth mother's murderer.

But if Elizabeth *was* responsible for their current situation, Zane might choose his mother's freedom over Bernie and justice. Turning his back on the law and all he believed, to protect his family.

Shaken, she finished dressing. Lacing up her rapidly deteriorating shoes over her last pair of clean socks, she muttered, "I'm going outside to search for food."

"I'll come with you. You shouldn't be out there alone."

A torch flared to life, revealing Zane's set expression. He rose, the burning torch in one hand then held out his other to assist her. A courtesy that never failed to touch her.

They gathered up their gear. Blinking, she followed him back to where the others were beginning to stir around the embers of the campfire. Piku was curled in a ball on a pile of palm fronds. Her eyes opened, but she didn't move as Bernie began to speak.

When advised of their intention to forage for food, both Tai and Ricky volunteered to assist.

"Good. I'll show you how to cut bamboo for water too. It will be cleaner than using water from the stream given we've got no water purifying tablets left. You don't want to risk a parasite infection." Bernie cleared her throat. "Zane and I are leaving for the dig this morning. We hope to be there by nightfall and back sometime tomorrow with help."

Silence. Piku sat up, her face expressionless as she listened.

Then Delroy spoke. "Yer leaving us here, sweet girl?"

"Yes."

He nodded slowly. "Ain't no other way. I guess this as good as place as any to die."

"There's no need for talk about dying. You've got kids here to look after," Zane growled. "We'll be back in thirty to forty hours max."

"Yo! What about me?" Ricky pranced forward, rifle already over his shoulder, an empty pack in one hand.

"You'll be needed here, Ricky. Your job is to guard the entrance.'"

Ricky puffed out his chest and pointed to his face. "I be your man, Zane."

"Cody. Please take Cody." The sound of Cheryl's weak voice startled them all. It had been a long time since she'd spoken.

Everyone shuffled about, avoiding looking at the woman on the stretcher except for Bernie and Zane.

Together, they crossed the cave to crouch beside Cheryl, her son snuggled into her side, his face innocent in repose. Cheryl's eyes were sunk deep in her sockets, but her smile as sweet as ever.

"Tai, I want you to go with them, save our son."

"I'll never leave you, Cher." Tai kneeled beside his wife and brushed a gentle kiss on her brow.

"My beautiful man," she murmured, her eyelids fluttering closed. "You must go. Promise me. Save Cody."

Tears glistened in Tai's dark eyes. "Neither of us are going anywhere without you, honey. Bernie and Zane will be back tomorrow. Before you know it, we'll be on a chopper and as soon as you're well, we'll finish our honeymoon."

Cheryl frowned. "Tai..."

"We'll slow them down, Cher. They'll make better time by themselves. This is the only way." Tai looked over at Bernie and Zane, who nodded. "Just get yourselves back here. Quick smart."

"We will." Zane held out a hand and Tai shook it.

Wiping the moisture off her cheeks, Bernie rose and led the way from the cave. Two hours later, they were back with sufficient supplies to last the others for several days. Bernie stashed one water bottle, her last two salt tablets, her first-aid kit, her plastic poncho and a *goiaba* into her small pack, then shrugged it on. She looked over to see Zane speaking with his mother who had an angry frown marring her face and kept shaking her head.

Elizabeth turned her back and after a few seconds Zane walked away from her. A muscle throbbed below his tense jaw, but when he reached Bernie's side, he didn't offer an explanation.

"Bernie and I will take a rifle each, as well as the revolver, machete and hunting knife. That leaves two rifles, a pistol and two knives for the rest of you. Be sparing if you need to shoot. The only ammo we have is what's in the chambers."

"I pray to the Lord above, there'll be no more killing," said Pearl in a sorrowful tone.

271

"Amen to that," her husband responded from where he sat propped up against the cave wall. "But I'll be taking care of our pistol, if you don't mind, Zane."

Elizabeth nodded. "Ricky and I'll take custody of the two rifles, son."

Without speaking, Zane doled out the weapons. He then turned his attention to stuffing a few meagre supplies into his duffle.

"Everyone will be safer if you remain inside the cave." Bernie paused. "Don't venture out unless there it's necessary. I found jaguar prints beside the stream."

Should she mention she'd also found animal tracks inside the cave? Her eyes met Piku's steady gaze. The Indian girl gave an infinitesimal shake of her head.

Hoping and praying she'd made the right decision, Bernie refrained from elaborating any further. "Keep a watch on the tunnel entrances." With a sweep of her hand, she indicated both sides of the chamber. "Good luck. We'll be back as soon as we can."

Piku rose gracefully. "I will show you the way to the professor. Then I return to my home."

Eyebrows raised, Bernie exchanged a glance with Zane who appeared equally stunned. "You know Professor Kowalski?"

Piku shrugged. "He digs in the dirt not far from my village. But it is many miles from here."

Bernie chewed her lip, hating the acrid bite of suspicion. Once she'd been more inclined to take people at their word, but the past few days had taught her everyone had secrets. She recalled how the Indians from the village near the runway had been executed, a brutal reminder of what would happen to any who crossed *El* Jaguar. To save her own people, Piku could be leading them into a trap.

"Where we found you is a long way from your village," Bernie said slowly as she processed this new development. "What were you doing so far from home?"

Piku shrugged. "I was here. With my father's father. We conduct ceremony for plentiful food with the return of the dry season. We fish in stream, hear gunfire and I go to see what is happening."

"And your grandfather?"

"He go home. He is too old to fight."

Tatum looked up from where she and Cody were sprawled on their bellies attempting to coax a finger monkey to come a little closer. "You don't dress like a native."

Piku plucked at her shirt and grinned. "I also will be schoolteacher. This is practice for when I go to college."

Bernie supposed it *was* possible the Indian girl spoke the truth. Troubled, she scratched at a bite on her arm.

"Let's go." Zane made the decision for her as he shook hands with all the men, even scooping little Cody up for a swift hug. Cody squealed, giggling when Zane tickled his belly.

One glance in Zane's eyes told Bernie he harbored the same doubts. With no other alternative, they'd follow Piku, but keep a sharp vigilance for any sign of betrayal.

"We will go this way." Piku shot Bernie a quizzing glance, before turning and heading down the tunnel she'd taken Bernie into the night before.

Blast. Hoping Zane wouldn't quiz Piku about the other entrance and learn Bernie had kept quiet, she picked up her rifle and staff. After taking one last look at the people who'd grown important to her, she followed Zane along the tunnel. She left such a heavy silence behind her, that grief re-surfaced. If they'd made the wrong decision, these people would die.

When she emerged from the hidden ruins, she found the morning to be uncomfortably muggy. Patchy clouds scudded across the sky with rays of sunlight bursting through the canopy now and then. It made a pleasant change from the menacing shadows cloaking the jungle floor.

Zane paused and studied the weathered carvings on the boulder then sent a loaded glance over his broad shoulders at Bernie. "Did you know about this other entrance?"

She shrugged, guilt flooding her face with warmth. Frowning, he turned away. Keeping a cautious lookout for mercenaries, they followed Piku as she led them in an easterly direction through the jungle until they came to the stream. Half a mile on, the stream widened into a gushing current with a large clearing on one side.

They skirted five black caimans basking on the sandy banks. One had to be at least twelve feet long. Nausea rose as Bernie's thoughts immediately winged to Melanie floating dead in the water.

Turning north they left the stream behind as they pushed their way through dense jungle undergrowth. Several times, Bernie thought she heard the distinctive 'whoop-whoop' of a helicopter, but the canopy above was too impenetrable to spot any aircraft. The constant buzzing of cicadas filled her head with white noise as she slogged one foot after the other. Monkeys' chatter and screeching sounded from the branches competing with the birds' whistles and chirps. What she wouldn't give for some quiet.

They stopped for a brief respite around noon. Bernie sank onto a fallen tree trunk with a thankful sigh then took several mouthfuls of water along with her last salt tablet.

Zane sat beside her. Perspiration gave his olive-skinned face a golden sheen. His damp auburn hair glistened like the embers of a glowing fire while the stubble lining his strong jaw glittered like specks of gold dust. Such a beautiful man. He winked, a grin tugging at the corners of his mouth.

And I'm staring at him, catching flies. Rolling her eyes, Bernie closed her mouth, then made a business of stashing her water bottle away.

Piku re-appeared and tossed over a couple of *camu camu* fruits. "We go."

Zane rose, wiped dirt from the fruit and handed one to Bernie. Picking up her rifle, she followed the other two. As she walked, she sank her teeth into the citrus fruit relishing the tartness on her taste-buds and the flow of juice down her parched throat. When they reached civilization, she intended to drink and drink until she was as bloated with water as a camel.

They struggled on. Often Zane had to slash their way forward with the machete leading Bernie to wonder whether they were even following an actual trail. But Piku kept reassuring this was the correct path.

After being consistently hounded by mercenaries, their absence made Bernie uneasy. They might have given up the chase if they'd rounded up the other passengers. Kit could be in their clutches right now, being tortured. And Bernie could do nothing to help.

Night began to spread its dark wings over the jungle. Shadows formed black pockets where danger lurked.

Wiping his forehead with the back of his hand, Zane called a halt. "How much further, Piku?"

"Still far."

Bernie checked her watch and compass. "I think we've walked a good seven or eight miles."

"We can't stop. How's the battery life of your flashlight?"

She retrieved it from her pack and switched it on. The beam was thin but better than nothing. "A couple of hours left, I think."

"My cell phone has a bit of power. We can use that when your flashlight dies. We need to keep going."

"Agreed."

"Ladies first." His smile was weary, but his face resolute as he waved her to walk in front of him.

Nodding, she set off after Piku. They couldn't stop. Lives depended on reaching the archaeological dig before morning.

～ 28 ～

Close to midnight Piku stopped and whispered, "Walk in straight line and you will find the professor. I go now."

"Piku, thank you." Zane went to clasp her hand, but she slipped away, melting into the night. "She's gone."

"Yes. Shall we continue?" Bernie's voice sounded heavy with fatigue.

He repeated the offer he'd made a few miles back. "I can piggy-back you, sweetheart."

She snorted. "What? And stagger into camp like I can't hack the jungle? I've got my reputation to think of here."

"Not to mention Professor Kowalski's opinion of you."

"On this dig, he's my boss. Plus, he carries a lot of weight in our field. I'd be crazy to do anything to jeopardize my career."

"Not even within sight of the dig and you're already thinking of him," he drawled, hating the acrid taste of jealousy souring his gut.

Having met Kowalski on that fateful dig in Mexico, Zane hadn't been impressed with the man's smug attitude. Kowalski gave the impression he knew something the rest of the world didn't and laughed up his sleeve at the lot of them. How Bernie thought the man worthy of admiration baffled him.

The memory of how the man would often place a possessive hand on Bernie's shoulder, rekindled Zane's anger. The man wasn't who the world believed him to be, and Zane intended to prove it.

She'd gone quiet. She'd already worked out that he had kept something vital from her. More snarky comments from him and he would drive her back to her initial suspicion and distrust. Maybe that would be for the best.

Then he'd never have to divulge that he came from not one killer, but a family of killers. Glumly, he flicked his cell phone flashlight over the thick screen of foliage surrounding them. The light lit a mere foot ahead.

"Power is almost gone."

She touched his arm. He glanced at her shadowy form, wishing he could see the expression in her eyes so he could figure out her thoughts.

She stepped closer, pressing her slight body against his and his heart flipped over. "You're right. Work should never come between friends and family. I won't make that mistake again."

Her lips brushed over his cheek then she whispered, "Shades of my father. That was the old me."

Sighing, Zane looped his arm around her waist, loving how she fitted so perfectly against his body. He rested his face on her soft hair. "I've got a tough decision to make." The words dried in his throat and he hesitated. *His family. Murderers.*

"I know. But don't leave it too long before you decide to tell me." She slipped from his hold, then her fingers found his. They inter-twined and she gave his hand a gentle tug. "Let's go before I fall on my face and you have to carry me."

His chest tightened. She hadn't rejected him. Not yet. After a quick check of his compass, he led the way, and twenty minutes later the jungle fell away into a hulking mass behind them.

Ahead, four lights stationed in a rough square glowed, powered by a humming diesel generator. The shadowy outlines of several tents of varying sizes signaled they'd arrived at the dig. A small fire burned in the middle of the camp site.

All was quiet apart from the generator. The closer they walked, the more the jungle sounds faded.

"Hello, the camp," Zane called when they came within shouting distance.

Mutterings came from a couple of tents. Canvas rippled as people moved about inside. Then a flashlight flicked on and someone stepped outside.

A male voice snapped, "Who goes there?"

"We need help. We've been lost in the jungle since our plane crashed."

"My God! Quick, Alf, James. Get out here." The man hurried toward them, shrugging into a shirt as he walked, flashlight bobbing up and down. As he came closer, Zane recognized him from his distinctive white hair, long curling moustache and goatee beard.

Kowalski to the rescue. Damn him.

"Look!" Bernie squeezed his hand and began to tug him toward a familiar shape. "They've got a chopper!"

"Hold on, Bernie. We can't hijack it without a pilot."

"Where there's a chopper, there's a pilot." Smiling broadly, she jumped into his arms. "We made it. Zane. We made it."

Explanations in Zane's opinion were long, tedious and took far too long. After Kowalski re-appeared from phoning through the news of their miraculous survival, he pressed food and water onto them, insisting on hearing the details of their find.

"Good news. Your families will be notified as soon as possible. The search and rescue teams will set out again tomorrow morning. Now, about the lost city. Bernie, you must tell me more."

They were seated in camp chairs around the spluttering fire. Overhead the stars twinkled larger and brighter than any Zane had seen in the city. The warm, moist air of a gentle breeze kissed the bare skin of his face and arms, a blessed relief after the heat of the day.

Slumped in her chair, Zane wasn't even certain Bernie was still awake until she shifted.

"Professor, we have to return to the ruins. Our friends are expecting us. We need your chopper." Struggling to hold back a yawn, she waved a hand at the helicopter as she repeated the request they'd both made earlier.

"Yes, how soon can you get us back there?" Zane added.

Kowalski rubbed his hands briskly. "As I've told you before, it's too dangerous to try and land in the jungle at night. I won't risk any lives or our only means of transport. We'll leave at first light."

Kowalski and Alf began to speculate about the treasures the lost city could hold. Zane's mouth thinned. This lot appeared more interested in the archaeological prospects than the fate of innocent people. It turned his stomach.

And didn't look as if the guy would change his mind. Zane pushed out of his chair. "We could do with somewhere to sleep."

"You can bunk down in the supply tent. Alf, show them the way, will you? I'll look at my maps and plot the quickest flight path to save time tomorrow." The professor patted his shirt pocket which held the notebook where he'd scribbled down the co-ordinates Bernie had given him the second they'd arrived at the camp.

"See you in the morning." Kowalski waved them off, a broad grin on his face.

"I wish we could leave now, but he's right." Yawning, Bernie took Zane's outstretched hand allowing him to help her upright. "I'm beat. I need a wash and sleep."

Leaning heavily on him, she walked beside him as they followed Alf, a middle-aged Londoner with a wizened face, rather like an old monkey. The supply tent was large and crammed with stacks of crates, but it had a zippered floor and sides.

Alf located a couple of spare sleeping bags, but no

bunks. Not that Zane cared. All he wanted was to be off his feet.

"Here, I'll give the both of you a shot of antibiotics. Just in case." Alf opened a first-aid box and retrieved two syringes.

As soon as Alf left, Zane zipped up the tent flaps. He placed the flashlight they'd been given on top of a crate and laid out the bags onto the ground, stuffing a couple of blankets beneath for cushioning.

Bernie swayed where she stood. Dark smudges beneath her eyes, seemed to highlight their beautiful and unusual color stark against the pallor of her skin.

Tutting, he helped her undress, tamping down his instant reaction to the sight of her naked flesh. Green crystal glittered between her breasts.

"What's this?" He touched the stone with his forefinger.

"I'd almost forgotten. I found the pendant in the cave."

"Now who's the thief?" He grinned to take any sting from his words.

"I'm only keeping it safe." Smiling, she made good use of the bucket of water and towels, even rinsing her hair while he stripped before taking his turn.

At last, clean and with their bellies full of food, they snuggled together on top of the sleeping bags. Zane covered them with a blanket a second before exhaustion swamped him. His last thought, *I don't trust Kowalski's smile.*

They were woken the next morning by Kowalski unzipping the tent and strolling casually inside.

Zane peeled open his eyes to find the tosser standing, hands in pocket and gazing down on them. A quick check ensured a blanket covered Bernie from neck to toe. He shifted onto his elbows. "Do you mind?"

"Not really. Pretty girl." Kowalski grinned.

Zane's hands fisted, but he refused to respond to the taunt.

Eyebrows raised, Kowalski shrugged. "You've got fifteen minutes before we leave." Then he strode from the tent.

"Bastard."

"What?" mumbled Bernie, attempting to snuggle closer.

Smiling, Zane banished the wanker from his thoughts, turning to look down at her. A tiny frown wrinkled her forehead, like she forced herself to remain asleep so she wouldn't have to face the day. Her dark hair with its blue-black highlights tumbled enticingly around her face and neck. His gaze dropped to her lusciously full lips and he groaned.

Fifteen minutes. Less now. Hardly time to visit Mother Nature and grab a bite to eat. Definitely not enough time for a 'good morning' romp.

"Rise and shine, beautiful."

"I hate you."

"No, you don't." He grinned and flicked off the blanket.

"Seriously, I do." Shivering, she dived for the blanket.

He wrestled it from her hands then leaned in low to plant a hard kiss on her pouting lips.

She wrapped her arms around his back, running her teasing fingers along the contours of his spine, whispering, "How long have we got?"

"Not that long," he said, his voice hoarse with need and regret.

"Blast." She gave him a rueful smile, rolled away and began to gather her scattered clothes.

Heart heavy and wondering whether they'd ever share another night together, Zane dressed in silence before leading the way from the tent and out into the early dawn.

He glanced around, noting the excavations undertaken to the east of the campsite. Had anything of significance been found here? There'd been no evidence of pottery or other artefacts in the supply tent although they could be stored elsewhere.

The man introduced last night as James, strode past, a cheroot clamped between his yellowed teeth. Zane frowned, his gaze following him as he made for the helicopter. So, he was the pilot. The bloke wore faded green army fatigues. Not that his clothes meant anything. Army disposal stores were plentiful these days.

Underfoot the tufted grass felt spongy and squelched when he walked. Squinting, he thought he saw the glint of water in the distance of the gently undulating terrain. He hadn't realized the dig was close to a river.

"Grub's up," shouted Alf, banging a spoon against the side of a pot.

Bernie already stood near the fire with a bowl in her hands. Digs weren't usually this sparse of people. When Zane had been in Mexico, the place had been crawling with them. But most had been officials or tourists, keen to witness history being unveiled or seeing value for the money they'd invested. Perhaps more people were due to arrive later.

"Scrambled re-constituted eggs and tofu sausages." Bernie offered him a plate.

"Thanks."

He dug in, wondering whether he should share his ruminations with Bernie. Then he dismissed the thought. The sooner they'd eaten, the quicker they'd be in the air. And the closer he'd come to deciding his mother's fate.

Rays of sunlight skipped over the surface of the stream, as if gleeful to be released from its prison of clouds. Although, Bernie doubted the sunshine would last long, if the heavy, bluish clouds billowing in from the east meant anything.

"Down there." Shouting to be heard over the whirling rotors, Bernie pointed toward the glint of water, while Zane made circular gestures.

Professor Kowalski gazed downwards. "Are you certain?" he yelled, a doubtful frown furrowing his brow. "I excavated along this ravine several years ago and found nothing."

Bernie nodded vigorously.

"Put us down," bawled the Professor.

The chopper tilted on an angle, turning as the pilot prepared to land. Pressing a hand to her roiling stomach, Bernie squeezed her eyes shut, grateful for the arm Zane threw around her shoulders. She nestled closer to him until the craft landed, even waiting until the engine died and the rotors stopped with a whine before opening her eyes.

"We're back." Zane's voice sounded strained.

Looking up into his face, her gaze locked with his. She knew his thoughts were centered on the friends they'd left behind and how they'd coped. She wanted to utter reassurances, but the same worry sat like stone in her belly. If they'd made the wrong decision... Legs shaking, she clasped his steady grip, the warmth of his touch stealing over her cold skin.

Zane draped his arm around her waist. "Are you all right?"

The concern in his dark eyes almost undid her, but she managed a nod before surveying the area. "No sign of the evacuation team. Professor?"

Kowalski looked around at her call.

"Did the search team give an indication of their ETA?"

He checked his watch. "They should be here within thirty minutes."

"Thank heavens." She shared a speaking glance with Zane.

Alf scrambled down from the chopper, carrying a first-aid box. He pushed past them, heading to the professor's side where they traded a low-voiced conversation.

A frown formed on Zane's face as his gaze dropped to the gun holster around Alf's hips.

Bernie elbowed him in the ribs. "Relax. We're carrying weapons too."

Kowalski swung around. "James, stay with the chopper. Which way?"

"It's a bit of a hike along the stream then into the jungle again." Lowering her voice, Bernie murmured to Zane, "Let's keep the knowledge of the second entrance to ourselves for the time being."

"I couldn't agree more." Zane gave a fierce grin.

Wondering where that sly whisper of doubt had come from, she shifted her rifle around to her front, placing her fingers close to the trigger.

She took a long moment to study the area. No sign of their hunters. No animals. No birds skimming over the stream surface searching for insects. No anything really. Only an ominous quiet that shrank the flesh over her bones. Her sixth sense warned danger prowled close by.

But from which direction, and when, would it strike?

～ 29 ～

Zane entered the cave first, his gaze sweeping the occupants, lingering on the deathly quiet forms of Cheryl and Nyle.

A ragged cheer rent the air and he smiled. He searched for his mother's familiar face, but didn't find her. She could have chosen to escape before he returned therefore ensuring he wouldn't have to make that terrible choice. Or she could be in another chamber. "We've got a chopper. And help is on the way."

Smiles lit the weary faces.

"Oh, praise the Lord!" intoned Pearl as she slipped her handbag over her shoulder.

Hand on the cave wall where she'd been sitting beside Delroy, she rose to her feet. Her smiled slipped from her face, as her gaze travelled past them to settle on the professor. A curious expression flickered in her eyes. Zane's skin prickled uneasily.

"Yo, man, I knew you could do it!" Ricky raced over and high-fived him before seizing Bernie in a hug.

"Weren't you supposed to be guarding the entrance?" Zane asked.

Ricky released Bernie, his delighted grin turning quickly into a grimace. "I thought I'd check on Nyle. I think he's in a coma."

Bernie sighed heavily. "This is Professor Kowalski and Alf."

Half-sobbing, half-laughing Tatum cried, "We're going home." Cody, sleeping on her lap, woke up and rubbed his eyes. A little finger monkey poked his head out of Cody's shirt pocket and blinked with big brown eyes.

"What have you there, Cody?" Bernie kneeled and held out her hand for the monkey to sniff.

"It found me last night. I'm keeping him. He's name is Micky."

"He's lovely." Bernie smiled and stood.

Tai, anxiety evident in the taut line of his body, strode over and wrung Zane's hand. "Cheers, mate. Are we leaving now?"

"Yes. Everyone get your gear together. Ricky and I will help with the stretcher. We'll probably need to make two trips. The sick and injured go first. Don't worry, Tai, you'll be with your wife."

"Alf? Bring the first-aid kit over here." Waving for Alf to follow, Bernie hurried over to Cheryl. "Perhaps there's something we can use to help Cheryl before we leave."

Zane dug in his pack and handed out the items he'd taken from the supply tent to Ricky. "Here's some protein bars and milk."

Grin back in place, Ricky walked over to share them with Tatum and Cody. "I don't know about you, *chica*, but fruit is no longer on my menu."

"Thanks, Ricky." Smiling, Tatum opened the milk and gave it to Cody, watching as the little boy drank a few mouthfuls. She replaced the milk with a protein bar.

"Yum," Cody said around bulging cheeks.

Tai shook his head. "Don't eat so fast, Cody."

Zane looked at Nyle still slumped against the opposite wall. The co-pilot's shirt was drenched with blood but as if sensing his gaze, Nyle opened his eyes.

"Still here," he rasped. But the man looked like he was fading fast.

After giving a cursory glance at their group, Kowalski pushed past Zane and headed for the crumbling walls. "What a fantastic find." He began to rummage in his knapsack, seemingly oblivious to the needs of others.

The man was a total bastard. Lips curled, Zane glared. "There's no time for that now, Kowalski. We've got people who need urgent medical attention."

Kowalski waved a hand behind him, like he shooed an irritating fly. "Let Alf see to them. That's what he's paid for."

Choking over his curse, Zane glared at the man's back. Bernie's voice pulled him up before he could go over and punch the bloke in the chops.

"Zane!"

He went swiftly to her side.

Bernie indicated Cheryl. "I think she's in a coma."

Alf nodded. "I've given her a shot of morphine. Nothing else I can do."

Tai turned his face to the wall.

"Nyle?" Zane's voice cracked.

Pulling at his lower lip with his hand, Alf sent a considering stare toward the co-pilot. "I'll take a look-see. Come on, missy."

"I know you," grated Delroy suddenly. "Hey! You there. The guy who thinks we're not worth looking at."

Frowning, Kowalski glanced over his shoulder. "Can't you see I'm busy?"

In three strides, Zane reached him. Grabbing the jerk by the shoulder he spun the man around to face him. "Look here..." His voice trailed off.

Kowalski held a gun in his hand. "Move back. All of you, get over to the side where I can see you."

"Professor, what are you doing?" Her face a picture of astonishment, Bernie slowly stood.

I never did trust this bastard. Zane raised his hands a fraction, ensuring he could still lunge for the rifle slung behind his back the second Kowalski took his eyes off him. "No one here is interested in these ruins. Trust me. The glory of this discovery is all yours."

He ignored Bernie's soft snort, continuing in his best hostage-negotiator's voice. "All we want is out of here in that chopper."

Kowalski shook his head. "Sorry, buddy. That is not going to happen. Ditch those weapons. Including the knife."

Lips thinned, Zane dropped his rifle and machete, placing the hunting knife in the dirt beside his feet.

"Now, move." Kowalski jerked the revolver sideways.

Jaw clenched, Zane shuffled a couple of steps backwards.

"Alf, forget that loser."

"Sorry, mate. Ain't nut'ting I can do for you, anyways." Pistol in hand, Alf kicked aside the first-aid bag ignoring when items spilled close to Nyle's thigh. He walked over to the right, covering the tunnel that led back to the entrance beneath the tree.

Just as well Bernie had kept quiet about the other exit. Zane flicked a sneaky glance around the chamber, certain he'd spied movement in the tunnel. His gaze swept over their group, lingering on Delroy whose face began to redden, his eyes bulging. *Shit! I hope he's not about to have a heart attack.*

"Bernie, lose that rifle you're carrying. Place it very carefully on the ground." When she hesitated, Kowalski barked, "Do it!"

Eyes blazing with fury, she obeyed. Taking her time, and ensuring the weapon lay between herself and Zane.

Kowalski nodded at Ricky, "You too, macho man. Come on, before I shoot all of you."

Ricky placed his gun on the ground while Tatum, white-faced and shaking, crouched over Cody sheltering him.

"Alf, I believe I hear our guest arriving. Good thing I switched on my tracking device," the professor said as sounds of male voices floated down the tunnel. "Go and greet him."

Alf trotted into the tunnel.

"What guest?" growled Zane, unable to hide his hostility.

"Someone who badly wants to meet your girlfriend." Kowalski bared his teeth.

Bernie gasped, her hand clutching at her throat.

Fucking hell, he should have gone with his gut and investigated the shit out of this chump last year. If he had, then maybe Bernie wouldn't be in danger now. Maybe none of them would be one step from death. Because his gut sure as hell told him that the bloke tramping down that bloody tunnel was going to be none other than the *Jaguar*.

Zane's fists curled as a man stepped out of the shadows and into the light of the burning torches. Of medium height with a pock-marked face, salt and pepper hair and an easy smile adorning his dark-skinned face, nothing signaled this guy out from the ordinary. Apart from his cock-of-the-walk posture, the white cowboy boots he wore and the leery watchfulness of three henchmen filing in behind him, armed to the teeth. Gold gleamed from the gun in the leader's holster when it caught the light. The odds of getting out of here alive shortened considerably.

"Bernadette Ashford. May I present to you Luis Rodriguez, aka *El* Jaguar." Kowalski gave a dramatic flourish with his left hand.

Unfortunately, the gun trained on Zane remained steady. *Easy does it, old boy. All I need is one tiny slip-up and I can make a move.* Regardless of the consequences to himself, that bastard would not leave the cave with Bernie.

"*Diablo!* You've evaded me for the last time." Rodriguez strode forward and grabbed Bernie by the upper arm. A vicious snarl to his mouth, he twisted savagely. "I will make you pay for these wasted days chasing you through the jungle."

Tears glittered in her eyes, but she didn't allow

them to fall. Tossing her head, she snapped, "As I thought, you're nothing but a coward and a bully."

Rodriguez shook her furiously. "You will beg to die, by the time I and my men have finished with you."

"I don't think so." Bernie looked down her nose and sniffed.

"We shall see. But first, *señorita,* you will tell your father unless he releases my son from prison immediately, you will be raped to death." He leaned closer and Bernie turned her head aside as if his breath disgusted her.

His son! Zane recalled how the state of Florida still upheld the death penalty. Rodriguez's next words confirmed his suspicions.

"My only son has five hours before he is executed. You will do as I say."

Bernie raised her chin, staring him in the eyes. "Your son will die. My father does *not* negotiate with terrorists."

"I admit our first phone call did not go well. *Diablo!* What father says his daughter must fend for herself?"

"One who knows I would never want or expect him to betray his principles or his country."

"Little fool!" Rodriguez roughly shook her arm then yanked her head back by grabbing a fistful of her hair. Bernie fell against him.

"Like father like daughter, eh? I like that you have spirit. It will make breaking you so much more pleasurable."

Muscles bunched, ready to attack, Zane shifted forward an inch.

Rodriguez's reptilian gaze swung toward him. "Do not be stupid, *señor*. My men have orders to shoot at the least provocation."

Bernie grimaced as she attempted to tug her hair free from Rodriguez grip. "No matter what you do, my father will not agree to your demand," she panted.

"Once I show him proof of life, he will do anything to save you." Rodriguez leaned closer to speak near her ear. "You see, *señorita*, the sight of a woman bruised, broken and bleeding has changed many a man's mind. Your father will be no different."

"You're wrong."

He laughed.

"Do whatever you want with me, but let the others go. They're innocent," Bernie pleaded.

"I admit I have no use for them. But I do not like loose ends." Rodriguez glanced at the professor. "*Muchas gracias,* Dick."

Kowalski smirked. "Isn't that what partners are for?"

"Partners?" Bernie attempted to twist around to stare at her former mentor.

"Sí. I am his partner." An evil grin spread over Rodriguez's face.

Thinking fast, Zane cut his eyes at the professor. Any moment now, he sensed one of them would start killing them off. He had to make his move soon.

"Richard, what's going on?" Pearl rushed forward a few steps, freezing at the click of a gun. She stared into Kowalski's face, flung a hand toward Rodriguez. "Who is this man?"

"I *knew* it." Spittle flew as Delroy pounded the ground beside him with his fist.

"Pearl, you are so predictable." Kowalski brought his pistol up, pointing it in her face. "A lousy lover, but a very efficient artefact smuggler."

Gasping, she stumbled backwards, tripped then sprawled on the ground, gaping up at him.

"You? You're the one responsible for selling artefacts on the black market?" Bernie glared at Kowalski.

He shrugged. "What can I say? I love money and beautiful objects. I've acquired quite an impressive private collection over the years. And no one ever suspected the most respected archaeologist of his time." He pointed to his own chest. "Me."

Pearl held a hand to her mouth. "Richard, why are you saying such things?"

"You just don't get it, do you, Pearl?" Kowalski rolled his eyes. "It was surprisingly easy recruiting bored, middle-aged housewives. Some wining and dining and sex, and they were putty in my hands."

Gasping, Pearl buried her face in her hands.

"Conceited tosser," Zane said, not liking how easily Kowalski spilled his soul. It could mean only one thing—none of them were getting out of there alive.

"I agree with you. Your greed will be your downfall, Dick, my friend." Rodriguez began to walk backwards, pulling Bernie with him. "I am glad I decided to cut our ties. I will not fall with you."

"What the fuck are you talking about, Luis?"

"You will know soon enough." His smirk faded as he indicated Zane with the muzzle of his pistol. "I have another surprise for you. This one here, he is Interpol. Did you not know?"

"What?"

"*Sí.* You slipped up, Dick. Get rid of them. I want no witnesses," ordered Rodriguez as he jerked Bernie so hard she stumbled, landing heavily against him.

Bernie cried out, bringing her left hand up as if to balance against him.

Zane tensed, noticing she slid her other hand toward the drug lord's knife sheath. He flexed his hands, digging his heels into the ground, ready to spring.

"Wait!" Pearl held up a trembling hand. "We can trade. We have samples of a rare plant which will make you rich."

"I am already rich," said Rodriguez in a bored tone.

Pearl turned to her lover. "Richard, please, save me. I'm pregnant."

For a second Kowalski appeared startled then he snorted. "So what?" He threw a loaded glance at Alf.

Looking bored, Alf aimed his gun at Pearl. He stood not far from where Nyle rested against the wall.

"I don't want to die." Shrieking, Pearl threw herself at Kowalski's feet, anchoring her hands around his ankles. She tugged.

Off balance, he staggered. And everything seemed to happen at once. Nyle threw himself forward and drove a syringe deep into Alf's fleshy calf. Alf screamed. His shot went wild.

Zane dove for his rifle, bringing it up as he rolled, firing at the closest mercenary and sending the man slamming into the dirt. Blood spurted from his chest. Dust rose forming a gritty haze in the air.

Delroy lurched to his feet, revolver in hand. His bullet drilled into the wall behind Kowalski who fired back, hitting Delroy in the thigh. Roaring in pain and clutching at the blood spilling from his leg, Delroy fired again as he crumpled.

Pearl screamed, kept on screaming.

Kowalski swore as the bullet grazed his cheek. He dropped to his hands and knees, and crawled around a half-wall.

Bernie twisted in Rodriguez's hold, driving her elbow into his groin. She kicked back with her foot into Rodriguez's face. Wrenching free, she hurtled the knife she held at the closest mercenary, catching him in the shoulder.

Cursing in Spanish, the thug let lose a stream of automatic fire. Everyone ducked for cover as bullets zinged around the cave, burrowing into the mud walls. Tai threw himself over Cheryl. Ricky shoved Tatum and Cody face-down on the floor.

Zane dropped to his belly and fired toward Kowalski, pinning him down. Rolled and fired toward Rodriguez's remaining henchman, hitting him in the leg.

The thug lurched, continued to fire. The noise deafening in the confined space as cordite mingled with the dust. A single rifle shot rang out from the direction of the tunnel, smacking into his forehead. Dead center. He folded.

Alf kicked Nyle in the head then began to return fire into the tunnel.

Mom. It could only be her. And she was being greeted with a hail of bullets.

Rodriguez had Bernie by the foot, pulling her backward. She kicked and thrashed for all she was worth. The swirling cloud of dust made it bloody hard to see.

Zane took a bead on Alf, squeezed the trigger. Nothing. Out of fucking ammo. Unable to help his mother, he dropped the rifle and launched himself on top of Rodriguez, kidney-punching him before locking his arm around his throat. The cartel leader clawed at the pressure being applied to his windpipe. On his knees, Zane dragged the bastard away from Bernie.

Bernie shimmied backwards on her belly and elbows. Rodriguez's eyes rolled up in his head. He sagged. Ears ringing, Zane released his grip. His gaze darted to Bernie who leapt for her staff. She charged off after Kowalski who'd taken advantage of the diversion, and run toward the tunnel entrance. *Shit.* Didn't anything stop that woman?

Bullets ripped into the ground around her feet. She flung herself sideways, bounced off the wall, then lay still for a few seconds, before she lifted her head to scan the cave.

Zane rolled off Rodriguez. Snatching the leader's pistol from him, he targeted the asshole peppering the area near Bernie with bullets. Fired. Shooting Alf's face off. The remaining mercenary flung panicked glances around the cave, shooting indiscriminately.

Squinting, Zane struggled to get a bead on the guy through all the smoke and dust. Pebbles crunched to his right. He whirled, blinked as he recognized his mother edging into the cave, bent over. Her blood-stained hand was pressed to her stomach.

Their eyes met. Her gaze slid past. She gasped.

He spun around. The mercenary stood behind him, gun raised. Zane pressed down on the trigger. It clicked over an empty chamber. *Fuck! Not again!*

His mother rushed forward, drawing the soldier's attention. The dick fired at her. Helpless, Zane watched his mother fly backwards. He dropped the revolver, swept up the machete and threw it deep into the bastard's chest, dropping him like a rock.

Silence.

The dust and smoke dissipated into a fine mist. Heart jackhammering against his ribs, his breath trapped in his lungs, Zane stared where his mother lay motionless.

～ 30 ～

Head pounding, her body aching, Bernie peeled open her eyes. Coughing, she pushed to her hands then onto her knees. The shooting had stopped.

Dimly, she was aware of someone crying. Quiet, heaving sobs. Tatum, she thought. Her gaze sought and found Zane stumbling toward his mother's prone figure. She moved, desperate to reach him.

A hand snagged her about the knee, knocking her off her feet. Dragged backward, she clawed at the ground. Grabbing a fistful of dirt, she twisted and flung it at the man she'd once revered as a mentor.

He spat, shaking his head. Barely recognizable, his face twisted with hate, he lashed out with his open palm. The slap snapped her face sideways, giving him the chance to haul her up against him and place a knife to her throat.

"Bernie," shouted Zane.

"Don't come any further, Mr Interpol agent." Kowalski dug the knife tip into her skin.

The blade stung. Blood trickled down her neck

and Bernie blinked the cave back into focus. Zane stood three yards away, hands held in a placatory manner. A large bruise had already begun to bloom where a fist had connected with his jaw. Cuts marred his face and hands. Fresh blood seeped from where the bullet had grazed his thigh the other night.

"Easy, Kowalski. Let her go and walk away. No one will stop you." His calm voice a balm to her tattered nerves.

Over on the ground, Rodriguez stirred, groaned. Trembling she watched the cartel leader roll onto his side, hacking and wheezing.

Any second, they'd be backed in a corner with no way out. Her gaze shifted to the others.

Poor Nyle lay unmoving. Delroy was on the ground, his hands clasped to his leg attempting to stem the flow of blood. His wife hid behind a pile of rubble, peering around the edge. Tai lay shielding his wife with his body. He lifted his head. Blood seeped from his head. Over in the corner, Ricky had herded Tatum and Cody behind him. It was a miracle none of them had been shot. But Ricky looked rattled, shaking visibly, a young man on the edge, about to lose his cool...big time.

Bernie bit down hard on her lip, using the faint stab of pain to clear her dizziness. The professor walked backwards, taking her with him. With a knife pressed to her throat, options were limited.

Rodriguez heaved to his feet. "You, boy." One hand braced against the wall, Rodriguez crooked his finger at Ricky. "I could use a *soldado* such as yourself in my crew. Come over here and bring that gun." His gaze dropped to the automatic weapon lying in lifeless fingers on the opposite side of the cave.

Sweat dripped down Ricky's face. Seconds ticked slowly past as she waited for the boy to cross the line and betray them.

"Stand fast, Ricky. Remember we're your friends." Zane switched his gaze to Rodriguez.

The ass shook his head sadly. "White *hombres* are no friends of yours, *amigo*. Come, join me. I make you a rich man."

Ricky inched toward the gun.

"Don't do it." Delroy's voice, reedy with the pain he must be feeling.

Time seemed to stop. Ricky scuttled to the gun, raised it.

"Wait," cried Elizabeth.

"Mom, don't move." Zane shot a glance over his shoulder.

Lying near the other tunnel entrance, Elizabeth twitched her feet, like she wanted to rise, but couldn't find the strength. She wheezed out, "He is your father."

Zane spun around. "Who?"

Bernie gasped for air, as if sucker punched.

"Kowalski...changed name... Dick Beresford. Black Betty always...checks out...marks."

Bernie finally remembered to breathe. She dug her heels into the dirt, making her body as heavy as possible.

"Fuck this," muttered Kowalski.

"Forget these *hombres*," Rodriguez wheedled. "Give me the gun, boy."

"Shoot him," screamed Pearl.

The gun wavered between Zane and the drug lord and back again. Ricky squeezed his eyes closed. A tear escaped.

Elizabeth muttered, "Zane."

"You!' Zane swung back, bounded toward Kowalski, his face thunderous. "You murdered my mother."

"Don't move," snarled Kowalski. "Or I'll slit your girlfriend's throat."

Zane stopped in his tracks. His chest heaved. His hands fisted by his sides. Agony and fury blasted from his eyes.

Kowalski snorted. "I don't believe it. You're that snot-nosed little tyke sniveling in the cupboard. I should have killed you too when I had the chance."

But Elizabeth wasn't finished. She rallied, her voice strengthened, "*El* Jaguar...hired me. Kill Kowalski. Believed he wanted...control...drugs..."

"Do not listen to her. My friend, never would I do such a thing," Rodriguez spluttered.

"Luis, what is this shit?"

Rodriguez limped forward a few steps, smiling. "My friend, the old woman is mad. Surely you will not believe the ravings of a lunatic?"

"No. But I do believe Black Betty. Save it, Luis." The professor shifted, his body tensing. "Consider our partnership officially over."

The knife left Bernie's throat.

Pushing her roughly aside, Kowalski hurtled the knife at his partner. It lodged hilt-deep in the drug leader's heart. Gurgling, Rodriguez made clutching movements at his chest. Disbelief spread over his features as his knees buckled.

Ricky, mouth twisted with disgust, dropped the rifle as if it was made of hot metal.

Catching Bernie by the arm, the professor locked his arm around her throat, and using her body as a shield scurried backward along the tunnel. He shouted, "Follow and I'll wring her neck."

Darkness enfolded them in the narrow passage until Kowalski switched on a flashlight. Ears straining, Bernie thought she heard a soft patter of feet and shuddered. Her heart pounded, her gut churned, hoping Zane followed them and not something else. They rushed through the last tunnel and stumbled into the small cave. Daylight glowed from the hole amongst the tree root bowl above their heads.

The professor removed his arm. Bernie lurched forward. His hands came around her neck. His fingers tightened. She pushed to her toes then slammed her head against his nose.

He howled, one hand going to his injured face while his other groped for her. She danced out of his reach, but not before Kowalski hooked his fingers into the necklace, yanking it savagely. The chain broke. He lashed out with his boot, slamming Bernie in the back of her right knee.

Crying out, she fell.

"*Bastard!*" Zane bounded out of the tunnel and shoulder-rammed Kowalski to the ground.

Panic rose at the sound of fists hitting flesh. Bernie's gaze darted about. She spied the flashlight and scooped it up, whacking Kowalski on the shoulder.

The men rolled over in the dirt. Bernie swiped at the professor again, this time on the back of the head. He swore, swinging wildly.

Zane grabbed the professor's head, holding him in a neck-hold, cutting off his oxygen until Kowalski lost consciousness.

Bernie pulled and tugged at Zane, until she got him to his feet. He swayed, wiped a hand beneath his bloodied nose and glared at the prone figure. "Bloody bastard. I should have killed him."

"Leave him be. You're going to hand him over to the police and he'll go to prison for the rest of his life." She led Zane away then tenderly cupped his bruised and battered face. "Your mother would never want his death by your hands."

Mouth compressed, Zane closed his eyes briefly before emitting a long sigh. "You're right. She was a gentle soul."

"That's the memory you need to hang onto." She brushed her lips tenderly over his before moving away and beginning to scour the ground. "I've lost the were-jaguar pendant. Can you see it?"

Leaves rustled as the wind picked up, sending the patch of daylight skimming over the sandy ground. Crystal glittered near the entrance to a small opening almost completely hidden by dangling tree roots. About to race over, Zane hauled her backwards.

"Don't," he whispered near her ear.

A satiny black paw stepped firmly on the pendant, pressing it deep into the sand. Three other paws quickly followed, and Bernie's horrified gaze travelled up the short muscular limbs to the snarling face of a jaguar.

"Move very slowly." Zane exerted pressure at her waist.

Together they shuffled backward. The jaguar's

unblinking eyes traversed the cave, coming to rest on Kowalski when he groaned.

"Professor, don't move," urged Bernie.

Ignoring her entreaty, Kowalski rolled onto his side. He saw the jaguar and stiffened. The jaguar emitted a rumbling growl. Kowalski turned his head, looking around for an escape route, his breath catching when he spotted a knife in the sand.

"Shit, my knife. It must have fallen out when we were fighting," murmured Zane. "Don't do it, man."

The big cat's haunches bunched. Kowalski lunged for the knife.

"No," shouted Zane.

Bernie wrapped her arms around him, holding him back when he would have leaped forward.

Raising his arm, Kowalski threw the knife, imbedding it in the cat's shoulder. Howling, the jaguar leapt, plunging its huge incisors into the professor's skull.

"Come on." Zane pulled Bernie away as Kowalski screamed and the jaguar thrashed him from side to side. "We need a gun."

They fled down the tunnel, bursting into the chamber and startling the stunned members of their group who were tending the injured.

Zane snatched up Pearl's pistol from the ground. "Stay here. Get a rifle and guard the entrance, in case it comes for the rest of us," he snapped before tearing back to the entrance.

"I've got two bullets in the chamber." Ricky hurried to Bernie's side and handed her the rifle. "What's going on, *chica*?"

"Jaguar." Trembling, she rushed to the tunnel

entrance, crouched and sighted down the barrel.

High-pitched screams reached her ears.

Ricky joined her, a blood-stained machete in his hand. He saw her glance and muttered, "Your gun is the only one with ammo."

The screaming stopped.

She waited for what felt like a life-time, hoping, praying. Her heart dying piece by piece as the long minutes ticked by until the soft thud of footsteps heralded Zane's return.

"It's me. Don't shoot." He stumbled into her arms, a haunted expression etched in the taut lines of his face.

She moved.

"No. Don't go there. It's over." Zane shuddered, pressing his battered and bleeding knuckles to his eyes.

"Oh lordy." Despite Kowalski's betrayal, tears fell. No one deserved to die like that, even a man who'd murdered his own wife. "The jaguar?"

"It's gone." Zane shook his head, then his eyes widened. "Oh God...Mom."

Zane rushed over to where Elizabeth lay on the ground, Bernie followed close behind. Someone had attempted to make her comfortable. A space blanket had been pulled over her body and a jacket placed beneath her head.

Elizabeth opened her eyes. Her breath rasped in and out of her mouth. Too slowly.

"Zane," she shuddered.

"I'm here, Mom."

"I wanted...best for my kids." Black blood ran from her mouth. "Tell Amelia...love her. Be happy, son."

↶ 31 ↷

Not wanting to tempt the jaguar to attack again, Bernie led the survivors out the other entrance. When they'd finally stumbled into the ravine, exhausted and weighed down by sorrow, they discovered James and his chopper had vanished. But Rodriguez's helicopter stood idle on the banks of the stream. Guns pointed into the pilot and the two load masters' faces, quickly persuaded them to yield to the inevitable. A good bluff; considering Bernie and her friends had no ammunition left.

Fifteen minutes later they were in the air where Zane broadcasted their location to the authorities who'd directed them to the nearest community.

With space limited on the chopper, they had to leave the bodies of the dead behind. But Bernie and Zane had every intention of joining a recovery team to retrieve them and send them home to their families.

Her back against the hard seat, Bernie sat tense, unable to relax, hardly daring to believe they were on their way home. Her fingers clutched Zane's tightly as her gaze traveled over her bloody and bruised companions. "Lordy, we look like we're straight off a battlefield."

"But triumphant." Zane gave her a quick smile then he beckoned the others to lean closer to be heard over the motor. "I suggest we keep quiet about Nyle's involvement in the plane crash. It will only hurt his family."

He turned to Tai. "But I totally understand if you decide otherwise."

Frowning, Tai lowered his head. After a few moments he looked up, his jaw set. "Nyle's paid the ultimate price for his mistake. I can let the crash remain an accident."

Delroy nodded. "Agreed. Let the man rest in peace. And I didn't hear nothing about what your good mother did for a living. That's another thing no one but us needs to know. We wouldn't be alive without her skills."

Pearl turned her face away while the others murmured their assent.

"Thanks, Delroy," Zane said gruffly.

Sighing, Bernie leaned into him and watched the jungle pass beneath their feet.

Around mid-afternoon, the chopper landed with a jolt on the tarmac at the small community of São Paulo de Olivença. They'd come full circle. A light drizzle of rain fell from the gray skies, forming a mist in the steaming air.

Paramedics, Brazilian soldiers and a private security force quickly surrounded the aircraft. She recognized the insignia on their armbands as belonging to a company her father had used in the past. Dad had sent in his version of the cavalry.

Several yards away, armed soldiers formed a perimeter, holding back the cluster of journalists already shouting questions and capturing the drama on their cell phones and cameras.

Leaning forward, Bernie scrutinized every face. No Kit.

Her gut clenched as she dug her nails into her palms. Her sister could still be safe. She could be waiting for her elsewhere, protected from intrusive journalists. She could be in hospital, recovering from her ordeal.

She could still be lost in the jungle.

As if sensing her thoughts, Zane patted her knee. Strong, kind, wonderful Zane. Returning from the deadly jungle without his beloved, adoptive mother. He'd been spared having to choose between right and wrong. He'd witnessed the agonizing death of his father—karma's end to the man who'd murdered his birth-mother. A life-changing event, they had yet to discuss.

With a soft whir, the rotors slowed then stopped as the engine powered down.

Blinking back tears, Bernie watched as eager hands reached for the stretcher and eased Cheryl from the chopper. She hadn't regained consciousness. The injured needed to be seen to first, then Bernie would be free to ask the question burning in her heart.

Before climbing down, Tai leaned over and planted a kiss on her cheek. "Thank you, luv. You too, mate. Regardless of what happens, Cher and I thank you both. Come on, son." He jumped out then lifted Cody onto the ground.

"Take good care of Micky." Bernie smiled. Her eyes misted. She'd miss the cherub, having grown quite fond of the little boy these past few days.

Cody nodded, his face solemn as he checked inside his shirt pocket for his monkey. Seconds later, the ambulance carrying the Miller family sped off, sirens screaming, with an army escort clearing the way.

"Thank you for saving us." Tatum scrambled over to hug Bernie. Disengaging, she gave a tremulous smile then turned toward the crowd. Her jaw dropped for a second, before she began to sob and wave madly. "Daddy! Daddy!"

A distraught-looking man broke through the ranks and rushed toward the chopper.

Her face awash with tears, Tatum looked back at Bernie. "I'll talk Daddy into taking me home to Wisconsin and go to college. Just like Mom wanted. Goodbye, Bernie. Goodbye, Zane. Come visit me sometime."

She slid a cautious glance at Ricky, before being helped to the ground where she was immediately enveloped in her father's arms. A soldier guided them away. One of the load-masters placed his arm beneath Delroy's and prepared to assist him out of the chopper.

Delroy, his sweaty face a landscape of pain, grimaced. "I know what yer intend to do, Zane, my man. I understand, but I won't thank yer for it."

Refraining from looking at his wife, he ignored Zane's outstretched hand and clambered down onto the tarmac. Two paramedics loaded him onto a gurney and Delroy sank down with a thankful groan.

"You ain't gonna leave me here, Delroy. Delroy! The baby is yours, I swear," screeched Pearl, flashing frightened eyes at Zane as she scrambled from the chopper.

Bernie and Zane climbed down close behind. Immediately, three soldiers stepped forward. Jaw tight, Zane handed a note to the captain and indicated Pearl. "Please send this message off immediately. Keep Mrs Lewis under protective custody until Interpol agents arrive. She's an internationally wanted criminal."

The captain nodded then issued a quiet order to two soldiers who stepped forward to escort a loudly protesting Pearl off the tarmac.

Ricky jumped out of the chopper. "What about me?"

Zane eyed him carefully, then offered his hand. "Try to stay out of trouble."

"Fuck yeah." A relieved grin spread over his face as Ricky pumped his hand. His gaze drifted to the pack Bernie still held. "Take care of that shit."

"I intend to." Bernie kissed his cheek. "What will you do?"

His cocky grin vanished, revealing the lost boy who lived inside, reminding Bernie, that for all his swagger, he couldn't be more than eighteen or nineteen years old.

Shifting his weight from foot to foot, he took out his crumpled cigarette pack. "Dunno. I got fifty bucks. Maybe get me a bus ticket to Manaus."

A weary Delroy raised his head, staying the paramedics about to wheel the gurney away. "There's a job waiting, if yer interested, boy. Ain't nothing fancy. Ye'll be starting at the bottom. Kitchen hand and a room at my place. I'll be taking yer board out of yer wages of course. No drugs. No drink and no smoking."

"Yo, man! Seriously?"

"I don't talk shit, boy. Now, git over here. I need a doctor." Closing his eyes, Delroy gestured to the paramedics to load him into the waiting ambulance.

Smiling like he'd been handed the world on a plate, Ricky squeezed Bernie's fingers one last time, tossed his smokes to a nearby soldier, then raced over to join Delroy. The rear doors slammed shut and a few seconds later the ambulance drove off with another army escort.

Bernie sniffed and blinked back her tears. A happy ending, of sorts. Most of them had lost something or someone, but a few had found a new direction in life.

A tall man with close-cropped black hair, a square jaw and dark aviator shades shielding his eyes, stepped forward. "Miss Bernadette Ashford?"

Bernie nodded, her heart hiccupped.

"Welcome home."

Pulse racing, she choked over the words, forcing them out. "My sister. Kit. Kitarna. Is she here?"

The guy shook his head. "We've located the plane wreckage and were about to head off for another search, when we received your radio call. Our intention is to make camp on the smugglers' runway, using that as our base while we perform a sweep of the surrounding area." With a jerk of his thumb behind him, he indicated a large black helicopter several yards away.

"My men will escort you to a safe house where you will remain until your private passage to Manaus has been organized. They'll keep watch until you're safely on a flight to the US, ma'am." He nodded to Zane. "Sir." Then he swung away, his long strides eating up the tarmac.

In seconds, he'd be in the air, on his way to resume a search of the jungle. Of their own volition, her feet followed, her eyes fixed on the security force's leader. She brushed past the soldiers and policemen waiting to lead her to safety. Heading in the opposite direction, she began to jog.

"Bernie!" Zane's hand caught her arm, bringing her to a standstill.

Eyes brimming with tears, she met his quizzical gaze. "I'm going back."

"I know." He fingered the straps of Colin's pack which she still carried. "You can't take this with you."

"Thanks for the reminder, I'd forgotten." With a quick smile, she handed the bag over.

Zane immediately turned and gave it to the army captain who'd followed them. "Inside are rare plant specimens and research notes. Contact Miss Ashford's father and tell him we need the best bio-scientists here. At once. Then and only then, give him the pack."

"*Si, señor.*" The captain took the pack carefully, looking from one to the other. "With respect, *señor*, we require statements from all the survivors."

Zane pulled out a folded sheet of paper. "This will serve as my and Miss Ashford's brief for the moment. I've also written the name and contact details of my boss, who will be only too happy to vouch for me. I'm certain Miss Ashford's credentials are without dispute."

"I understand." With a half-smile on his face, he gestured to his men and they walked off leaving Bernie and Zane alone.

Bernie shot a yearning glance at the chopper. The rotors were whirring into motion while several men loaded equipment into the aircraft's belly. She didn't have much time. But how to say what could be her last goodbye to the man who owned her heart?

A wistful smile tugging her lips, she placed trembling hands on Zane's threadbare shirt. His skin burned hot through the thin fabric. His heartbeats were steady and sure. She longed to escape to that hotel room and spend her life in his loving arms. But she would never leave the jungle until Kit was found.

"No rest for the beautiful," Zane murmured, lowering his head until his mouth was a whisper from hers. He weaved a hand through her hair, gently massaging her nape. "I made a promise, Bernie."

"What promise?"

"That we'd keep searching until we find your sister."

Her chest expanded. Love, respect and admiration swelled. "And you're a man of your word."

"It's more than that and you know it. Who else is going to make love to you in a tree?"

Her heart rolled over as her fingers clutched his shirt. "We were lucky. We may not make it back this time."

A tender smile glowed in his dark eyes, he ran his thumb over her lower lip. "I'm not spending another

SCENT OF THE JAGUAR

minute without you. Whatever happens, sweetheart, we'll face it together. And that's another promise."

"I love you," she said, her voice thick.

He quirked an eyebrow. "I know."

She narrowed her eyes. "And?"

"I love you, too, sweetheart." Sincerity rang deep in every word.

"I know," she said and grinned.

A broad smile chased the fatigue from his face. "Cheeky. Besides, you're going to need my charming influence to get you on that chopper."

She gave a mock frown. "You're such a tosser."

Zane laughed. "I love it when you talk dirty. Come on. Or they'll leave without us."

Hand in hand, they ran across the tarmac where, after a heated discussion and Zane resorting to pulling rank, they boarded the Black Hawk. A few minutes later, the chopper lifted into the sullen clouds and roared off toward the hulking dark mass of the jungle.

Bernie nestled close to Zane, taking comfort from his solid body while she gazed at the canopy passing swiftly below them.

We're coming, Kit. Hold on. This time, we'll find you.

∽ Epilogue ∾

Bernie lay face down, limbs sprawled wide, in the pillowy softness of a real bed. The air-conditioning pumped delicious cold air into the darkening Manaus hotel bedroom and it was blissfully quiet. No constant chirping of frogs, crickets or other insects. No squabbling monkeys. No squawking birds. No people. No heat, humidity or constant rain. It was heaven; exactly as Zane had promised.

She pressed her fingertips into the crisp, cotton sheets, enjoying the coolness against her skin and the knowledge she didn't have to move unless she wanted to. No need to forage for food, no need for vigilance against their hunters.

The nightmare was finally over.

Kit was alive and safe. And in this very hotel. Bernie couldn't wait to tell her sister about the lost city and introduce her to Zane. But first they'd had other matters that needed immediate attention.

Upon their return with the private security force, they'd been assessed by health officials. Next, they'd been transported to the police station where they'd given their official statements. Bernie had made phone calls to her parents while Zane contacted his sister. Afterwards, she and Zane had hopped onto the chopper again, and headed back to the ravine. Several hours later they'd retrieved the bodies of their fallen companions and brought them to Manaus—except for one.

Elizabeth's body had disappeared.

With a click, the hotel room door opened.

Bernie smiled, picking up the soft pad of Zane's footsteps as he crossed the room. The mattress moved as he sat close to her. Peering through lowered lids, she saw him deposit a tray on the bedside table. A glass decanter of iced water, with slices of lemon and lime, two empty champagne glasses and several small cardboard boxes.

He bent over her, tenderly brushing aside hair from her face. "I know you're awake, so stop pretending. I've brought us a snack before we go downstairs for the party. Every type of chocolate I could lay my hands on."

"Sounds perfect." Anticipation buzzed at the knowledge she'd soon see Kit and she hugged herself inwardly. She leaned into Zane's hand, then pressed a kiss to his palm. "How did the debriefing with your boss go?"

"Not bad, all things considered." He shrugged. "Mainly, a few pertinent facts no one but us needs to know."

"I'm glad." She sat up. Tingles fizzed over her skin when Zane's gaze travelled slowly over the filmy, turquoise dress she'd donned after her mammoth shower. There, she'd scrubbed every inch of her body, lathered every strand of her hair until the past six days of despair and death had disappeared with the dirty water down the drain.

He added, "Have to front my boss in person first thing tomorrow morning when he flies in from Mexico City. I could tell by his voice, he wasn't satisfied with my account of what happened."

"About?"

"My mother." Zane looked toward the window, swallowing. "I'm fairly certain he knows I'm withholding information."

"It didn't help that we couldn't any trace of her." Frowning, Bernie chewed her lower lip.

"I'm sticking with the paw prints near where she fell. With luck, he'll dredge up some sensitivity and leave well enough alone." His voice rasped, harsh and thick.

She touched the side of his face with her fingers, trailing along his cheekbone. "I can't help wondering what happened."

His jaw worked for a few seconds. "All I know is that she's gone from my life."

"I'm so sorry, Zane." She moved onto her knees and with her fingertips, turned his face to meet her gaze.

A world of confusion and desolation shimmered in his velvety brown eyes. While she'd agreed not to relate certain aspects of the past few days to the authorities, where Zane was concerned she had to have total disclosure. Today and in the future. "We need to talk."

"Now there's a phrase guaranteed to strike terror into a man's heart."

Sliding her hands from his face to around his neck, she whispered, "When I showed you that piece of paper I found on the runway, did you know what it meant?"

"I swear that was the first time I'd seen it or heard about the contract." His hands found her waist.

"And what about your mother?"

His lips twisted for a moment. "She confessed she was a hit-woman when Ricky and I were drawing off the mercenaries from the ravine."

"You didn't tell me."

"I couldn't find the words. I wanted to, but I was shit scared you'd reject me." The intensity of his gaze could not be denied.

"You really thought I'd do that?" She drew back. "Why?"

"Because you're a woman bound by honesty and honor. I thought you were like Mom, but she turned out to be something entirely different. How could I expect you to tie yourself to a man whose father is a killer? And whose adoptive mother kills for a living."

"Is that all? We can't choose our parents. We just accept them for who they are. Like they have to accept us." She tugged on a lock of his hair. Hard. "Men. Were you ever going to tell me?"

"Yes. When I finally had you somewhere safe, I planned to tell you everything and then walk away."

"And you say, I'm the one with honor. From now on, we share everything." She ran her hand over his chest, then began to unbutton his black, linen shirt. What was it about guys wearing black? So sexy. "I still find it hard to believe Professor Kowalski was a major player in a drug-trafficking ring. And that he was your father. I can't imagine what you must be going through."

"To be honest, relief that I finally have closure. There was a moment in the ruins where I had a stupid longing for him to tell me I was mistaken. That my mother's murder was a bad dream. That he wasn't involved."

Bernie pressed a tender kiss to his chest. "Understandable. We all want parents we can trust."

"I quickly realized my mistake." Zane's voice turned cold. "I pieced together a lot of information today. When the bastard fled England after murdering my mother, he and Rodriguez came into each other's orbit as small-time drug dealers. They built up quite an empire together. Beresford re-invented himself as Kowalski then attained a college degree. Transporting equipment and supplies to and from digs was merely one of the ways they funneled drugs into the US."

"Thank heavens, that's one drug ring smashed."

"Not quite. There's still a lot of work to be done identifying all Rodriguez's allies. All of which is the main reason, my boss is flying into town. Unfortunately, that translates to my new career being delayed a while."

"No problem from my end. It may take a while to obtain funding and the government's consent to excavate the ruins. Is that the only reason?" She leaned back to study his face, noting with relief the haunted expression in his eyes had dissipated.

"Yes. I'm not wasting any more of my life chasing ghosts."

"I'm glad. We'll leave the past where it belongs." She wound her arms around his neck and nestled close.

He kissed her fiercely then said, "Any news about Cheryl?"

"I phoned the hospital an hour ago. Tai said, she was out of surgery and in an induced coma. The prognosis is positive. They said she wouldn't have made it if not for Colin's herbal mixture which had slowed down the internal bleeding."

"That's great. The Millers are good people." He dipped his head and trailed his lips along the sweetheart neckline of her dress, murmuring against her skin, "Now, about that life together. After all that's happened, are you still game?"

"I'm in. I'll never change my mind, Zane, and that's my promise."

"As soon as we're done with all the formalities, we'll organize our first dig together. And excavate those ruins you found." He leaned back and examined her face. "You and me, a team. Forever. That's my promise, too, Bernadette Ashford." He smiled before pulling her down onto the bed and rolling on top of her.

"Now, this is heaven." She slid her tongue over his earlobe, her fingers sliding through his soft, clean hair.

"Beats making out in a tree. Or a cave."

She giggled. "Oh, I don't know. I thought we didn't do too bad, considering the circumstances."

He grinned. "Full marks to us for ingenuity."

"Where there's a will..." She allowed her voice to trail off while she busied herself undoing his belt buckle.

"You talk too much." His lips claimed hers in a kiss that blazed a fire through her body and a tremor through her heart.

Someone rapped loudly on the door.

"I don't believe it. Interrupted. Again," muttered Zane, grinning as he pulled away and attended to his clothes.

Bernie planted a loud kiss on his cheek. "Don't be so greedy."

"I'm insatiable where you're concerned." He winked, indicating the door with a jerk of his chin. "I met a special person downstairs. Someone who's very impatient to see you."

Her breath snagged in her throat, her heart bumping crazily against her ribs. She sat up, feeling her eyes grow wide. The knocking paused then thumped out a familiar beat. Relief. Love. Excitement fizzed in her veins making her dizzy.

Scrambling to her feet, she squeezed Zane's hands. "I'd know that tune anywhere. Kit!" Half-laughing, half-crying, Bernie flew to the door to embrace her sister.

The End

Reviews can help readers find books and increase a writer's visibility. I am grateful for all honest reviews. Thank you to any who have the time to let others know what you thought of the book.

If you'd like to know more about me, my books or to connect online, please visit my website at http://www.segilchrist.com/

ACKNOWLEDGEMENTS

To my partner-in-adventure, fellow romantic suspense writer and lovely friend, Erin Moira O'Hara, it's been a pleasure working with you on such an exciting venture.

My heartfelt thanks and appreciation to Juanita Kees for her great editing and clear-cut directions that helped make my story shine.

Thank you to Fiona of Fiona Jayde Media for the gorgeous book covers and Amy Atwell of Author E.M.S. for her formatting expertise. A special thankyou also to critique partner, Susanne Bellamy for her thoughtful suggestions.

ABOUT THE
DEADLY FORCES SERIES

A Note from S. E. Gilchrist

Around two years ago, I had an idea for a romantic suspense, group venture series centered around survivors of a plane crash. Each author would take a group of passengers and write an adventure-filled story about their struggle against a hostile environment—preferably a jungle. The venture was placed on the back-burner for a while until early this year I teamed up with special friend, romantic suspense writer, Erin Moira O'Hara to write this series. We make a great team. We had a ball—brainstorming our premise and fleshing out our individual ideas. The research was wonderful. I came away with a new-found respect for the amazing world of the Amazon Rainforest.

My research highlighted how important this region is for the world's survival.

Both Erin and I incorporated into our stories some of the Amazon's amazing creatures and plant life. I hope readers of our books will also find the Amazon just as fascinating.

Our books can be read as stand-alone, but if reading in order of 'time', Erin's book, *Beat of the Jungle,* comes first.

We hope you enjoy our *Deadly Forces* series—
adventure twisted with drama and suspense and,
of course, romance.

~

Books in the Deadly Forces series:

Beat of the Jungle – Erin Moira O'Hara
Scent of the Jaguar – S. E. Gilchrist

Discover Kitarna Ashford's adventures in Deadly Forces
Book 1, *Beat of the Jungle*, by Erin Moira O'Hara.

Excerpt from

BEAT
OF THE
JUNGLE

A DEADLY FORCES NOVEL

ERIN MOIRA O'HARA

~ 1 ~

Screeching, tearing and grinding erupted around and under the plane. Ripping metal competed with terrified screams. They were traversing downward, off the side of a mountain, but into what?

The sudden explosive impact threw him back in the seat. The plane swiveled to the right. A horrendous tearing surrounded them. Jack flinched, praying he was wrong, but only a giant tree made such a spine-chilling noise before it crashed to the ground. And God only knew where it would fall.

The crash sounded like a cannon firing, but after spending eight months working for a logging company, he knew better. A savage blow hammered the plane. The sound of tearing metal screamed throughout the plane. Debris flew around him. The acrid smell of rain, rotting forest and hot metal filled his nostrils.

Powerful vibrations shuddered under his feet. The stench of vomit assaulted his airways, filling his lungs until the acid taste of bile rose in his throat. An oxygen mask caught the edge of his eye with a sting worthy of a wasp. Hysterical screaming dragged him back into the past, to the carnage he could have prevented with one extra bullet.

Shearing metal competed with torrential rain and the roar of jet engines, which didn't make sense. This plane was a propeller job.

He lurched sideways, confirming his worst fears. A deluge of water poured through jagged cracks, thanks to an enormous tree trunk, which had crushed the middle section of the plane like an aluminum can.

ABOUT THE AUTHOR

S.E. Gilchrist can't remember a time when she didn't have a book in her hand. Now she dreams up stories where her favourite words are...'what if' and 'where'? After several years travelling around Australia and Asia, SE settled in the Hunter Valley, Australia with her family and pets. Several of her books have finalled in writing contests and her first published work was in December 2011. She loves combining romance with action, adventure and suspense across many different writing genres.

SE takes a keen interest in the environment and animal welfare and loves bushwalking, reading and spending time with her family.

Published by Escape Publishing (Harlequin Australia) and Pan MacMillan Australia, SE is also an indie author.

http://www.segilchrist.com/

www.ingramcontent.com/pod-product-compliance
Lightning Source LLC
Chambersburg PA
CBHW071049250626
47159CB00002B/420